HOLLOW CITY

A Max Strong Thriller

MIKE DONOHUE

For Mom –

You always skipped to the ending,
but you were always reading.

PROLOGUE

The man in the driver's seat looks over at his passenger. His face is slick with sweat. His hair is matted at the temples. They have been driving in the dark for a long time. They'd passed the state line three hours ago. The driver can finally see the brighter lights of the city softening the sky on the horizon. It won't be much longer now.

The passenger gives a strangled cry and his arm locks up and grips the air as if desperate to hold something. Or hold something back. The driver doesn't know. They haven't talked about it. They've been on the road for five days. Taking the smaller roads. Sharing cheap rooms. Saving cash. Taking it slow. Being careful. There is no rush. Not yet.

The driver doesn't wake the man or try to comfort him in any way. He knows it won't help. The driver has his own demons. Better to wrestle them down in your own way.

The passenger finally drops his arm to his lap, whispers something, maybe a name, and slumps back into the seat. He does not look rested.

The driver thinks the nightmares are getting worse as they travel. The cheap motel rooms offer little privacy and he's watched the other *man thrash in his sleep as if he's desperate to get to the surface. As if his life depends on it. Maybe it does.*

The driver turns his attention back to the road. Another half-hour passes and the headlights catch the reflective paint of a roadside sign.

Entering Boston.

CHAPTER ONE

Max stood in the shadows and eyed his watch. He figured ten minutes, at the most. The Celtics had played the Lakers earlier that night. It wasn't Sox-Yanks, maybe back in the '80s, those days were long gone. Still, it got the natives restless. Max figured by now, with the clock circling midnight, the crowd would be pretty well oiled. He kicked off the wall and started toward the door. A group of five guys stumbled through the door and out onto the sidewalk. He revised his estimate. Seven minutes, tops.

He nodded to the bouncer, keeping his chin tucked and face turned slightly away. He wanted to do this inside, not out on the sidewalk. He pushed through the scarred door and into the heat and funk of Kelly's Tap. It was crowded and tight with bodies. He paused in the doorway, letting everyone in the place, and the camera over the door, get a good look if they cared, then headed to the bar.

The bartender made his way to him, wiping some water marks as he approached.

"Bass," Max said.

He was a young guy, gelled up spikes of bleached hair on top, carved facial hair running along his jaw, and a bland smile. Max guessed he would be too young to be any help. He probably came to town for college and never left. Max had learned that youth had no sense of history. If it didn't happen to them or it didn't happen in the last five minutes, it didn't matter. It wasn't their fault. Perspective came with age. It was evolution at work.

Spike put down a cardboard coaster and placed a dripping bottle of beer on top. "Four."

Max slid a five across, turned around to survey the room, and took a pull from the bottle. It was ice cold and numbed his back teeth on the way down. He and Kyle had been sitting in the car for most of the last three hours listening to the game absently and waiting for the crowd inside the bar to build up.

He gave the crowd another long, slow look. He picked Kelly's for a reason. Most of them looked like locals. T-shirts, jeans, well-worn baseball caps. Mostly men, mostly younger than him, but with a few exceptions. Three grizzled old-timers sat on stools on the short side of the L-shaped bar. He looked them over slowly and thought he saw a glint of recognition from one of them. Satisfied, Max turned back around, nursed his beer, and kept watch over the room from the bar mirror.

It took eight minutes. Max recognized him. Fat men changed at a glacial pace.

Bobby Briggs, a couple of inches over six feet, fleshy all over with short cropped hair, now receding back toward his ears, and a waist size higher than his IQ. He wasn't connected, at least not back when Max was running a crew, but he always liked to think he was. Bobby was always grasping, but never quite catching on. He was big, dumb and mean enough to get himself hooked up as local muscle for a couple hundred bucks a pop, but he never went higher. He had a big mouth and liked to fill it with talk and booze. The Bobbies of the world had a place in life and tended to stick to it like water finding its level. Max guessed the man's vanity and love of gossip hadn't diminished in the time Max had been gone.

He was perfect.

Bobby looked big; hell, he was big and could loom with the best of them. Max was sure Briggs's services also came with a halfway decent sneer, but it was all smoke and mirrors, a tough guy veneer that would crack at the slightest pressure.

The one time Max had seen Bobby in action had been the time Carter had called in a favor and gotten the Dropkick Murphys to provide entertainment for a New Year's Eve party and things had gotten predictably out of hand. Max remembered watching Bobby try to wade into the mass of people and restore some order near the makeshift stage. Bobby's most effective weapon, by far, had been his gut. He'd gotten into the middle of the melee and promptly gotten punched twice in the head and gone down. The drummer hadn't missed a beat. Max and Danny had to pull his titanic ass out by his ankles before he got stomped to death.

At least he had the good sense to take care of his best asset, Max thought, as he watched the prow of Bobby's gut now cut a clean swath through the crowd toward the bar. Along with the blubber, Bobby carried a pool stick and an empty bottle of Bud in the other.

Max finished his bottle of Bass and turned around. The move brought Bobby up short. Max kept his hands at his sides and his mouth shut. He just looked at Bobby Briggs with the hooded stare he'd learned in the prison yard.

Max didn't know what Briggs had planned, some tough guy posturing or maybe the coward would have just cracked him with the pool cue while his back was turned, that actually would have been the smarter play, but smart was a long way down the list for Bobby Briggs. Turning around and facing him seemed to have thrown Bobby completely off script. He looked at Max for a moment, seemed about to say something, then swallowed the words. He veered to the right and parked his gut against the bar rail.

"Another Bud, Sean."

"You should probably think about switching to light," Max said.

The insult had the intended effect.

"Whaddija say?"

"You heard me, Bobby. I mean, a light beer is still a beer, not a miracle worker, and you are seriously packing on the pounds. If I come back in five years, I'm pretty sure you'll be working on your second heart attack."

Max felt the room's attention swing in their direction.

Bobby was clearly a regular and was used to being the biggest guy in the room. He still was. He had at least a hundred pounds on Max, which made the confrontation and promissory violence an attention magnet for all the other drunks in the bar.

Bobby felt it too. The room went still.

Kelly's Tap wasn't a big place. A warped bar along the left, eight stools plus the waitress station. Two scruffy pool tables in the back and four tables in the middle that could be moved out the way if people felt like dancing to the juke. Three sagging booths filled out the room against the right wall under dusty neon beer signs and faded pictures of long-forgotten local softball teams. Max had first thought about going to McGann's; he thought he might catch a smile or a kind look there, but decided against it. He wasn't back for sympathy.

Max waited, and Bobby slowly came to a predictable decision. He swung the empty bottle in a short arc toward Max's face. Max shifted back and let the bottle whistle past his nose. Once Bobby's bulk got moving in one direction it wasn't easy to stop. Max stepped into the opening and easily hit Bobby with a short, precise chop to his Adam's apple. Something else he'd learned in the yard. Bobby dropped the bottle, and his hands went to his throat. He started gagging. In his panic to find oxygen, he slipped on the beer-soaked floor and went down. Max watched the man's face begin shifting from its natural red to a florid purple.

He looked up at the sound of a chair scraping. Two guys were headed in his direction. The one in front had another pool cue, held upside down, and he looked smart enough to use it. The second guy had the squat build and cauliflower ears that told Max he wasn't a stranger to fighting.

Max had some size and was decent with his fists from his hockey days, but two against one wouldn't likely end well for him. Luckily for him, the cramped bar played to his advantage. The pair had to make their way single file through the four tables scattered in front of the bar to get to him. Max stepped away from the bar and closed the gap before they could flank him.

The first man swung the weighted butt of his pool cue. Max deflected the blow with his shoulder, but still felt the impact run down his arm, his hand going numb. Max clapped the guy hard on his ear with his left palm. More than a few beers into his night, the shot to the ear made the guy dizzy and he toppled over into the group sitting at the table. He was down for the moment in a tangle of arms, chairs, and legs.

The second guy tried some sort of judo move, perhaps hoping to catch Max off guard, but forgot either how much he had to drink or just how slippery a dive bar's floor is when last call is near. He slipped halfway through the move and fell to the floor, his head making a crack on the concrete that made the crowd wince.

Max checked in on the first guy, but he seemed disinterested in continuing.

"Guys, do me a favor. When at least one of you can walk and talk again, tell Carter that Michael Sullivan would like to speak to him."

Max said it loud enough so that he was sure most of the bar could hear him. He then turned to the bartender who took an involuntary half-step back. "Sean, get some ice on that for Bobby and keep it there. If you don't stop the swelling, he's going to suffocate to death."

Max saw one of the old-timers pull a phone from his pocket. Even if Bobby missed the message in his panic to keep breathing, it would get delivered. He turned his back on all of them and walked out. No one else tried to stop him.

He took the first left, walked down two blocks, and jumped in the passenger seat of a late model Ford Taurus. Back when he was planning jobs, Max always had a fondness for the boxy, anonymous Taurus. This one, bought for cash and few questions at a rust bucket lot in Delaware, lacked AC and power windows but ran just fine and no one would give it a second look.

"All good?" Kyle asked.

"He'll get the message."

CHAPTER TWO

State Police Detective Colleen Adams took the frozen dinner off the top of the stack, orange chicken with green beans, popped it in the microwave, and tried not to think about how it would taste. Her name was scrawled in black marker on the front, but she doubted the food was a temptation for most in the office. She included herself in that. She ate it solely for the energy and to keep her dad off her back about her weight, or lack of it.

A wave of fatigue rolled over her and she stifled a yawn. It had been a long day of chasing whispers and rumors with little to show for it. She hadn't left her chair except for the bathroom, but all her muscles ached from the concentrated stillness of intense study. The coffee pot next to the microwave was half-full, but also smelled burnt; there was a good chance it had been made more than five hours before. Even when it was fresh, it was only barely tolerable. The microwave beeped and saved her from another bad decision. She slid the black plastic tray out and peeled back the cellophane wrapper. The lumps of varying grays and green didn't exactly match the picture on the box. She swirled a fork through it and took it back to her cube.

It was past ten and the office was quiet. Her favorite time of the day. Just about every agent she knew was a morning person and the office was always buzzing by seven-thirty or eight. Or so she was told. She liked the nights and found it more productive to work late, after the others had left.

She stabbed a piece of what she hoped was chicken, sampled some green beans, then pushed it away. She needed to eat some real food. She made a promise to herself. She would read and annotate two more field reports, then she was going home. No excuses. No exceptions.

Her stomach rumbled, and she glanced at the congealing food. It couldn't look less appetizing. She pulled a sleeve of saltine crackers from her bottom drawer and grabbed the Min folder from the corner of her desk. She really did need to finish this one before she could go home. Creeger had a stick up his ass about this one and wanted it on his desk when he walked in tomorrow.

She spent the next ninety minutes reading local law enforcement reports and witness statements from the Min's Hair Salon murder in Chelsea. She had already read them through twice before. Two weeks ago, Min Lee, 42, and her employee, Chang Heng, 34, were shot and killed after closing the salon. It wasn't late, just after seven p.m., and the strip of stores that included the salon was well trafficked, even at night. The bodies were discovered quickly by someone walking past, but no one saw the actual shooting.

Tragic as it was, that type of crime, in that type of neighborhood, happened twenty times a year in and around Boston and might have slid under the radar except for a few off-key statements that didn't exactly line up. The local Chelsea cops had asked for some help. She saw the same thing. It's what people that were interviewed *weren't* saying that hinted at something darker and more sinister as the motive behind the murders. No one seemed all that surprised that Lee was killed. So, what was it? Drugs? Smuggling? Prostitution? They simply didn't know. They'd gone through the salon with a fine-tooth comb. They'd had forensic accountants look at the books. They'd run down Lee and Heng's backgrounds. It was all clean. They'd hit a wall. After letting it slip, the community now seemed intent on putting the lid back on.

But Colleen wouldn't have lasted as one of the few female state police detectives if she were so easily put off. She was confident they would figure it out. It was about pressure. Keep applying steady pressure until something cracked. But there was nothing else she could do tonight. She made notes on the photocopied reports and added a typed summary and recommendations on their next steps to the front of the file, then walked it down to Creeger's office at the end of the hall.

Her lieutenant's door was shut. The frosted glass pane with his stenciled name and 'Commander' was impenetrable. The blinds covering the window view of his officer's cube farm were closed up tight. She could see nothing inside. It wasn't unusual. Creeger wasn't a bad boss. Far from the worst she'd had, but he kept his cards close to his vest. Adams didn't like secrets. It was one reason she became a detective. She reached out and tried the knob. Locked. She turned around, dropped the folder in his assistant's inbox, and returned to her own workspace.

She popped her iPod buds in and figured she could finish the second report in a half-hour and be home by midnight, twelve-thirty at the latest. She put on some ambient house and smiled remembering the time Jackson had ridden in her car and discovered her penchant for pulsing house and techno. He gave her a cross-eyed look and was now convinced she spent her downtime in abandoned warehouses going to secret raves. In truth, she'd never been to a rave or a night-club. In college, then law school, and later during her six months of academy time out in New Braintree, she found the music had an odd and trance-like way of helping focus her attention.

Twenty minutes later, she was halfway through the report when Ted Rabalais popped his head over the cube wall. Colleen shot back from the desk and brought her hands up. With the music going, she hadn't heard him approach.

Rabalais brought his palms up and stepped back, smiling. His hair was wet, and his tie was off. The strap of a gym bag was slung over his shoulder. Rabalais wasn't in her group, he worked mostly fraud and computer crimes, but they both worked on the seventh floor and were friendly. She had the feeling he liked her, but either wasn't forward enough to ask her out or he was by the book enough not to date his co-workers.

She pulled the buds from her ears. "Jesus Rabies, you scared me. I thought I had the floor to myself."

"You did. I just popped back in after working out to pick up some files for bedtime reading."

"What's up?"

"Nothing. Heard the phone ringing and saw your light. Just wanted to say hey. You have a message." He pointed at her phone. "I could hear you jamming out," now he pointed at her ears, "and figured you missed it. Didn't know if you were waiting for it or something. Didn't want your boyfriend getting upset or anything ..." he trailed off.

She looked over at the missed call number showing on the phone's display. "Not my boyfriend, but thanks."

"No problem." He waited a beat. She just looked at him. Then he tapped the top of the cube. "Alright, have a good night, Adams." He gave her a wave and headed for the elevators. She watched him go. He had nice shoulders, she decided. There were probably a lot of other nice parts of Rabalais, too. She smiled to herself and then quickly shook off the thought. No time for that.

Her cell phone vibrated, also indicating a missed call and a message. She happily chucked the thoughts of her barren social life aside and checked the call log. It showed the same number as her office phone. Local area code, but she didn't recognize it. She listened to the office one first, then grabbed her coat and ran for the elevator.

As she waited impatiently, her cell chirped again. She punched the down button until the car finally arrived.

She pulled out of the agency's underground garage in her personal car, a charcoal gray Mini Cooper. Not exactly a practical choice in Boston winters, but having a car at all in the city wasn't practical, so if you were going to have one, she figured, it might as well be fun to drive.

A city whose downtown streets were originally laid out as cow paths was a recipe for constant gridlock during rush hour, which in Boston extended from seven a.m. straight through until seven p.m., but now, creeping up on one a.m., midweek, the streets were virtually empty. A few delivery trucks, a couple of cabs and Ubers cruising for fares, but little else to get in her way.

She drove fast, let the engine cycle up, and took the corners hard. She put both windows down and let the night air blow through the car and revive her. She tried to focus on the cold air on her skin, fingers gripping the wheel, and the tires biting the road. Nothing else.

She couldn't do it. Her mind was restless. It jumped from the Min file, to another case, to Rabalais's shoulders, to the phone message. She couldn't let things lie. It was her biggest strength and weakness. There could be only a few reasons for Foxx to call. She turned onto Summer Street and accelerated up and over the small bridge that spanned the Fort Point channel. The wind shifted and swirled and buffeted the little car. It seemed to be warning her, whispering in her ear. Hold on. A change is coming.

CHAPTER THREE

The screen was a soft fuzzy glow. Carter sighed and told himself that it was late and his eyes were tired, not that he was old and his eyesight was going. He'd lie to himself even in an empty room.

He pulled the laptop closer and, after a moment, boosted the magnification up another notch. He then carefully ran his finger down the column of glowing figures and found the row he wanted. He used the mouse to select the numbers in the cell and cut and pasted them over to a new sheet he'd started. The tallies reconfigured with the new information, and Carter was satisfied to see that everything now tied out.

He did one last quick double-check. If you were going to kill someone, it was important not to make an adding mistake. It was all there. Cheating and robbing in neat, orderly rows. Carter shook his head. It didn't happen often, but occasionally someone came along who thought they were smarter or found a better way.

Carter closed the laptop then stood, ignoring the popping of his joints and the stiffness in his back, and put the laptop back into the wall safe behind the signed photo of himself and the late Boston mayor, Raymond Curley. The story behind that photo always made him smile. He had top of the line encryption on his laptop and he'd filled all the ports with glue. It wasn't going to connect to the internet. It was for business only and his eyes only. He closed the safe and spun the dial before swinging the photo back in place.

He dropped the scraps of paper he'd been using to confirm the leaking money into the garbage can next to his desk then stopped and pulled one back out. He used his lighter to set it on fire and drop it on top of the others. The pile flared for a second before dying back to ash.

He knew some people called him paranoid. Hell, maybe they were right, but paranoid men lived to see the next sunrise and, more importantly to Carter, stayed out of jail. He'd been proving that for over 20 years. So, no, he didn't think it was paranoid. He thought it was good business practice.

He left his office and walked down the hall. He could see plaster dust pooling at the edges of the hall. He was having renovations done on the first floor, but that stuff had a way of getting everywhere. He passed the stairs that led up to the third floor and his bedroom and continued down to the next door. It was closed, but he could hear muffled voices. He opened the door and saw the big screen TV tuned to the Celtics post-game show. He didn't think Daniel Hogan actually liked basketball, but he didn't complain. He walked into the room. It was empty, save for Hogan. The night nurse must have come and gone already. He knew another would be in soon to take the overnight shift. Carter lowered the volume and looked at his friend. Hogan's eyes were open, but it was difficult to know what he was seeing or taking in. The man once nicknamed The Ghost, who was whispered about with fear, was becoming more and more true to his nickname. Just in a different way. Carter dropped the remote on the table next to Hogan's chair and left, closing the door behind him. Hogan never moved.

It had been a mistake to go in there. It had left him feeling off balance. The indignation and fury that he'd felt like a wire in his blood as he confirmed Barboza's cheating had burned low. Now, he just felt old and tired. He knew he couldn't go downstairs feeling like this. He pulled out the small pillbox and tapped a fingernail on the top. Was it worth the cost? Even half a tablet would have him wired half the night. He decided it was. Appearances were worth preserving at the cost of some lost sleep. He took out half a pill and used the back of the box to crush it to powder on the small hallway table before snorting the pop up his nose. He knew it was a placebo effect and it would take at least ten minutes to really feel the effects of the drug but he already felt better, his heart kicking in his chest as he came down the stairs and found Little John sitting at the kitchen table. The big man had his hands wrapped around a cup of tea that looked like a thimble in his big mitts.

"Find what you need?" he asked.

Normally, Carter wouldn't take any questions on his business or his methods but, with The Ghost fading away upstairs, he didn't mind Little John stepping into his place.

"Yes. It's no mistake. We ready?" he asked.

The big man nodded and stood up. "Yes. Downstairs."

"Who else is here?" Carter kept his inner circle tight and let even fewer people into the house. Tonight, he wanted to keep it to the minimum.

"Jimmy and Legs."

"Good. Let's do this. You know where you're taking him?"

"Yes, it's all set up."

They went down the stairs into the house's narrow basement. The wall near the stairs was cluttered with construction materials for the first-floor renovation. Buckets, ladders, tile, paint, drop cloths, and other materials. Carter made them clean and pack it all up and put it down here each night.

There was an old cold room under the stairs, leftover from when his mother initially lived here. He hadn't been in there in years. It was probably still full of old Ball jars or sixth generation potatoes. A separate door was opposite the cold room. Other than that, it was just the typical boiler, water heater, and furnace.

And the chair.

A man was currently tied to the chair. He wasn't the first. Probably wouldn't be the last. The chair was in the middle of a square of clear poly sheeting, probably taken from the remodeling supplies.

Jimmy and Legs stood behind Barboza, within easy reach. Barboza himself was older, likely close to Carter's own age, with slicked back salt and pepper hair and fleshy jowls framing a large nose that was holding up even larger glasses. The man was sweating, and his glasses had slipped a bit. Carter was disappointed to see the resignation already in the man's eyes. It would take some of the fun out of it.

Steve "The Accountant" Barboza wasn't a made guy or an explicit member of Carter's crew, he was Italian after all, but he'd worked Carter's loansharking books and parts of the laundering business for more than a decade. He was trusted. Until the spreadsheets started kicking up red flags. Barboza wasn't stupid but neither was Carter.

He could feel the drugs humming in his veins now. It was a drumbeat in his ears. His hands ached. He got on top of it and controlled it. That was the key.

"Gotta say. I didn't see this coming, Stevie."

"Just got tired. Wanted out."

"Why didn't you just ask?"

"I was getting to it but didn't have the nut saved to just walk away."

"You saying I didn't pay you enough?"

Barboza tried to wave an arm, forgetting it was tied down. "Not that." He paused, and Carter realized he was embarrassed.

"Ponies?" Carter asked.

"Nah. Worse. Poker. And the sports book. Ironic, I know." Carter didn't even need to prod him. The rest of the story, sad and short as it was, tumbled out. "First, I was skimming to get out but that was going too slow. So, I started putting some of the skim toward a few bets. Lost more than I won and … well … you know how that story ends."

Carter shook his head. "You should have, too." He took a cigar out of his pocket and a clipper from his other pocket. "This is usually the part where I take out my cigar and school some stupid schmo sitting in your spot about the genius of Red Auerbach and what it meant when he lit up his stogie. But I'm guessing you know that story as well as I do."

"Victory cigar. The Celtics had the game in the bag. I miss the old Garden."

"You and me both. I miss a lot of things about this city. It's changing." Carter cut the end of the cigar. He took out an old burnished silver lighter. He told people it was his father's from the war, carried all over Europe. The only thing he had from the miserable old man. Even that was a lie. In truth, it was nothing special. Something he'd stolen when he was eleven from Max's Drugs when it used to be on L Street. He held the flame to the cut end and got the cigar going.

"Tell me something. You got any of it left?"

"Ten or fifteen at the condo. In the closet. Shoebox."

Carter imagined he could feel the Adderall now mixing with the pungent smoke of the cigar in his blood, all of it pushing him on like a dog snapping at its tether. Everything felt sharp. His heart galloped and he couldn't keep his leg from jumping. When he reached out to take Barboza's glasses, he noticed the tremors in his fingers. He folded the glasses and put them in his pocket. No reason to cut up his knuckles.

Some discreet part of his brain watched all this happening and wanted to shut it down. A bigger part knew that if he let this slide, or just had the boys take care of it, then rumors would start spreading. Carter was going soft. Carter was losing it. You couldn't unring that bell. The whispers would ripple out and, sooner or later, Carter knew they would erode the foundation of all he'd built.

So, he turned that discreet part of his brain off and lashed out a fist and bent Barboza's ugly nose into a new shape. He pulled back his fist again and again until he was dizzy and breathing hard. Barboza's face was a mottled canvas of blood and bone. He took a step back and tried to catch his breath. No one moved, least of all Barboza. Carter stripped off his shirt and wiped his face and hands before throwing it onto the plastic sheet. He noticed a splotch of blood on his pants and added those. He then turned and headed up the stairs.

Halfway up, he heard a phone ring and Little John answer.

"Boss, you need to hear this."

CHAPTER FOUR

She slowed as she took the second bridge across Fort Point, over the reserved channel. Summer Street turned into L Street and Fort Point became South Boston. She knew the general neighborhood and the street but not the exact bar. It took her another five minutes to get to 6th and P Street. Finding the bar wasn't hard. Three squad cars were still flashing at the curb in front of a small brick bunker with a carved wooden facade on top and a neon Bud sign in one of the two small windows that faced the street. An ambulance passed her as she approached, she pulled over to let it pass, then squeezed the Mini into a space in front of a hydrant. She doubted anyone was looking to write parking tickets, but she dropped her PBA placard on the dash just in case. She put the window back up, took a deep breath, and stepped out.

Facing the bar from the street, she could now read the weathered facade on top as the bar's signage. Kelly's Tap, spelled out in a curling script and surely painted at one time but was now just a cracked and brackish brown, like old dock pilings.

There was no crime scene tape, but a city uniform stopped her near the bar's door.

"Ma'am?"

She badged him. "Detective Adams. Sergeant Foxx called me."

"State?" He gave her a puzzled look. She didn't offer more and he was too new or too smart to argue. He wrote her name on his clipboard along with the time and held the door open for her. "Sergeant's inside."

He didn't have to tell her where. The bar was a simple square box and Foxx would have stood out in a room three times its size. He was short, maybe an inch or two below Colleen's own five feet nine inches, and he was easily two hundred pounds heavier. He seemed to add a layer, like a growing oak tree, each time Colleen saw him. There were only three people inside. A city plainclothes was interviewing a skinny, greasy guy in a white shirt and black pants, presumably the bartender, at the far end of the bar. Foxx was at the other end, balancing his wide ass on a stool.

"Detective Adams," he bellowed. She made her way over. "You made good time," he said before crushing her in a bear hug.

"I was at the office."

He raised an eyebrow. "Age hasn't weaned your enthusiasm, I see." He settled back on his stool. He was sipping from a rocks glass half-full of ice, which he crushed between his teeth with every sip. It could have been whiskey or ginger ale. He gave her a look and knew he wanted her to comment. She didn't. She knew it would take at least a gallon of Jameson before you noticed a tremor or a stutter. Even fall-down-drunk, he was sharper than at least half the Boston city cops she knew.

"Can Sean get you something?" He waved a hand at the

greasy guy with sculpted hair being interviewed at the far end of the bar.

"No, thanks."

He shrugged. "Suit yourself."

She took the stool next to him.

"How's the old man," he asked.

"He's doing alright. The physical therapy has really made a difference. The last six months he seems like a different person. You should come by sometime."

"That's good to hear. Really good." He rolled the glass between his palms. "Maybe I will come by. It would be nice to catch up."

She didn't blame him for the white lie. Cops were loyal to the core but were also just as superstitious and weird about injuries. They'd visit a guy in the hospital when something happened, take up a collection for him, look out for his family, wish him well, but most cops wouldn't come around to socialize if you pulled the pin due to an injury. It cut too close to the bone.

To be a cop and go out into an increasingly violent and unpredictable world, day after day, takes a certain fearlessness and a certain obliviousness. An injured or impaired officer punched through that bubble and reminded them of the reality of their vocation.

She got that, she did, even as his daughter, it was never easy for her, but it still didn't make it any less heartbreaking to see her dad so lonely every day. Her dad hadn't been cut down by a bullet or shanked by some crackhead in the line of duty. He'd had a stroke. A plain vanilla brain burp between roll call and lunch and suddenly he's a pariah because half his face is frozen, and his right arm is rusty. In her dark moments, she thought maybe it would have been better if he had been shot. Maybe then, his precinct buddies could understand it, rationalize it. A stroke was too ordinary and too random.

She let it drop. "So, what happened here, Foxx?"

"I'll let Sean tell it. I think Chuck's almost done with him. Better to hear it straight from his mouth but, trust me, you'll want to hear it, Adams."

They sat in silence and listened to the murmurs from the other end of the bar. Foxx reached over and grabbed the fountain gun and filled his glass with ginger ale. Colleen tried not to look at herself in the bar's wavy mirror. She looked at the bottles instead and was beginning to regret that she turned down Foxx's offer of a drink when the detective at the other end put his pad away, gave Foxx a wave, and left. He never glanced in her direction or showed any interest in who she was or why she was there.

"Sean, come on over here and tell us your story one more time."

"Sergeant, come on. I've been over it four times already. I'm beat."

"I know, but, Sean, it's such a good tale. Humor my friend here. Besides, it's barely past last call, if none of this had happened, you'd still be on the clock sweeping up this lovely shit hole, so it's not like you were expecting to be somewhere else."

Colleen had learned a long time ago that arguing with Foxx was futile. Sean appeared to have enough functioning brain cells to come to the same conclusion.

"Fine." He wiped his hands on a dish towel that was tucked into his belt. Nervous tic or an addict, Colleen thought. Cooped up with the cops, he was starting to itch for a bump of something to keep him sane. He kept his eyes down and started talking.

"It was a regular night. Nothing special. Typical crowd. Usual drinks." His eyes flicked up to hers. "As you can see, this ain't exactly Faneuil Hall. There aren't a ton of random walk-ins. People find their way to the door, it's on purpose. I've only been here six months, but I already know most of the guys, and it's usually guys, by face, if not name."

"Get on with it, Sean." Foxx said.

"You wanna tell it?"

Foxx made a spinning gesture with two fingers on his hand and sipped his ginger ale. "Just keep it moving. I'm losing feeling below the waist."

"Fine."

He wiped his hands on the dish towel again. He'd be a terrible poker player, Colleen thought.

"Like I was saying, it was a regular night. Celtics game so maybe a few more townies than usual packed in. No reason to think I'd end it by talking with you types though. About midnight, game's over, crowd is starting to thin out, a guy walks in and takes a spot at the stick. I'm pretty sure I've never seen him before. Just an average guy at first glance. He orders a beer, a Bass, and just stands there nursing it. Doesn't talk to anyone, doesn't look at the TV. Just stands there. He turned around at one point like he was looking for someone but mostly he just stood there staring at himself in the mirror. It was odd, but I mean, whatever, we get our fair share of crazies in here, too.

"So, he's zoning out there for maybe ten minutes. Beer's gotta be getting warm and I keep giving him the eye, but he just shakes me off. Then, I notice the room. It's gotten quieter, tense, like at a hockey game when you know the next line change is gonna result in a fight. Charged, right?

"The next thing I know Bobby Briggs has sauntered up behind this guy and he's carrying a pool cue. Guy finally moves, turns around. Quick. Now they're kind of toe-to-toe. Guy doesn't give an inch. You know, Briggs?"

"She knows the type," Foxx said.

"Right. Well, he's not the type of guy that's used to other people crowding his personal space. I mean this new guy wasn't big, not Bobby big, but he had some size on him, still, I bet most of the folks in the bar would have put their money on Bobby.

"They're standing there like two prizefighters at a weigh-in and you could feel everyone holding their breath, then Bobby leans around him and calls for another beer. I breathed out, the whole room did, but before we could laugh it off, this new guy actually starts giving Bobby shit about his weight. I mean, Jesus Christ, the balls on this guy. He backs Bobby down in his own bar and now he thinks it's a good idea to twist the knife? Bobby backhands the empty he's still holding at the guy's head. The guy dodges and, a second later, Bobby is flat on his back, turning red, gasping for air. I was two feet away and staring right at 'em and I don't know what happened. It was nuts. I've never seen someone take down Bobby or anyone else that fast. And it was just with his hands. Just crazy."

Colleen's back was tightening up from sitting on the bar stool; the stale smell of body odor and beer was giving her a headache. She looked at Foxx with a frown. "You pulled me down here to listen to a story of some local Bruce Lee take out a two-bit hood?"

Foxx just smiled. "He's getting to the good part. Tell her the rest, Sean."

"Right. Two of Bobby's pals tried to have a go at the guy but pretty much got the same treatment. When all three were laid out, this guy stands over Bobby, but you got the idea he was speaking to the whole room, and says, 'Tell Carter that Michael Sullivan would like to speak with him.' Then, he tells me to get Bobby some ice for his throat so he doesn't die and walks out the door. That dude was a fucking badass. You know him?"

He looked at both of them, but they didn't answer. He pulled a face, then grabbed the dish towel from his belt, and moved off wiping down the bar.

Colleen tried to take it in, couldn't do it. She looked at Foxx.

"I thought you might want to hear that story."

CHAPTER FIVE

The bottles gently knocked against each other in the passenger footwell as Kyle braked the Taurus to a stop at the intersection. It was late and the streets were mostly empty. This was still a mostly working-class neighborhood where alarms went off before dawn. They'd driven the route twice and only passed two cars and a group of drunks off the subway stumbling toward home. They might be seen, likely would be, but it couldn't be avoided. It actually might help in some respects.

Max leaned down and tucked the wicks deeper into the necks of the glass bottles. Earlier, after the stop at Kelly's Tap, they'd driven a few miles across Southie and found a liquor store still open. They'd bought a six-pack and emptied the beers into the gutter. A second stop at a nearby gas station, they bought a quart of motor oil and a gallon of gas. Finally, they'd raided Kyle's duffel for a cotton T-shirt to provide the wicks.

Max knew the bottle bombs wouldn't do much in the way of destruction, but that wasn't the point. Just like laying out Bobby Briggs wasn't going to get him closer to Carter. The point was to create chaos. To make Carter angry. To make him look like a fool in his own neighborhood. To get him to make a mistake. Max hoped that would give him the opening he needed.

"You made the calls?"

"Yes. Two connected. Gave them the message. One was never answered."

"The salon?"

"Yes."

"Makes sense. Should be long closed at this point."

They were idling at the corner of 8th and Springer. They were targeting three businesses, a hair and nails salon, a bar, and a flower shop that was a front for a sports book, in a short two block radius. Max knew he'd need to get some up-to-date intelligence on Carter's operation soon. He'd been away too long to think at least some things hadn't changed. Just driving through all the new construction in the city tonight was proof enough that the world moved on, whether you were ready or not. But he was confident that these three places were still on Carter's books. One maxim that didn't change? Once Carter owned you, he never let you go. These three places had been part of Carter's rackets when Max was still in the loop. He didn't think that had changed.

"Cameras?" Max asked.

"On a couple lights. I didn't see any others. You?"

"No. They don't want the ins and outs recorded. Works for us. Let's go."

Kyle pulled away from the curb and turned right. The flower shop was halfway down the block. Both sidewalks were empty. Earlier, during their reconnaissance circuit, they'd stopped briefly near Carson Beach and grabbed some fist-sized rocks from the shoreline. Max picked up a rock, along with a bottle, and jumped out. The flower shop was dark. It was small and Max could see all the way through to the back.

He tossed the rock through the shop's plate glass window and then quickly kicked open a bigger hole in the glass.

He paused and listened to see if the noise had stirred up any activity, inside or outside. Nothing. He lit the strip of T-shirt on the molly and tossed it inside. The bottle didn't break, just rolled along the floor near a display of greeting cards to pair with a flower arrangement. There was a pause as the makeshift wick's flame threw shadows over the ceiling, then there was a soft whump as the fire ate into the neck of the bottle and met the gas and motor oil mix. The bottle exploded, splashing the liquid onto the cards which quickly started to burn. Max jogged back to the car.

Around the corner on 8th was the bar, The Abbey. Of the three, it was the one that Max was most worried about. He didn't need any more innocents on his conscience. He had enough old blood on his hands. Carter was one thing; injuring or killing someone just out for a drink or working a shift was something he wanted to avoid. But Kyle's warning call seemed to have the intended effect. The bar was just as dark as the flower shop. It was close to last call and midweek, so that likely helped. He'd take any luck he could get in the next few days. He'd need it.

Max repeated the same process. This time using the rock to clear out the glass from the top half of the bar's battered front door and getting the bottle deeper into the room behind the bar. The effect was much bigger with the bar's alcohol stoking the flames higher. They both could see the orange glow growing quickly as they drove away.

"Gotta hurry. That's going to get someone's attention."

Kyle didn't respond but pressed the accelerator down a little further.

Healthy Glow Hair & Nails was on G Street and would give them quick access up Columbia to the boulevard and then onto the expressway to get clear of any official response to the fires. The salon occupied the corner spot of a short strip of stores that fronted a commercial block. Pulling up, it looked like the first two, dark and empty.

Max jumped out a final time. He looked through the window and surveyed the place. It was a simple set-up. Reception desk and waiting chairs up front, styling chairs and rinse stations to the left, pedicure stations aligned on the right. A central aisle ran down the middle and led to an unlabeled door. He assumed the door led to supplies and maybe a restroom.

Satisfied it was empty, he cracked the big plate glass front window with the rock until it broke and cleared a hole wide enough to toss the bottle. He lit the wick and aimed for a product display of hair and nail products that ignited almost immediately and created a fireball hot enough for Max to feel from the sidewalk.

He started to turn back toward the car when the light came on. He watched in horror as the door in the back opened and a small woman came out, blinking in confusion. The fire was spreading quickly, gobbling up the old carpet and finding fresh fuel at each beauty station. Worse than the heat was the noxious cloud of black smoke the fire was throwing off. Even now, it was filling the room, diffusing the lights, making it difficult to see the woman on the other side.

"Go out the back," Max shouted.

The woman didn't move. Maybe she was in shock. Maybe she didn't speak English. Maybe there wasn't a back door.

Max turned to Kyle. "Check the back," he said before turning around and climbing through the broken window.

He felt a shard of glass slice along his ankle as he climbed inside. He had to force himself not to back out again. The heat was intense. The smoke was worse. He tried to breathe, coughed, and felt the burn in his throat. He'd lost sight of the woman. He swiped at his watering eyes. He pulled his shirt up over his face and bunched his hands inside his sleeves. It was the only protection he'd get. He couldn't wait any longer. He plunged into the store doing his best to stay in the center, away from the worst of the flames, but he still felt the heat singe his hair and neck with every step.

The smoke was thicker in the back without the broken window to provide some relief. He couldn't see more than a foot in front of him. He got his feet tangled up with the legs of a chair and fell over. It turned out to be a good move. There was less smoke down on the floor. He spotted the woman ten feet away, curled up in a ball in the corner. Her eyes were glassy and vacant. She was in shock. She would be roasted alive if she didn't start moving. They both would.

He crawled across the floor and grabbed for her arm, intending to lead her through the door and out the back. The smoke was a thick, billowing wall above them and was pressing lower by the second. Breathing would be impossible soon. He had turned back to find the door and found that he'd lost touch with her. She'd pulled away. He could see she was crying and whimpering and intent on staying in the corner. If she'd had a blanket, he was sure she would have covered her head and tried to hide like a child. In the real world, that blanket would melt only to her face.

He grabbed her elbow, more firmly this time, and pulled until she was forced to crawl across the carpet in his wake. He found the doorway she'd come through and pushed them both through on their hands and knees. They were in a narrow hallway. There was smoke here, but it wasn't as thick and bilious as in the front of the store. He closed the door. It wouldn't do much, but it might buy them a few precious minutes.

He stood and pulled the woman to her feet as well. There were two doorways on the left and right facing each other. Max looked in the first. An employee break room. Counter, refrigerator, stained coffee maker, cabinets, and an old round chipped table. Against the wall, behind the table, there was a fold-up camp bed with a green sleeping bag on top. That explained the woman. More importantly, there was no other exit.

He backtracked across the hall. He could feel the temperature already rising in the small hallway. He glanced back and saw the smoke threading its way under the door. He pulled open the second door. It was a small bathroom just big enough to fit a toilet and a sink.

And a small window.

It was placed up high, abutting the ceiling, and its primary purpose was likely for ventilation. It was an awning-style window operated by a crank that hinged open from the top. Max was not an overweight or large man. His years in prison, and then on the run, had left him with little excess fat, but he quickly realized, even if they could find enough leverage to break the window and push out the frame, he was not going to fit.

But the woman might.

He quickly cranked it open to the max and then almost screamed as a hand appeared on the sill. Kyle. In the heat and confusion of the fire, Max had almost forgotten he wasn't alone in this.

"Only way out," he said. He wasn't sure if it was a question or a statement but got his answer when Kyle just nodded.

"If we can force the window clear, there should be enough room for her to slide through."

Kyle nodded again and then disappeared. A moment later, Max heard a grinding screech and then the top of a flaking green dumpster rolled underneath the window. From the outside, the window's height was just as awkward. Kyle had the same issue with leverage on the outside as Max had on the inside.

Behind him, the woman coughed. Max turned. She had slumped down onto the floor, back to a mostly comatose state. Max could see the smoke in the hallway now. With the window open, the fire was sniffing out fresh oxygen. He stood on the toilet and pushed, while Kyle pulled from his spot on top of the dumpster. Both men strained to their limit and the metal extension arm snapped out of the frame and the window flew out, held in place now just by the top hinge. It would have to be enough.

Max stepped off the toilet and waved to the woman. "C'mon, climb up. You can get out." He pointed out the window. He still wasn't sure if she spoke English. Outside of the dusky smoke, she looked Asian or Indian, but some primal survival impulse had finally overridden her shock. She clamored up without a word. Max helped boost her up onto the windowsill and Kyle pulled her the rest of the way through.

Watching the waif-life woman just clear the edges only confirmed Max's earlier thought that he would only manage to get himself stuck if he even tried. He stood on the toilet. Kyle's face appeared in the window. Max could hear sirens now in the distance, likely for one of the first two places they'd hit. Even if they were coming straight here, he didn't think it would be in time.

"Get her some help. She's in shock. She's probably got some burns in her throat and lungs, too. Maybe carbon monoxide poisoning. I'm going to look for another way out. Gotta be another exit."

Kyle just looked at him. Max knew he'd likely come to the same conclusion that Max had. A secondary exit was unlikely. He hopped off the toilet and didn't look back.

The hallway was thirty degrees warmer. Max could see the doorknob glowing a dull orange, and the thin door appeared to be bowing outward with the stress of the heat. He would not be making a mad dash back out the front door.

He crossed the hall into the break room, cast around for a miracle. He saw a narrow door in the corner that he'd missed the first time and ran to it, but when he pulled it open it was just a narrow supply closet with a well-worn broom, mop, and bucket.

The smoke was thicker now. It had breached the ceiling tiles and was drifting down in a poisonous cloud. He tried to think. Tried to figure out some way out. He'd always been good at planning. Most of his jobs for Carter had gone off without a hitch because he could see and anticipate the angles. But that was when he had time. Now, he couldn't see anything and he felt panic eating away at what calm he had left.

The smoke and heat forced him to his knees. He crawled back to the hall and away from the door, but nothing magically happened. Nothing changed. The hallway still ended in a wall. He put his back to it.

Who didn't build in a back door? Max almost laughed because he knew the answer. Carter wouldn't kill him. Not directly. But his cheap-ass, not-up-to-code, cut every corner construction methods might.

It was getting difficult to breathe. His throat and nose felt raw. He was starting to feel dizzy. He closed his eyes to stop the floor from tilting. At least he hadn't let another innocent die.

CHAPTER SIX

Colleen leaned against the bar and tried to make sense of it. Her mind resisted. The memories of Michael Sullivan and what he did to her family were radioactive. She'd locked them up tight and thrown away the key. She knew if she opened that door, she'd be right back there reliving it all over again.

She heard Foxx say something to the bartender. What was his name? Patrick? Conner? It was something Irish, she was sure. Foxx put a drink in her hand. Something amber. She sipped it, felt a hot burn in her throat, but didn't taste it. She was drifting away from herself. She felt like she had plunged underwater. Hearing his name, here and now, in Boston wasn't possible. She was fighting against it. How could he be back?

"Why would he be back?"

"I don't know," Foxx said.

Colleen wasn't aware that she'd spoken aloud.

"I heard he was in the wind. I followed that story from Iowa, like everyone else. I'm sure you did, too."

Colleen nodded. She actually hadn't followed it that

closely. After the story broke, the most she did was read the headlines. You'd think with her connection to the case that she would have been all over every detail, but she found herself surprisingly indifferent. It wasn't going to change anything. She realized, one morning, while browsing the Globe's coverage, that she was mostly checking to see if he'd been killed yet.

She looked down and noticed that the bartender had refilled her glass at some point. Sean. That was his name. She took another swallow to steel herself and tried to think back to the time she knew Sullivan, but all the doors slammed shut. She couldn't do it. She didn't *want* to do it.

"Is there any video?" She asked.

Foxx grimaced. "Some. One camera just inside the door. Gets everyone coming in or going out. The front door anyway."

"That's it?"

"Not the type of place where security is high priority. Guessing it's there to cover its ass for insurance. Sean, you mind if we take another look?"

"No problem. You need me to show you how to use it again?"

"Nope. I'm all set."

Foxx led her around the bar door, just past the waitress station. He pushed the door open and led her into a room that could marginally be called a closet. There was a desk, fashioned roughly out of a door cut in half, with an old desktop computer perched on top. There was a small safe in the corner and a particleboard bookshelf, straining under the weight of multiple three-ring binders. Foxx squeezed his bulk behind the desk and took control of the mouse. The program to watch the recordings was already on the screen, probably from the detective or Foxx himself watching it earlier.

"Don't get your hopes up."

Colleen wasn't sure what she was hoping to see. She latched onto the possibility of the video to steer her mind away from the past.

Foxx enlarged the video player window to full screen and used the mouse to drag the play head backward. She watched people enter and exit in high speed. Foxx found the time and clicked a button to play it in normal speed. The video was in black and white and wasn't the best quality. The system was probably several years old. She watched two men wearing matching Sox hats enter. Then, a single older guy grinding a butt out on the sidewalk. The bulk of the bouncer to the left of the door was the only constant. A group of four men entered, then two women.

"Coming up," Foxx said.

Colleen watched a man enter and pause in the doorway. He seemed to want everyone to see him. He even glanced up at the camera at one point. She leaned in trying to squint some more quality into the video. The man continued and walked out of the frame. Foxx backed it up again and froze it with the man looking up.

"What do you think?" He asked.

The highlights were washed out and, damn, she wished the owner hadn't scrimped on the shitty camera. It was like looking through rain-streaked glass. "I don't know. Definitely could be him. The face doesn't feel right. It's close but doesn't totally match up. Almost like a relative."

"Been almost ten years. Probably ten mostly hard years. People change."

She stared at the image on the screen. Was it him? She closed her eyes and winced as her mind involuntarily flipped through a painful rolodex of memories looking to match up this man on the screen with the man in her memories.

There was a pause in the little room, and she realized

Foxx had asked her a question. She opened her eyes again and found Foxx looking at her. "What was that?"

"I asked if he ever contacted you? After everything happened."

"Me? No. Why would he contact me? I'm the last person that would want to talk to him."

"I don't know. He might. Everyone reacts differently. After something like that, people sometimes reach out. She was your sister. There was a connection."

Colleen felt a burning rage bloom at the base of her skull. "He killed my sister. I wouldn't call that a connection."

"C'mon, you know what I mean."

"No, I really don't," she almost shouted.

Before the argument could escalate further, the uniform on the door poked his head inside. "Sarge, you might want to turn on your radio. A lot of chatter about multiple 101s in the area."

Foxx frowned and reached for the radio on his hip. Growing up with a cop for a father, Colleen was well versed in the radio codes but 101 was an unusual one and she couldn't immediately recall what it meant.

Foxx must have seen it on her face. "Tsk, tsk, Officer Adams. Fire, explosion, possible building collapse."

There was a fresh burst of chatter from the radio. There was a lot of crosstalk and Colleen quickly lost track. She gave up and waited for Foxx to fill her in. Or not. With the news of Michael Sullivan, she couldn't muster up the energy or attention to really care about a fire. The radio went quiet and Foxx put it back on his belt.

"Care to go for a ride?" he asked.

Colleen knew it was an olive branch of sorts after their brief disagreement. She didn't really want to tag along to a fire, but she also knew she wouldn't find much peace at home.

Maybe this would distract her and tire her out enough to sleep. She doubted it, but it was worth a shot.

"Sure."

She followed Foxx out and squeezed into the passenger side of Foxx's patrol car. He didn't typically ride with a partner and the dashboard computer, a jacket, and various takeout wrappers littered the passenger side. She shoved the computer toward the center and raked the rest of the crap into the footwell. She didn't miss being stuck in a car.

Foxx slid his bulk behind the wheel and the car rocked on what felt like a well-worn suspension. He draped his big hands over the well-worn steering wheel. "I've probably spent more time in squad cars than in my own bed."

"By choice."

"Ah," he flipped his hand, "true enough. I like being on the streets. I would have gone crazy if they tried to kick me up to management." He started the car and pulled away from the curb. "Wouldn't have lasted more than a week. I do not have what they'd call a silver tongue."

"Would have been fun to watch though," Colleen said.

Foxx gave a wicked smile. "Would have felt good to get a few things off my chest."

They drove less than half a mile. Foxx's mental GPS guiding them through a narrow alley and then two rights before emerging behind a phalanx of fire trucks and a single ambulance. The EMTs were leaning against the front grill of their vehicle.

"EMTs looked bored." Colleen said. Even with the doors and windows of the squad car shut tight, she could smell the dank odor of burnt insulation, plastic, wiring, and other building materials. She opened the door and it rolled over her in a wave.

"Good sign," Foxx replied. Bored EMTs meant no bodies.

"Or crispies."

"Always the optimist, huh, Adams?"

They stayed in the car. Colleen could feel the energy, or lack of it, just by watching the guys milling around, looking for something to do. The fire was out. No bodies. Nothing hazardous to deal with. Nothing left to do but pack up and go home.

"Huh." Foxx said, looking it over, as well.

"What?" Adams asked.

"Nothing. If I remember correctly, this was a little flower shop."

Colleen doubted Foxx was wrong. "Odd target. Insurance, maybe?"

Foxx just grunted a noncommittal response and scratched his nose, going quiet for once.

After another minute of watching, Foxx backed up around the ambulance and reversed course through the alley, this time taking a left and driving a short distance before finding the second fire site. It was now a husked shell of what looked like a bar or restaurant.

"The Abbey." Foxx said. "Decent bar. Good shepherd's pie."

It would be awhile before they were serving anything again. Through the windshield, the results of the second fire looked much like the first. Like the flower shop, the bar was a one-story building. The firefighters had vented the roof, but there was a lot of smoke and water damage. Colleen could see through the missing front door from her vantage point. The worst of it looked to have chewed up the right side of the building. She guessed that was where the bar had been with bottles of liquor to stoke up the initial blaze.

Even without the close timing, there was little doubt that the two scenes were connected.

"We getting out?" Colleen asked.

"Don't think so. You want to?"

"What's going, Foxx? I know that look on your face. It's the same look you'd get when you were cooking up some scheme to get us in trouble during those cop BBQs at the house. You know something."

"Could never get anything past you or your sister."

Colleen winced at the mention of Cindy again but refused to be sidetracked. Driving around with Foxx had turned her cop brain on and allowed her to bury anything personal. At least for the time being.

"Spill it."

"These first two, and I'm betting the third one as well, are owned, for all intents and purposes, by Carter."

"No shit."

"It's not on paper, of course, but the bulk of the profits are definitely going in his direction."

"You think it's Sullivan?"

"That lit the match? Who else? It's not random, clearly, and way too much of a coincidence after his bar cameo." He dropped the shifter into drive. "Might as well take a look at the last one."

Foxx angled his squad car to curb next to an ambulance. The last site was a corner building in a commercial strip, and it looked a lot more damaged than the first two. This time, they both exited. They each gave quick nods to the two EMTs leaning against their ride and continued around a ladder truck to a space in front of the ravaged building filled with wet, deflated nylon fire hoses.

Colleen couldn't make out what type of business it had been. Any signage had been destroyed, and there was nothing inside the blackened shell that immediately gave it away, either. Just melted and smoldering hunks of wood and plastic. Either the conditions inside were better here for the fire to spread or it was deliberate, set with more fuel to burn hotter. The side of the building was partially caved in, leaving a crumpled hole with a view into the back half of the structure.

She looked over at Foxx.

"Yeah, it's his. Healthy Hair or something. A salon."

One of the firefighters rolling up the hoses noticed Foxx and came over.

"Foxx what brings you out?"

"Hey Jonesy, that you under there?" The firefighter was short and thickset. His squat stature was amplified by his bulky black fire coat and matching helmet. He pushed the helmet back on his head. He had bright blue eyes that stood out against his dark, sweaty hair.

"Yup."

"We," he waved a hand at Colleen, "were down the street at Kelly's handling a thing. Radio blew up as we were finishing. Didn't want to miss out on any fun."

"Yeah, this is one of three. Strange night. What I'm hearing is they are all pretty similar. Feels like we got a potential firebug on our hands. You think it's connected to your thing at Kelly's?"

"Probably not. That was just a routine thing. Too much to drink. Too much ego. Guys blowing off steam." Colleen glanced at him, but kept her mouth shut. She was just riding along. "What happened here?" Foxx asked.

Jonesy shrugged and turned back to look at the front of the building. "Looks like someone tossed a Molotov cocktail through the window. Probably looks and smells worse than it really is. All those hair and nail chemicals was good fuel. But structurally the building is fine. They'll need to rebuild that wall, but all the load-bearing stuff checks out. They'll have to gut it but no need to demo it. More a nuisance, a costly one mind you, than anything else. Even without our help, with that hole in the sidewall, it would have likely burned itself out without jumping down the block."

All three of them now looked at the shell of a building with the perforated hole in the bricks. Now that she knew it was a hair salon, Colleen could see the shape of each station in the melted chairs and hip high counters running along the edge.

"Saw a couple EMTs picking their noses back there. No bodies I take it?" Foxx asked.

"No. Not here or at the other two either. We did find one thing that was a bit abnormal."

"Oh yeah? What's that?"

"Toward the back in what looked like a break room there was a trapdoor that led to some sort of storage space or basement. One of our guys almost fell through."

"What's odd about that? Gotta keep all that extra hairspray and nail polish somewhere, right?"

"Sure, but they weren't keeping it there. It was empty. Just an empty space about half the footprint of the whole building. Not sure why it was there or what they were doing with it." Jones shrugged. "Like I said, a strange night."

"Strange in all sorts of ways. Thanks for the info, Jonesy. Stay safe."

"You too, Foxx."

Back in the car, Colleen asked, "You mind sending me copies of the incident reports on all this?"

He looked at her.

"Relax, it won't get to you," she said.

"Not what I'm worried about."

"I won't step on anyone's toes."

"Also, not what I'm worried about."

She knew he was worried about her and wanted to talk more about Sullivan and her sister, but she wasn't going there.

"What do you think?" she said instead, waving a hand at the scene outside the windshield.

"I think Sullivan really wanted to make sure his message got through. If Bobby Briggs got cold feet and didn't deliver his message, these three fires certainly wouldn't be missed."

"Ok, I buy that, but I'm still stuck on why now? What brought him back?"

"Maybe the itch for revenge just got too strong to resist?"

"Maybe, if he came back right after all the Essex stuff but that was over a year ago. Where was he? What was he doing? Again, why now? Sullivan was always a planner, but he also always had a reason."

"Don't give him too much credit. He was still a two-bit criminal."

"He was definitely a criminal, but he wasn't some brain-dead soldier. He was smart. He wouldn't come parading through the neighborhood again without an endgame."

"Pretty sure the endgame is to take out Carter."

"How much juice does Carter still have?"

Foxx blew out a breath. "That's a loaded question."

"I thought the RICO stuff in the '90s took down most of the organized crime in the city."

"It definitely did some damage and did a lot of good over-all, but it didn't stamp it all out by any means. More like reconfigured whoever was left, and Carter was smart enough or lucky enough to still be on the outside when it was over. Funny you mention that. There's rumors that the new chief is gearing up for another go."

"Really? Why?"

"C'mon, don't be naive. You know how it works. The mob, the outfit, organized crime, call it whatever you want, is nowhere near what it was 25 or 50 years ago but it still brings the headlines. Easy glory. Easy way to make political hay. These days, most of the crime and trouble is driven by street gangs and cartels. But the OC is still around. There's just more parity now.

"As for Carter specifically? Is he a national player? No, I don't think so. In New England? He's respected, if you want to call it that, by certain people, but he still doesn't have a lot of pull. Even in Massachusetts, he doesn't have a lot of juice. But in this city? Yes, he's got plenty of power. Boston gets talked about like a big city, but it really isn't. It's a fraction of the size of most major metropolises. There's money to be made, sure, but it's small potatoes compared to other places. Boston just isn't big enough for the major players to care that much. And it's way more provincial. Everyone sticks to their neighborhoods and ethnicities. It's like the friggen' Balkans."

"You always did like the colorful metaphors."

"Similes."

"What's that?"

"Similes use the word like. Metaphors are direct. Love is a battlefield."

"Not as dumb as you look."

"That's my big secret."

"So, what about Southie?"

"Southie? Carter owns Southie."

CHAPTER SEVEN

L ittle John stood back and listened to the water splashing up on the shore. Jimmy and Legs were almost done planting Barboza, but Little John knew his night was far from over. He'd let the guys go, but he needed to start working on Sullivan.

It was hard to imagine, now in the dark with the smell of the nearby oil tanks drifting on the wind, but the thin strip of sand just to the south was a moderately popular beach in the summer heat.

They were on a rocky outcrop partially covered by low brush and dotted with the stunted trees that had managed to get a foothold in the shadow of the Southeast Expressway. He supposed it was still technically Tenean Beach, but they were far from the public beach access.

It was not the first time they had visited.

"Too many goddamn roots," Legs complained. Legs was a talker. He was whippet thin and almost vibrated with nervous energy. Jimmy was built like a beer keg, if kegs had a fondness for old-fashioned pork pie hats. He was the quiet one and mostly kept his mouth shut unless he was chewing something.

"You want to put him down in the soft stuff where a kid might dig up a finger," Little John replied.

"Boss took care of that possibility," Legs said, and then they all fell silent as they remembered the scene in the basement.

Little John had no illusions about his job and the violence it often entailed. He didn't exactly enjoy it. He wouldn't go that far. He simply did it. None of it affected him. Give him a job and he would get it done. He was a pragmatist.

He knew he was missing something in his brain that others had but what was he going to do about it? He often felt like he was observing life rather than actually living it. Carter? Carter was something else. A psychopath? A sociopath? Little John didn't know the technical term, but he knew Carter was missing all sorts of pieces. Carter liked a good murder.

After he'd gotten the phone call from Old Sean about Sullivan and the fires, Carter had lost himself. That's how Little John had come to think of those times when Carter became more animal than man. Most of the time, Carter was good at keeping the mask on and bullying or charming his way through the day. When something went wrong or he was provoked, the mask fell away like a snake shedding its skin.

Carter had taken a pair of pliers and pulled all the teeth out of Barboza's head and then used his cigar clipper to wrench all the guy's fingers off at the knuckles. At some point, Barboza had died. Little John had seen Carter's face and, even hopped up on whatever drugs he was taking, he could tell Carter was enjoying himself.

Little John wasn't scared of Carter, not exactly, but he knew normals would be. Normal people could probably smell the scent of crazy on Carter. It was the first time Legs and

Johnny had really seen Carter go off his rocker. It made an impression. You no longer wondered why or how he'd risen to the top.

"So, what's the deal with this Michael Sullivan?" Legs asked when he'd found his voice again.

Little John sometimes forgot that not everyone knew the history. Legs and Jimmy were young and were transplants from Philly.

"He worked for Carter back in the day."

"Doing what?"

"Heists and hijacks mostly. Anything with logistics. Sullivan was good with a plan. Give him a target and some time and he'd get it done."

"What happened? He get greedy?"

"No, he got allusions of a different life. Met a girl, wanted to get out, go straight. Thought ratting out the boss to the Feds was the best way to do it."

Legs whistled. "Not too smart for a smart guy."

Little John didn't want to mention it might have been a little more complicated than that. Better to keep things simple for Jimmy. "No. Never a good idea."

"So, why's he still walking around?"

"We took a shot and missed. Bad luck. Got his family instead. " Little John looked out into the blackness. "Tried another time. Got his brother. Man's a survivor."

Little John could see Jimmy shake his head in the dark.

Legs said, "So now he's back. And he's motivated."

"You could say that."

Forty minutes later, they managed to get the plastic wrapped Barboza into the hole and had it covered up again. Back in Southie, he cut Jimmy and Legs loose for the night and then started hunting for Sullivan.

He drove north out of Southie. He knew the man probably still had friends in the neighborhood who might help,
but it was simply too small to hide in. It would be suicide.
Even the sidewalks had eyes in Southie. He'd have to hole up
somewhere else. That was fine. It might take a little longer,
but they would find him. Carter had friends throughout the
city.

He glanced at the glowing clock of the Custom House
Tower as he drove through the empty streets. Nearly four
a.m., no longer late, it was now officially early, at least for
normals. Most of Carter's properties were the type that trans-
acted the majority of their business between midnight and
dawn. The early hour wouldn't change Little John's approach.

He continued through Boston's Financial District and
over the bridge into Charlestown. Just past the Navy Yard,
he pulled in diagonally next to the curb in a loading zone in
front of Cash, Carry and Convenience. It was one of the
oldest businesses that Carter ran. It was also probably the
most legitimate, other than the underground numbers
racket and small book it ran. Marty Duran paid a small
percentage to Carter every other week and was largely left
alone. The little convenience store was like a rent-controlled
apartment.

Little John went inside and found Marty's son, Dave,
behind the counter. The place was open twenty-four hours
and made most of its legit profit money cashing payday
checks, selling cigarettes, stale pastries, and single cans of
beer. It was empty of customers now. Dave was watching the
Keno game on the television mounted up in the corner. A
stack of old tickets was by his elbow. He didn't look up as
Little John's shadow fell across the counter. He must have
pegged him on the security camera.

"Hey, LJ. What are you doing here?"

Dave's topics of conversation were limited to Keno,

scratch tickets, buffets, and tits. Little John skipped the small talk.

"You remember Michael Sullivan? Part of Carter's crew a few years back."

Dave stood up and brushed some crumbs off his chest. "Sure, I remember him, I guess. Didn't really know him. He was younger than me. I knew him enough to nod at him if I saw him in the neighborhood. Not enough to stop and chat."

"He's back in town." Little John slid a fifty across the scarred counter. "If you're the first to call, there's more."

"Guy must be a sucker for punishment."

"Don't talk to him. Don't try anything. Just call me. Got it?"

"Sure, sure."

Little John left and drove to a hair and nails place nearby on North Street. Salons were great fronts for laundering money. Carter probably owned a dozen or more. This one was closed, but he knew Kim lived in a small apartment in the back. He knocked on the back door until she answered. He told her the same thing he told Dave.

He stopped at three more places in Charlestown, then drove north on Route 1. Carter's influence waned quickly outside Southie, the city proper, and Charlestown but money still talked. He made a quick stop at an all-night copy shop and had some business cards made up with a phone number on it, then had a stack of copies made of Sullivan's face. It wasn't a great photo, but it would give him something to leave behind.

He pulled into any motel or low-end dive that caught his eye. He doubted Sullivan would try checking into any chain hotel. Too many ID and credit card requirements. Better to stick to places that would take cash.

He repeated his story each time, left a card and a face, and spread around Carter's cash.

He turned back around when he hit the town of Lynn. Rush hour was well underway at this point and it took Little John over an hour to fight his way back into the city. He made a stop at the big newsstand inside South Station.

"You have any papers from Chicago?" he asked the woman behind the counter.

"Just the Tribune. We get it a day old. On the end." She pointed to a rack off to the left. "New ones come in the mail around noon."

Little John found the Chicago Tribune along with various papers from LA, New York, and Washington. He picked it up and walked back to the register. "You have any of the older editions? Past few days?"

"Maybe. We bind up the old ones weekly for recycling, but it probably hasn't been picked up yet. Hold on a second." She rang up another customer than disappeared around a half wall at the back.

She reappeared two minutes later with three more papers from Chicago.

"All I can find."

"I'll take 'em."

He paid for the papers, then drove the rest of the way back to Southie to a diner near his apartment. He ordered eggs, bacon, and pancakes, then read through the stack. He ordered more coffee. Caffeine never had much effect on him; he just liked the taste. He read the front and the metro sections of each edition, front to back, but found nothing on the bank robbery or Frankie's death. The story was ice cold. Cold and dead like his old partner. It wouldn't be solved but maybe he could balance the scales a little before it was all over.

He paid, left the papers, and drove home to catch a little sleep.

Later, he'd check if any of his hooks had a fish.

CHAPTER EIGHT

Max opened his eyes and looked at a coffee-colored water stain that vaguely looked like the state of California. He turned his head left and saw brown paneling that dated from at least the '70s. He looked the other way and saw an empty twin bed, a small circular table, one chair, a battered AC/heater combo unit, and some ugly orange tartan curtains. It didn't take a genius to make it all add up to a cheap motel room. Max was something of an expert in these types of rooms.

He slowly rolled himself up to a sitting position. His stomach lurched unpleasantly, and he felt a pulsing beat behind his eyes that caused the edges of the room to shimmer. He was still wearing the same clothes from yesterday, down to his boots. Everything smelled strongly of smoke and burnt wire. The clothes would have to go.

He peeled off his shirt and went into the bathroom. He took a long, lukewarm shower, the hottest he could get it, and was surprised to find only superficial injuries. A couple of scrapes, a few bruises, probably from the bar fight, but nothing on the outside that wouldn't loosen up or heal in a few days.

The inside was a different story. Max's throat and chest felt like he'd been gargling sandpaper and glass. Each breath felt like he was scraping oxygen out of the bottom of a jar with a rusty knife. The tepid steam from the shower had loosened things up a little in his chest, and Max coughed up some black wads of mucus that he was happy to see disappear down the drain before he could contemplate them further.

He found his travel bag at the foot of the bed. He changed into a fresh T-shirt and jeans that didn't smell like he'd slept on the grates of a BBQ grill and went outside.

The sudden burst of sunlight almost made him stagger. He held up a hand to shield his eyes and groaned. Kyle glanced over and indicated a takeout coffee sitting on the railing. He was sitting in the chair that matched the interior table, drinking his own coffee, and staring out at the landscape behind the motel. It wasn't much of a view. The room was on the second floor. Their elevated position showed a swampy marsh, clogged with lily pads and a skein of vibrant green algae on the surface, then a stand of trees, before yielding to what looked like a small, anonymous industrial park. Max could hear the insistent white noise of traffic, so they weren't far from a major road.

"Let me guess. You've already run five miles in your boots, changed the oil in the car, and cleaned the bathroom with your toothbrush."

"Correct, except I used your toothbrush."

"What time is it?"

"Almost eleven."

Late enough that news of last night would be spreading. The small-town features of Boston might make it hard to maneuver and definitely gave Max limited time to pull off his plan, but it did help in certain aspects. News and rumors didn't stay secret very long.

"The money?"

"In the closet, above the ceiling tiles."

"Alright."

Due to circumstances outside of his control, mostly Carter, Max had been forced to rob a bank in Chicago in an effort to save his brother Danny. It hadn't ended well, but Max did end up with the money.

As they'd made their way across the country toward Boston, they'd stopped and rented out safety deposit boxes at different banks. It had lightened the load, but they still had a bag of cash. Max was planning to put it to good use.

He looked left and right down the hallway. No one else was moving. He wondered if there was enough business to keep a maid busy. Kyle was the only evidence of the place not being abandoned. There were approximately twenty rooms on each floor. He could see an ice maker and an old Pepsi machine at the far end near a set of stairs leading down.

Their room was in the middle of the row. He went to the rail and glanced down. The Taurus was parked tight against the building next to the dumpster and rotting wood fence that made up the property's border. Not invisible but hard to see unless you were looking. Max could see damage to the front quarter panel on the driver's side.

"Gonna need a new ride, huh?"

"Better than the alternative."

"Good point."

He watched a car in the distance navigate the road up to one of the parking lots outside a bland tan and taupe build-ing. Max dragged the other chair out of the room and sat down.

"What happened to the girl?"

"Took her to church."

Max was getting used to extrapolating what was left unsaid from Kyle's blunt conversational skills but this one brought him up short. "Come again?"

"She barely spoke English, but she kept holding up the crucifix she had around her neck. It took a few stops, but the third church was a hit. She jumped out before the car even stopped."

That answer constituted a damn soliloquy. "What church? Do you remember?" Max asked.

"Saint something."

"Catholic church? Off Third Street?

"They all look the same to me. We didn't drive far. Near the water."

Max had never been a regular churchgoer, but the parishes were still good landmarks or a good identifier when you met up with new kids on the street.

"Maybe Saint Brigid or Saint Monica's?"

Kyle just shrugged.

The woman might not have needed medical attention, but she was probably righteously freaked out. No matter why she was there, she woke up to an inferno in what amounted to her bedroom. Max hoped she'd be alright. He wondered if he'd ever find out or if she'd be another ghost joining his dreams. He hoped not. It was getting crowded in his head. He dropped it for now. He'd find out soon enough.

"Where are we?"

"Don't know. South of the city. Got off the highway, took a few turns, found this place. Dragged your ass upstairs. Figured it would hold for one night."

"If it's got coffee, it can't be all bad. Food?"

"Diner across the street."

The address on the plastic-covered menu the waitress

dropped on the table told Max they'd ended up in Quincy. Max knew it was about a half-hour south of Boston. Far enough that he could relax and eat breakfast, at least.

Sunny's was a narrow place built mostly for singles. Commuters driving to work or delivery guys looking for a quick bite. The right side was a counter jammed with mismatched stools. A door at the far end led to the kitchen in the back. Two four tops were opposite the counter. At this time of day, it was empty save for the waitress and a cook. Kyle and Max were seated at the table farthest from the door, closest to the kitchen.

The food came quickly; the cook knew his way around a griddle. Swallowing was painful, but it couldn't distract Max from the scrambled eggs, light buttery pancakes, or crispy bacon. Max had done a spell working as a short order cook. This was good.

He passed on more coffee. The cup Kyle had brought had cooled and was manageable going down. He definitely craved more caffeine, but he didn't think fresh, scalding hot coffee would help his throat. He wasn't a total masochist. When he finished the last bacon strip, he pushed his plate back. His stomach now full, he definitely felt better than when he woke up. After years of eating cold, powdered eggs in prison, he would never take a hot breakfast for granted again.

Kyle took a sip of coffee and asked, "What's next?"

"I figured I'd do what I always do. I'll get a stick and poke it into a hole. See what happens." Max wiped his mouth with a paper napkin. "No good? It's worked pretty well in the past." He couldn't goad Kyle into a response. Kyle took another sip of coffee. "Fine. The first part was to let him know I was back. We did that last night. Word will be getting around by now. I didn't think it was going to be possible to sneak up on him. He's always been a bit paranoid, so let's use that. I doubt that's improved with age. Let's get him seeing ghosts. Let's get him off balance. Second, let's inject some emotion into it. Let's get in his personal space. Let's mess with his business. I want him thinking about me, getting angry, getting out of his routine, and eventually slipping up. He does that and we have our opening. We just need to be ready."

"Safer to set up somewhere and pop him from half a mile."

"I don't want to take him out from some rooftop. Or shoot him in the back. Or blow him up by remote control. This is personal. It has been from the very beginning. I want him to know it's me and I want him to see it coming."

"Dangerous way to operate."

"Yes. I won't argue that. You can bail if you think my emotions are clouding things. I know you don't have the same stakes."

"I'm in until it's done."

Max nodded. "We keep it controlled. We push him, but we do it methodically. We harass. We needle. We jab. We hit his rackets, hit his stores, take his money, take his product. Mess with all of it until he snaps. Then we take him."

"What's first?"

"First, we just watch. Then, maybe we talk to a guy. Finally, we get some guns."

CHAPTER NINE

The place was a rundown rat trap. He could occasionally hear something moving in the darker corners. Max wouldn't be surprised if Carter owned this building, too. Being back in the neighborhood, he could almost feel the man's tentacles writhing and twisting through each street.

They were up on the third floor of the building across the street from Clover Cleaners, the dry cleaners and front that Carter used as an office. Earlier, they'd driven by Carter's house, as well, but agreed the dry cleaners offered better cover and potentially more useful intel on Carter's day-to-day business.

The ground floor was a Chinese takeout place; the smell of vegetable oil, ginger, and soy sauce permeated the entire building. The second and third floors were mostly gutted, but unfinished apartments. Rough boards and plywood framing filled the space, but it was clear from the collected garbage that the space was now mostly used for addicts and the homeless. The cheap door at the back that they entered through wasn't much of a deterrent. Max guessed the developer had gone bankrupt or ended up in court. Either way, the place was empty now and the second-floor window gave them an unobstructed view of the comings and goings at Clover Cleaners across the street.

So far, however, there hadn't been much to see. People, very normal-looking people, came in and dropped off or picked up various shirts, pants, and blouses. It looked like a mildly successful business on a high traffic street in a working-class neighborhood. The only thing that smelled a little off was the squat guy sitting just inside the door wearing a pork pie hat and reading The Herald. You didn't typically find him at most dry cleaners. Not the legitimate ones.

They passed an uneventful morning, switching places each hour. The Chinese place opened for business at eleven and the greasy smell of noodles and cheap chicken grew even stronger. They had stopped at a Walmart on their way into the city and bought a few supplies: a digital camera with a decent kit lens, a couple of cheap disposable phones, a thermos-sized bottle of aspirin for his aching throat, a case of water, some jerky, and a black canvas backpack. Everything but the water went into the backpack. So far, other than a few test shots of Pork Pie, the camera remained on the floor and the jerky was opened. But it was early.

At one point, Kyle had quietly disappeared and then reappeared carrying two lawn chairs, coffees, and a newspaper. Max didn't ask. He set up the chair and resumed watching. The coffee irritated his throat like he knew it would, but it perked him up. It was an ugly street and boring work. The pain from the coffee was a fair tradeoff.

They couldn't see into the back of the store, just the front counter, part of the rotating garment conveyors, and the side profile of the man in the hat. They hadn't seen Carter, but the store butted up close to the residential buildings behind it. There was a narrow alley just big enough to slide a car through, but they could see both ends of the alley from their vantage point on the second floor and no one had arrived or left. Kyle had walked past earlier and said there was a black Lincoln parked near the rear door. Max was confident Carter was inside.

Things picked up in the afternoon. More foot traffic started entering the store. Guys carrying Clover garment bags that didn't look like they were carrying just shirts. Pork Pie had moved behind the counter, joining the woman who worked the garment belt and the register.

As they watched the fifth guy enter and drop his bag on the counter and then continue out of sight down a hallway, Max said, "Why go and collect your extortion? Waste of gas. Make them come to you." Max shook his head. "The man always did have a good head for business. For being a well-adjusted human? No. For pinching pennies. Definitely."

They changed positions at the window. The shadows switched sides of the street. It was getting close to closing time for the dry cleaners. Max tried unsuccessfully to get comfortable in the lawn chair. He watched as a plain white panel truck passed by and then circled the block before parking illegally at one end of the alley. A man got out and walked toward the front of the cleaners. Pork Pie moved quickly out onto the sidewalk to meet him. Max couldn't hear the conversation with the building's window closed, but it didn't appear friendly.

"Might have something here," Max said. Kyle moved to the window. "Guy in the red shirt talking to Pork Pie got out of that unmarked truck on the corner."

"Pork Pie looks pissed."

"Yup. Someone screwed up," Max replied.

With a two-handed gesticulation that might have conveyed annoyance or frustration, the guy turned around and headed back to the truck.

"Follow it?" Kyle said.

"Yeah. Might as well. It's the most interesting thing to happen all day. Might be cleaning supplies. Might also be heroin. Take one of the phones. I'll stay here."

Kyle left and a minute later Max watched the beat-up Taurus pass in front of the window and turn left to follow the truck. The car still ran fine. It was a tank, but they'd need to swap it out soon. It was too memorable with the damage to the front.

Max picked up the newspaper and flipped through the tabloid, looking to see if the late-night fires made the paper. He found it on page five, a short piece in the left-hand corner. His eyes scanned the story and then slid to the accompanying photo. Fire stories always had photos, he thought. Then he stopped. His heart kicked in his chest. It was like looking at a ghost. She looked so much like Cindy. Max felt a catch in his throat. He took a deep breath. Even at a distance and in low light, Max knew it was Colleen. What was she doing there? He read the caption, but it was generic copy about the buildings and the incident and didn't give any names or descriptions of the people pictured.

Colleen was six years younger than Cindy and hadn't been around much when Max and Cindy were together. First, busy with the end of high school, and then off at college. He hadn't seen her since the funeral and then the trial. The only time she'd looked at him was to try to spit on him as they led him through court the last time. He didn't blame her for it. He thought much worse of himself.

Twenty minutes later, the phone vibrated next to his folding chair.

"Didn't go far. Couple of miles, maybe. Back toward the city. Followed it down to the water. Someone was waiting.

The truck pulled into a building. Looks like a warehouse in a shipping yard. Maybe an old dry dock."

Max thought back to another time with Carter that had brought him to the docks. "I'm pretty sure I know where you are."

"I'm on the street, but I'm going to have to move soon. Not a lot of traffic or civilian cars down here at this time of day."

"Stay on it as long as you can."

"Will do." Kyle hung up.

Max wasn't sure what it was, but he'd take all the info he could get. Given what they'd seen today, he was sure Carter was still in the extortion racket, but he wasn't sure trying to disrupt that business was the best play. It would take a lot of time and effort to make an impact. They could hit it quick and fast to annoy him and get the whispers going on the street, but, if Max wanted to really get up Carter's nose, he knew he needed something bigger. Maybe this truck could do that.

Max's best guess would be the truck was carrying drugs of some kind. That would explain some of Pork Pie's reaction. No one got that fired up about dry cleaning supplies. He was sure Carter would have control of any drugs in Southie. No way he'd let someone else run product through his neighborhood. But if the truck was a dead end? He had to find out what else Carter had going on. Max knew Carter thought of himself as a businessman, a man of finance, and those were some of the biggest criminals out there. Carter would need other schemes to delude himself out of thinking of himself as nothing but a common criminal. Max just needed a way in. For now, all he could do was watch.

Day was bleeding into night. The streetlights would pop on soon. Max would have to be careful he wasn't caught in the window. The dry cleaners had closed. A small security light was on near the door, but the rest of the place was in shadows. The chair was empty. Pork Pie was gone. Maybe he'd gone to get dinner. Max thought that sounded like a good idea. Just not Chinese food. He thought it might be a while before he ate any of that again.

The phone rang again. "Got movement. Truck is pulling out again."

"Any chance of getting in the building for a peek?"

"No easy windows. I'd be a little blind."

Max caught movement down the street to the left. The black Lincoln pulled out and turned right. Carter punching the clock for the day.

"I've got movement on my end, too. Looks like Carter is done for the day. At least at the dry cleaners."

"Truck or Carter?"

"Stick with the truck. I know where Carter lives. We can pick him up later and we can always come back to the warehouse. Whatever is inside, they might move it quickly or be storing it there. A chance we'll have to take. But figuring out where the truck came from might be a shortcut to an answer."

"On it." Kyle disconnected.

Max's stomach reminded him again that he hadn't eaten anything but jerky since the eggs and pancakes at Sunny's that morning. He looked across the street. All quiet and likely to remain that way. Without the car, Max was stuck. He could take a bus or taxi over to Carter's house and hope to find a spot there to take up the watch and try to get more details on his operation, but that would leave him awfully exposed in unfriendly territory. He knew Carter had eyes on the street, especially in Southie. It wouldn't take long for someone to sell him out. He'd be disappointed if it did.

He could see a sign for a pizza place just a block south. Better and smarter to get some food and continue to hole up here until Kyle returned. He took four more aspirin for his aching chest and throat. He put the camera and phone in the backpack. No one had bothered them during the day, but Max wasn't sure if squatters might show up later. Better to take the bag than risk having it stolen.

He went down the backstairs and out into the alley, trying to decide which topping would be easier on his throat, mushroom or pepperoni. The blow caught him on the shoulder and neck and knocked him sideways into the restaurant's dumpster.

Max went to a knee. His vision blurred, but he could hear the person shuffling closer for another strike. He instinctively raised an arm and a moment later felt an electric jolt run up his wrist to his elbow followed by a splintering crack. Max thought it was the sound of his arm breaking but it wasn't. The piece of wood that someone was attempting to bludgeon him with had broken in half.

"Shit," he heard someone say.

Max took the opening. Using the sound of the voice to get a sense of where the guy was, he pivoted and swung the backpack up as he stood. The digital camera was small and cheap, but with the lens it had some weight. Max whipped it in an upward arc as hard as he could. The bag hit the guy's arm and clipped his nose. His pork pie hat flew off his head and skittered under the dumpster.

It wasn't a knockout shot, but it stunned Pork Pie. "Fuck," he said as he stumbled back and brought his hands up to his nose. "I think you broke my fuckin' nose."

Max wasn't going to waste time chatting with the guy. He pressed his slight advantage and rushed Pork Pie, wrapping him up around the middle and driving him into the brick wall of the Chinese restaurant. He felt the air go out of the man's chest with a grunt. Pork Pie brought his hands down in a hammer fist to Max's back. Max ignored it, dragged Pork Pie backward and drove him forward into the wall again. Max heard the backdoor to the restaurant open and then quickly bang closed again. Someone would call the cops soon. Or maybe not. In this neighborhood, you couldn't be sure. Either way, with his litany of existing injuries, Max was tiring. He couldn't keep this up. It had to end.

He could feel Pork Pie scrabbling now, reaching for something in his coat pocket. Probably a gun or a knife. Max dragged him back, but instead of driving him forward into the wall again, he hooked a foot behind Pork Pie's ankle and pushed. Pork Pie stumbled back, tripped on Max's foot, and fell. He hit the brick wall with the back of his head, the impact making the soft cracking sound of a splitting melon. His eyes fluttered and shut before he had slid all the way to the ground.

Max leaned over and checked Pork Pie's pulse. It was steady. He'd have a major headache, maybe a concussion, but otherwise be fine. Max reached into the man's jacket pocket and pulled out a gun. Why go for him with a piece of scrap wood rather than the gun? The only reason Max could figure was that he wanted some glory. Or he had no idea who Max was. He'd spotted someone watching the dry cleaners and thought he'd handle it. Maybe shine up his rep with Carter.

The pressing question now was what to do with him? It would be good to get him somewhere quiet and get some information about Carter's operations. That might be an even better shortcut than the truck and much better than spending another day watching the cleaners, but Max didn't have a car to transport him or anything to bind him with. In the end, the sirens gave him his answer. He grabbed the backpack and the gun, hoping the camera wasn't busted and walked out of the alley, careful to keep the buildings between himself and the approaching sirens. Pork Pie was on his own.

CHAPTER TEN

The nurse came out of the room and bent to lock the door.

"You can leave it open. I'm going to sit with him for a while."

She started. "Sorry, Mr. Carter I didn't hear you." She reversed the key in the door and gently pushed it open.

She wore a light teal scrub top over jeans. She was probably close to thirty, with coffee-colored skin. She didn't wear makeup. Her hair was pulled back in a tight knot at the nape of her neck. Even in work clothes, she was attractive, and Carter felt a pull to try to do something about it but checked himself. He'd learned that home nurses had a thankless job and good ones were hard to find. This woman had been around for at least three months. That was an eternity in dealing with Daniel. He must like her. Keeping her around was worth keeping his libido in check.

She stepped back to let him go through the door and he could smell the slight scent of jasmine mixing with the harsher smell of antibacterial soap on her skin.

"Have a good night, Mr. Carter."

"You, too."

He couldn't remember her name, despite seeing her almost every day, and he felt an unexpected blush of shame as she turned and walked down the hall to whatever else her life contained.

What the hell was wrong with him? He physically shook his head as if he could shake off the feeling. Visiting Daniel always made him feel off-kilter, but he did it because he felt even more guilt over keeping his friend locked up in this room.

It had started with little things. Daniel would forget to make a pickup or try to make the pickup on the wrong day, getting the date confused. He would misplace keys or forget when or where he was meeting someone. It was easy to shrug off at first. The Ghost had been his right hand for so long it was easy to make excuses that he would never make for others. It was just part of getting older. You get a little more forgetful. Nothing to worry about.

Until he killed the wrong guy.

By that point, things had been going downhill for a while, but Carter didn't want to see it. He'd taken to letting Little John deal with Daniel as much as possible, but when he had killed the wrong Angello brother, he knew he couldn't avoid it any longer.

There were four Angello brothers. Three of them were tied up with what little of the La Cosa Nostra still operated out of Prince Street in the North End. They'd come to Carter and borrowed money, hoping to break out a little on their own. They decided later they didn't like the terms of the loan. After repeated warnings, they still weren't convinced. Clipping any of the three would have made the point. You'd think the odds were in Daniel's favor to deliver the right message. Instead, he'd killed the one brother that was a kindergarten teacher and community activist. Carter had barely avoided a war with the Italians and getting squeezed by the cops. He'd had to forgive the loan and call in a lot of favors to stay out of prison.

He'd also pulled The Ghost off the streets. Daniel had seemed just as relieved as Carter. He couldn't figure out what was going on inside his head either. They'd gone to all the top doctors at Mass General and beyond, even flying out to the Mayo Clinic. CT scans, MRIs, cognitive tests, neuro-psychobabble. It all added up to early onset dementia. No reason. No cure.

That was five years ago. Anyone else but Daniel and Carter would have had them taken out and put down. That was the safest play. Daniel had been his closest ally and confidant for so long that everything Carter knew, Daniel did too. If Daniel started talking to the wrong people, he could take down Carter and his whole operation with just a few sentences. Yes, the safest play, really the most empathetic thing to do was put a bullet in that damaged brain and be done with it. But he found he couldn't do it. And he couldn't let anyone else do it either. It was a weakness but something he'd come to accept. Some small sign that he was still human.

So, he took The Ghost off the street and kept him locked up in a room on the second floor of his house. Only a few people in Carter's organization knew The Ghost was still alive. As far as the rest knew, the man who had long haunted the Boston streets really had become a ghost. That was fine with Carter.

Carter stepped into the room now. The smell of the nurse's jasmine faded away and was replaced with the strong smell of disinfectant, stale air, and body odor. The once legendary hitman sat in a padded reclining chair with a blanket wrapped around his thin legs. The television was on but muted. The Ghost was asleep. His breath rattled slightly in his chest.

The room was large and comfortable. Hell, if he was going to put Daniel in a prison cell, he might as well make it a nice one. There was a big screen television on one wall with two reclining chairs, making a small space to the right. In the middle was the treadmill, massage table, and exercise equipment for the physical therapy sessions. On the far side was a large bed with another, smaller, television positioned at its foot. An en suite bathroom was tucked into a corner.

Recently, Daniel seemed to have moved into a new phase of this strange and untreatable disease. Before it was mostly about memory loss, poor judgment, and general confusion about time and place. Recently, his personality appeared to have shifted. He'd always been very level-headed, displaying an equanimity that left many wondering if he was more machine than man. In the last month, he'd begun to display disturbing mood swings. Nothing violent yet, but Carter could sense that was coming. He'd already had some complaints from the nurses. What would he do then? If he couldn't put down an old reliable dog, would he be able to do it when it had gone rabid? He wasn't sure he wanted to know the answer.

He carried his laptop over and sat in the other chair. The Ghost didn't stir as he sat, and he was relieved, then immediately felt his cheeks burn with embarrassment, even in the otherwise empty room. Why was he doing all this? What was he hoping to accomplish? He didn't know. He only knew he felt compelled to do it and would keep doing it as long as it took to reach some sort of conclusion. He hated these mixed emotions. He liked things in black and white. He might keep Daniel alive up here, but he would never let anyone else know what it really cost him.

He opened his laptop, determined to push his mind back from that emotional black hole. He might be getting older, but he was careful to keep up to date on technology. It wasn't just vanity either. It was about adapting with the times. To succeed, it wasn't enough anymore to keep the old way going. Prostitution, drugs, loan sharking? Increasingly dangerous and Carter was happy to cede those to the street gangs. Globalization, cybercrime, prescription pills, and other new industries were the future. He was a venture capitalist and cybercrimes, like hijacking, ransomware, phishing, and spamming, were lucrative and low risk, at least for him, if not the guys doing the hacking.

He had one guy, Jackson Mitchell, a graduate student at MIT, who had the unfortunate bad habit of being terrible at picking against the spread and had racked up a nice debt that he was now working off for Carter with his computer skills. He'd set up Carter's current laptop and network security. He was the one who told him if he truly wanted security for his spreadsheets, he needed to get off any network and remove any chance of someone putting it on a network. The kid knew jack shit about gambling, but Carter trusted he knew about computers. He knew they didn't let dummies into MIT.

Carter had sent Little John over to the campus earlier in the day for a visit. It was always good to send a personal reminder. Sometimes, these guys spent so much time with machines that they forgot the damage an actual person can do. So far, the money they'd spread around Route 1 motels and dive bars hadn't yielded anything on where Sullivan was holing up. It hadn't even been twenty-four hours yet, but Carter hated waiting. He had another idea. He'd sent Little John to ask Mitchell to check out the traffic cameras around the fires and the ones from the salon to figure out what Sullivan was driving. Little John had stressed to Mitchell that it was important. Carter didn't ask what that meant exactly. How the man carried out his job was his business. Whatever it was, it had worked. There was an email in his inbox with three attachments. The message was brief: "This is the only car that passes all three cameras during the requested times."

He opened the first one. It appeared to be from a red-light camera. Typically, it would only take a photo if it sensed a car going through against the light, but it also kept a forty-eight hour record for emergencies. That was what Mitchell had pulled. Carter watched. It was a six-second clip. At first, it was just headlights, but as the car went under the light you could make out more details. Carter watched it twice. It was an older Ford sedan. The exact details were difficult to see, but the license plate was clear. Carter ran it back one more time, slowly advancing it frame by frame. Was there another person in the passenger seat? The angle and the poor resolution made it difficult to see. Could Sullivan be getting help?

He opened the next clip. It was another traffic cam and added little to what he already knew, but the third clip was more interesting. It looked like it was from the salon's own surveillance system. The two cameras had been destroyed in the fire but uploaded to a remote server via wi-fi every half-hour. Carter wouldn't be telling the police that fact, but he'd certainly take advantage of any useful footage for himself.

Unfortunately, it looked like the camera in front of the shop hadn't uploaded before it was destroyed. This last clip only showed the back alley and part of the side of the building. At first, Carter wasn't sure why Mitchell had pulled it, but he kept watching. Carter watched as smoke and fire slowly broke through the tar paper roof. Eventually, he watched the lower corner of the building explode outward and the front portion of the old Ford poke through from the brick rubble. Sullivan had apparently rammed the building for some reason. Carter frowned. Why? A minute later, the car backed out of the frame and disappeared. The clip went to black. An older model Ford, probably a Taurus, Carter thought, with significant damage to the front panel. They'd have to switch vehicles soon but if they were still driving around it couldn't be hard to find.

If they could pinpoint the car, he could get some of the cops on his payroll to get the word out and really put Sullivan's balls in a vice. With the automatic plate readers and cameras dotting the city, Carter didn't think it would take long to find him. He was feeling better already. Carter knew how to handle a cornered rat.

CHAPTER ELEVEN

Max decided to keep walking out of Southie. He knew he could be waiting a long time for Kyle to return and he thought South Station, the city's train and bus depot, would give him enough cover to loiter around without drawing attention to himself. It was open late and there would be plenty of people.

He knew there was some risk that he'd be spotted as he walked. Southie was Carter's home turf and it was a small, tight-knit community with a long memory. Gentrification and new money were slowly changing it, Max only had to glance around at the renovated homes and trendy shops, but he was sure plenty of people would remember him. But would they recognize him? He'd been away for a long time and his face had been changed. Not a lot, the government's dime only went so far, but maybe enough.

One police car passed him going the opposite direction, with lights flashing, he kept his eyes forward and kept walking. It didn't slow and soon the cacophony of its siren faded into the rest of the city noise.

He weaved his way north through the neighborhood's

smaller side streets. It would have been faster to just head up the wider thoroughfare of West Broadway but that would have put more eyes on him and, while he thought the possibility of being spotted was low, why increase the chances at all? He took his time. There was no rush. He circled the block a couple times to see if anyone was tailing him. He thought Pork Pie acted alone, but he could be wrong. He rubbed his neck and moved his arm. It felt okay, but he knew that was still mostly from the adrenaline of the experience. It would be sore tomorrow.

"Add it to the list," he mumbled.

He'd been lucky it hadn't been worse. And that Pork Pie was an idiot. Most importantly, a short idiot. If he'd been taller or had better aim with that two by four, it would have been lights out, game over. He knew his luck wouldn't hold forever.

When he reached A Street, the unofficial border of Southie, he turned right. Half a mile later, he passed the convention center and figured he was mostly in the clear. Ten minutes after that, he crossed over the channel and walked into the bustle of South Station.

The building was a shell of its former self when rail travel ruled the world, but the structure had somehow avoided total demolition and still retained a few nice neoclassical touches like the high windows and three-door arched entryways.

Max walked through the lobby and went to the right toward the concessions to finally get that pizza. He took the two slices and soda up to the second level to an empty table. He spent the next two hours eating and re-reading the newspaper Kyle had bought earlier in the day. He also double-checked that the digital camera still worked after using it as a weapon. It did.

At eight o'clock the phone buzzed in his pocket.

"I'm on 91. Still going north. Just passed a place called Fairlee."

Max knew 91 straddled the border between Vermont and New Hampshire. "You thinking Canada?"

"Yes."

"Me, too. Probably Montreal."

"You want me to come back?"

"Would be interesting to know exactly where and who, but I'm not sure it matters. Might be enough just to know it's coming from Canada for now. Why don't you turn around? Some things have happened down here." Max filled him in on the altercation with Pork Pie and then disconnected.

He glanced down at the newspaper. He'd left it open to the page about the fires that showed Colleen Adams. The burner phones they'd bought were simple and didn't include a data plan so he couldn't look her up on the internet. He dialed information and asked for the number for the state police. He was connected to the general headquarters and then bounced to the Boston barracks before finally landing at the detective unit and getting her voicemail. He hung up without leaving a message. He wasn't sure why he'd called. He saved her number in his phone.

He glanced up and was surprised to find that most of the upper concourse had emptied out while he'd been talking to Kyle and then tracking down Colleen's number. He was the only one still sitting at a table. As he gathered up his trash and put the newspaper back in his backpack, three people came up the far set of stairs, two men trailed by a woman. One man glanced at a sheet of paper in his hand before folding it up and putting it in his pocket. They continued toward Max's table. He looked over his shoulder at the nearest set of stairs. A third man was standing on the top step. He was leaning against the wall with his hands in his pockets. He grinned at Max, showing an array of gray and yellow teeth. Max put the tray and backpack down and waited for the first group to approach.

The taller of the two men took the lead as they neared his table. The other man drifted to the right. The woman hung back a few steps. Up close, they might have been homeless or living rough. The whole group looked like they could use a shower and some clean clothes. Even with the ill-fitting and baggy clothes, Max could tell the first guy had some muscle or bulk to throw around.

"My friends and I could use some food. Maybe you could help us out?"

Max stayed silent, looking them over some more. They might be wearing old, dirty clothes but they didn't look hungry. Together, at least, they were likely used to getting what they wanted. Or, more likely, taking what they wanted. Max checked the third guy on the stairs. He hadn't moved. The woman was constantly looking around. She was the lookout. There were Amtrak cops and other law enforcement always drifting through the station. Train depots were still high-risk targets. Whatever they planned had to be quick, fast, and quiet.

"Sure," Max said and pulled out his wallet. He held out a twenty. He saw the flicker of surprise pass over the guy's face. Either they usually didn't get any money so easily or they usually didn't get this much money. He took the bill and put it in his pocket.

"You got that much to spare, maybe you got more?"

"I think that's enough for the four of you to get some food downstairs."

"Maybe we want dessert, too." The man smiled as he said it and Max noticed his teeth weren't much better than his buddy's.

"Sorry, friend, can't help you out with that."

"What if we just take it?"

Max shifted slightly. He was standing between two tables with his back now to the wall. He could see the guy on the stairs along with the other three.

"I guess you could try."

He checked the faces of the other two men. They still hadn't spoken. He'd given them some money. Now, he had the confidence to stand up to them. Were they willing to push it further?

"You like your odds? Four against one?"

"I gave you some money. Even a generous amount. So, I guess it's more the principle."

The first man started forward. Max watched the guy on the stairs start to move, too. He was relieved to see that his hands were empty when he took them out of his pockets. A knife would have escalated things. Max guessed they didn't want to risk being caught with weapons. Or maybe they didn't think they would need them to mug a few hapless commuters.

The third guy fell in line between the first two. The woman stayed in place, keeping watch. So, it wasn't four against one. It was really three against one and Max knew even that was false odds. He had the wall at his back and the tables on his flanks. He wasn't going to move so they'd have to come to him one at a time.

The first guy waded in and started throwing haymakers. It was clear he wasn't an experienced fighter and probably relied on his size and aggression to get what he wanted. He would have starved if he had to rely on his fists. Max ducked two wild punches and then brought his arm up, hand flat and stiff. It looked as awkward as the guy's haymakers, but it was much more controlled and effective. One of his cellmates at Lewisburg had been big into MMA. You couldn't have classes or spar in a prison yard for obvious reasons, but he'd shown Max a few things during their downtime in the cells.

The guy staggered back, clutching his neck, his face quickly turning a deep red. Max grabbed him by his sweatshirt and pushed him back into the second guy, the one that had been standing on the stairs. Max kept one hand on the sweatshirt and grabbed the greasy guy's hair and swung his head back. He heard a satisfying crunch as the first guy's head collided with the second guy's face. Broken nose and some chipped teeth. Honestly, it might be an improvement. He kept pushing the first guy backward until the two of them went down in a heap. Max stepped over them and squared up to the third guy. He glanced down at his two friends and raised his hands, palms out, in surrender. He and the woman retreated to the far stairs. Max let them go.

Max grabbed his backpack off the table and returned to the two injured men. They were still tangled up, both moaning in pain. Max reached into the first guy's pocket and took his money back. A folded sheet of paper fell out. Max picked it up and unfolded it. Max was surprised to see his own face staring back at him.

"Where did you get this?" Max asked, but the man was too distracted trying to breathe to answer him. Max looked around. He couldn't stay here. It wouldn't be long before someone came up and found these guys. He couldn't be here for that. He realized he knew the answer anyway. It was Little John. He was out hunting, and he had a lot of help.

Max kept the paper and took the stairs the rest of the way down. He ducked out a side door onto Atlantic Avenue and back into the Boston night.

Maybe it would be safer to just stay on the move.

CHAPTER TWELVE

I t was late when she opened the door to her townhouse in the Fens. It was always late these days when she got home. Despite moving him into her house, she wondered if she was just as guilty as all the other cops when it came to avoiding her dad.

She glanced down the hall and wasn't surprised to see a crease of light from under his door. Her dad had a stroke; it had almost paralyzed the left side of his face and his left arm, but it had done nothing to his mind. He'd been forced to retire, but he was just shy of sixty. She knew he missed the action and the challenge of being a cop. He struggled to fill his days. She knew he haunted these dark hours as much as she did.

She took off her gun and badge and put them with her keys in the drawer of the table. She sifted through the mail piled in the small bowl. Ads, circulars, and things masquerading as important documents but were really just more ads and circulars in disguise. She didn't know whether to feel relieved or depressed that the pile was so blandly innocuous. She left such a little mark on the world that she didn't get a single piece of meaningful mail. She shook her head. Christ, she must be tired, getting maudlin over junk mail.

She carried the pile into the kitchen and dumped it into the trash. She pulled a small frozen pizza out of the freezer and popped it in the toaster oven before heading back down the hall. She knocked lightly and stuck her head around the door. Her father was awake and watching the Red Sox game on television. The Globe and The Herald were separated, folded, and stacked next to his chair. He read each paper, plus the New York Times on the weekend, cover to cover. It filled up the time.

"Who's winning?"

"Tied. 4-4." The words came out slow and slightly slurred, but she'd long ago adapted to his new speech pattern and she understood easily enough.

"Who're they playing?" The game had gone to a commercial before she could see.

"Royals. In Kansas City."

That explained the quiet neighborhood. The townhouse was practically in the shadows of the old stadium. She usually could see the big stadium lights lit up. Sometimes even hear the crowd during a particularly raucous home game.

He patted the neatly made up bed with his right hand.

Her townhouse was comfortable but small. Her father's room held his bed, his chair, television, and an attached bathroom. She'd gotten lucky. She'd bought it during the housing crash. It wasn't in the best area of the city but in the ten years since her purchase, the ever-creeping gentrification of the neighborhood and the expansion of the nearby hospital had pushed values back up. Way up. She somehow now found herself living in a very desirable area.

She went and sat down on the bed. She knew what was coming. After her late night with Foxx the previous day, she'd rushed out this morning with just a quick shout to her dad. She was still sorting out her own feelings about Sullivan's reappearance. The fires had kept her distracted but didn't help clarify the bigger issues in her mind. Why was he back? How should she feel? She hadn't wanted to deal with all of that and with her dad at the same time. So, she'd bailed. She knew the papers had a small piece about the fires, despite it happening so late, but hadn't mentioned anything about Sullivan. Still, she was sure the old blue network would have worked overtime. Her dad had probably known all about it before she'd even left the house. Or even woken up.

She looked at him. Nowhere left to hide. "Yes?"

"Is it true?"

She picked at a hangnail. "The rumors are certainly real. But other than the people in that bar, no one has actually seen him. Could be bullshit."

"What do you think?"

This was always his way as a cop and as a dad. Ask questions. Poke. Prompt. When she was younger, she often thought he was less a cop and more a professor. "If it's not him, I don't see the point. Or maybe it doesn't matter."

"Why?"

"If Michael is really back or if someone is just using his name as a convenient bogeyman, they both are going after Carter."

"How do you feel about that?"

She was tired. It was late. She suddenly felt frustrated by his calm teacher routine, the need to interrogate her, even the time it took him to form the words. "How do you think I fucking feel, Dad? I'm pissed off. I'm mad. I'm confused."

He didn't react. Just took a beat and then asked, "At who?"

"Carter and Michael. The two of them. They're both responsible."

"What are you going to do about it?"

She looked him in the eye for the first time since sitting down. Her father's eyes blazed in the lamplight with a hot intensity; she recognized the feeling and felt her stomach churn.

What could she tell him when she didn't know herself? She'd been honest when she said she was confused. She was mad. She was scared. She'd worked hard to bury these feelings. She'd been young when it happened. She'd felt the rage she still saw in her father's eyes, but also crippling sadness and grief. That volatile cocktail of emotions almost swallowed her. It definitely warped her. It twisted her into someone she ultimately didn't recognize so she put it all in a box and tucked it away in the darkest corner of her mind. It was the only way she thought she might still find a way to have a life.

What would opening that box do to her now?

She stood and went to the door. What was she going to do? "I don't know."

"I think you do."

She no longer felt like eating. Even cooked, the pasty looking disc of pizza didn't look particularly appetizing. She tossed it in the trash and went to bed. As she lay in the dark, she listened to the familiar settling sounds of her house and tried to wipe her mind clean. It didn't work. Thoughts of Michael and her sister and the path her life had taken swelled in the silence.

She had almost given up on sleep when her phone rang on the nightstand. She leaned over and grabbed it. She didn't recognize the number but that didn't mean anything. She had little in the way of a personal life, so she didn't have separate work and personal phones. It could be a source, a colleague, a forgotten friend, or, most likely, a wrong number. She welcomed any distraction from her swirling mind.

"Hello?"

A moment of hesitation and she guessed it was an overseas telemarketer screwing up the time change, dialing multiple numbers, waiting for one sucker to pick up. Then a voice.

"Colleen?"

She drew in a sharp breath. She hadn't heard it in years, but she knew.

"Michael."

"Yes, I'm sorry to call so late. Did I wake you?"

She was so stunned by the call that their banal small talk didn't register. She didn't respond, momentarily lost in the sound of his voice and all the memories it dredged up. He filled the silence.

"I saw your photo in the paper. I didn't realize you became a cop."

Why was he calling? What possible reason could he have to contact her? She had made it very clear what she thought of him at the trial and that she never wanted to speak to him again. He was still talking, but she wasn't listening. She interrupted. "Why are you calling?"

"To apologize. To ask for your forgiveness."

"My forgiveness? What did you ever do to me? Why do you need my forgiveness?"

"I took away your sister."

"You killed her."

"Cindy's death is the worst thing that ever happened to me. I lost my wife and child, but I know it must have been equally hard for you."

"You don't know anything."

Like her father, he didn't rise to take the bait. After a beat, he responded, "I might not know exactly how you feel but you lost a sister, a friend, someone you loved. I know that pain. I know what it can do."

She felt her throat swell and tears prick the corners of her eyes, but then she let the anger override it. "Is that right? You can't have it both ways, Michael. You can't come back asking forgiveness with one hand and looking to get revenge with the other."

"I need to finish it."

"Well, just know you're not doing it for Cindy or Kylie. They wouldn't have wanted that. You're doing it for yourself."

"Yes, I know that."

"Good, if you know that, then you also know you aren't calling to really ask my forgiveness. Forgiveness means you've made amends and changed your behavior. You haven't done that. You're just looking to ease your own guilt."

She hung up before he could respond.

She tossed in the sheets, turning the conversation over in her mind. She knew forgiveness wasn't something you do alone. You need the cooperation of the person that had caused the pain in the first place. But could she forgive Michael when he showed no signs of changing? If she did forgive him, did she just become a doormat? Maybe. She also feared it might set her free.

CHAPTER THIRTEEN

L ittle John watched the caretaker from the kitchen window. He must be close to seventy. He could see tufts of white hair sprouting from the sides of a battered straw hat. He was tall and bony. His clothes were thin and stained, his back permanently bent like a bough after a winter covered in snow. He was hunched over, pushing a lawnmower up and down the long, orderly rows. Occasionally, he would stop the mower and wave his arms or gesture at something before shaking his head and continuing to mow.

As far as Little John could see, the man was alone amongst the headstones.

It had been three days since they'd gotten word Michael Sullivan was back and they hadn't heard a thing. Boston wasn't that big and Little John was certain they'd flush him out eventually, but Carter was not a patient man. He wasn't stupid either. He knew Sullivan had a soft sentimentality for family, even deceased family, and told Little John to find out where his sister was buried. If there was anywhere he was guaranteed to visit, it was her grave.

The caretaker's house was set off in the southeast corner

of the small cemetery, just inside the main gates. It was a white two-story cottage that reminded Little John of the rural farmhouses he'd seen driving through the Great Plains states.

He'd walked through the rooms on the second floor, two bedrooms and a bathroom. It looked like one bedroom was no longer used. He picked up a framed and faded photo from the dresser showing a man in dress blues and a petite blonde with a plain but pleasant face in a wedding dress. He checked the bathroom cabinet. Heart pills, aspirin, antacid. Nothing interesting.

The first floor had a living room to the left of the front door, a dining room, and a kitchen. There was a half bath off the kitchen. The kitchen looked like the only room that got regular use. A single plate, fork, knife, and coffee cup were drying on a towel next to the sink. He flicked up the lid on the trashcan. Coffee grinds, some scant food scraps, and three empty pint bottles of Wild Turkey.

He opened the cabinets next to the sink. Bachelor staples filled the shelves: cans of beans, vegetables, some rice. The second cabinet held more Wild Turkey. He opened the refrigerator: ground beef, hot dogs, a flank steak, a carton of milk. The freezer held a couple of ready-to-heat meals. Little John was getting the picture. Minus the alcohol, it wasn't that much different from his own place.

He slipped out the door and waited in the shade of a thin dogwood at the end of a row. He'd noticed that, in addition to the pruning and gardening tools on the man's well-worn work belt, he also carried a gun, tucked into a hip holster. He really didn't want to sneak up on this guy.

The guy eventually looked up, checking his line, and saw him standing there. He paused, studied Little John, then continued pushing the mower closer. Little John stayed where he was. He kept his hands in plain sight. He was aware of the effect he could sometimes have on people. Intended or not. Right now, he needed this guy's help, so he tried to make himself look timid and unintimidating. It wasn't an easy ask but he did his best. He even tried to smile. It felt a little strange on his face.

When the caretaker reached the end of the row, he let go of the bar and the mower's motor sputtered to a stop. He pulled off his gloves and wiped at his brows with a red bandana that he'd taken from a back pocket. "Help you?"

Up close, he didn't look too crazy. If Little John hadn't been watching from the window, he would have said the guy was eccentric. Of course, to Little John, most people seemed eccentric or weird. Weird was normal. He was okay with that. It was eccentric with a gun that had his attention. "They talk to you?"

"What's that?"

"I saw you mowing and ... it looked like you were talking to someone." Little John looked around and flipped a hand at the headstones. "Was wondering if you're one of those people that can talk to the dead. Maybe why you work here."

"Christ, if that were the case, do you think I'd choose to work in a place where they would constantly be bitching at me?"

"I guess not."

"Damn straight. I was just talking to myself. My Martha died thirteen years ago. The dead don't talk and not many people visit, so sometimes I talk to hear the sound of my own voice. That a problem?"

"Not at all. Didn't mean to offend. You been the caretaker here for a while?"

"Almost fifty years now. It's not just a job. Not anymore. About all I have left."

"Alright." Little John liked that the man took pride in his

work, but he also thought it might make securing his help a little more difficult.

"What's the piece on your belt for? Doesn't seem like something you'd need in here."

"Just for rats and vermin mostly. Raccoons sometimes. Sometimes bigger vermin. People try to get in occasionally after the gates are closed. I'm not as young as I used to be. Doesn't hurt to have a little protection. I got a permit. Now, you gotta lot of questions, fella. You need something specific or are you going to let me finish mowing?"

"You know Mary Sullivan? She's buried here."

"Which one? We've got two. Both died young, but one died in 1917 and one died in the early 2000s ... 2003, I think."

"2003 Mary."

The man didn't hesitate. If he was losing his mind, he wasn't losing his memory of the cemetery. "Plot J-24. Follow the path there and take your fourth left. She's over by the fence under the smaller oak. Not a bad spot, most days."

Little John figured if you worked here as long as this guy had you got to know your constituents. The man started to turn back to the mower.

"One more thing." Little John pulled the photo of Max out of his jacket pocket and handed it to the man. "You seen this guy around?"

The man held the photo close to his face, just a couple inches from his nose. "Living or dead?"

"Still walking among the living as far as I know."

"Haven't seen him." He tried to hand the photo back.

"You can keep it."

"Well, as I said, I don't get many visitors. Plots are almost all full, so I don't get many new neighbors either. If he'd come around, I would have seen him."

"He might have slipped in after hours."

"Unlikely."

"Why's that?"

"Couple of years ago, the town had a problem with vandalism. Bunch of stones were knocked over. A couple of the mausoleums were tagged with graffiti. They won't give me decent rat poison, but they managed to find the money to install a security system around the perimeter. Now, anything bigger than a beaver tries to get through, I get a goddamn earsplitting wake-up call."

Little John took one of the business cards he'd had made up and handed it to the caretaker. "Keep the picture. If he does stop by, give me a call at this number."

The man took the card but studied Little John a little more closely.

"The living still need a living wage, right? Even here, you got certain expenses, right? If they're tight with the poison budget, I can only imagine what they pay you. You see this guy and give me a call there's a finder's fee."

The man eventually nodded. He folded the photo and put it, and Little John's card, in a pocket before turning back to the mower. Little John let him go. He spotted the outline of a bottle in his back pocket along with the red rag. You need money for bourbon. If he saw the man, he'd call.

A phone rang as he was walking back to his car. He searched his pockets. He was typically carrying two or three at any time. Phones had become disposable. He'd taken to labeling everything other than his personal phone. It was the burner he'd setup on the business cards he'd been handing out while looking for Sullivan. He didn't recognize the number on the display. He glanced back at the caretaker to see if it was him, but he was bent over his mowing.

"Yes?" He answered.

"This is Anson with the H7. Heard you might be looking for someone."

Little John knew the H7 was the state police barracks down in Milton. He also knew he hadn't handed out any cards to any cops. "I think you might have the wrong number."

"Are you sure? I think we might have some mutual friends."

He didn't know all of Carter's contacts. It was possible this was legit. "That right? Who do you think I'm looking for?"

"I might have misspoken there. I don't know who you're looking for, but I'm looking at an old Taurus sedan with front panel damage. That any interest to you?"

"It might be. Where are you?"

"Out in Quincy across the street from some fleabag motel."

"Give me the address."

CHAPTER FOURTEEN

Anson liked carrying a gun. He really liked it. He liked the weight of it. He liked the feel of it in the holster on his hip. He liked the way people looked at him and the power it transferred to him. Putting his gun on in the morning was often the best part of his day. He unconsciously moved a hand down to the butt of his Smith and Wesson M&P. He'd never fired it in the line of duty. Plenty of times at the range, of course; he was a regular there with his department-issued semi-auto pistol along with a number of personal weapons, but he'd never needed to pull it while in uniform.

He was twenty-six years old and been on the police force for almost five years. He'd rarely left Massachusetts, even on vacation, but was starting to contemplate trying to transfer to a different state patrol. Someplace where there might be more action. One where the weather was nicer, maybe warmer winters, but definitely one with a concealed carry permit available.

He'd have to give up some of his, uh, extra income if he

moved states, but he was pretty sure he could find similar opportunities in most places.

He looked through the windshield of his cruiser at the motel parking lot. The car wasn't visible from the front, it was parked around back, but he'd been sitting down the street since he'd spotted it and no one had come or gone from the lot. The hotel looked like a real piece of crap, Anson thought. He wouldn't be caught dead renting a room. It was maybe a half step up from a rent-by-the-hour place. Whoever Carter was looking for must be a real deadbeat.

Where was this guy? Anson was close to going off shift. If this was going to happen, it had to happen soon. He'd been carefully maneuvering around all the incoming radio calls. He couldn't keep it up indefinitely. His finger tapped out a pattern on the wheel of the police SUV.

Screw it, he was tired of waiting. He'd do this himself. How hard could it be? And if he got it done solo with no fuss, he'd probably be in line for a little sweetener. He put the SUV in drive and pulled out, already thinking about what new handgun he might buy with the extra money.

He pulled up close to the office and went inside.

The office was a square box and didn't look like it had been updated since the motel opened sometime in the middle of the previous century. There was a leaflet display rack with yellowed brochures on the far wall next to an old Coke machine that rattled ominously. To the left of the Coke machine was an ice maker with a handwritten out of order sign taped to the front. Just inside the door, to the right, was the check-in desk with an old boxy monitor perched on top and presumably an equally old computer somewhere down below. There was a closed door behind the short counter.

The guy behind the desk did a quick double take when he caught sight of the uniform and dropped the magazine he was reading on a shelf behind the desk, out of sight. Probably porn, Anson thought.

"What can I do for you, Officer?"

"Trooper."

"Excuse me?"

The man was doughy and an indiscriminate age between thirty and fifty. His black hair appeared greasy and stuck to his scalp. He wore a white T-shirt that had a reddish-brown stain on the sleeve. His fingernails were chewed down to the quick. His sour body odor filled the small room. Anson didn't bother to hide his feelings. "I'm with the state police. It's trooper, not officer."

A look passed over the guy's face that Anson couldn't quite place before it disappeared and was replaced by a toothy smile. "Sorry, of course. How can I help, Trooper?"

"The Ford in the parking lot. The old Taurus. I'd like to know what room he rented."

"Oh jeez. I might have to call the owner about that. I'm not sure I'm supposed to give out guests' personal information."

"I'm not asking for any personal information. Just the room."

"Hmm. Yes, that's true, but I'm still not sure. I don't want to get in trouble. I need this job."

"I'm sure you won't get in trouble for helping in an active police investigation."

"Still, I don't know. My boss is a real stickler for the rules."

Anson was losing his patience. He leaned in a little closer, ignoring the fried onions on the man's breath. "If I have to call this in, I'll tear this whole place to the studs, starting with whatever is behind that door."

The guy glanced behind him as if just noticing the door

for the first time. Then he smiled. "That's just the john. Terrible design having it right there. Sometimes the sme—"

Anson hit the man in the ear with his open palm. The man staggered to the side and clutched his head. Whatever look had been on his face before was now replaced by one that Anson was familiar with: fear.

"What room?"

"Fourteen. Second floor, around back."

Max woke to the sound of splintering wood. The motel's walls were cheap and built to maximize profits, not privacy. He rolled off the side of the bed. He heard the heavy tread of a man running and then a shout. He came fully awake and realized it wasn't in his room. He got to his knees and looked over the edge of the bed. Kyle was standing by the window and looking through the curtains. He'd never heard Kyle move. He didn't look remotely sleepy. He looked awake and alert.

"Cop," Kyle said.

"Just one?"

"All I see."

Max came over to the window and Kyle stepped back. He looked out the thin sliver between the curtains. He could see the dark and light blue front end of a state police SUV blocking in the Taurus. A door on the far side of the L-shaped motel was open. He could see the maid cart down below on the first floor, but the maid herself was staying out of sight. There were a few other cars parked around back but no other movement. The people who stayed in these types of places knew to keep their heads down. As he watched, the trooper came to the door and looked around. He was on the short side, but big, muscled in the arms and shoulders, stretching the uniform's fabric. His gun was out and held down by his leg in his right hand. He turned and went back into the room.

"One cop. Gun out. I didn't hear any shouts before the door got kicked in, did you?"

"No."

"So that tells us something."

"Not really a cop."

"Oh, he's a cop. He's just Carter's cop first."

The trooper came back out carrying a small blue gym bag.

"Found the bait money."

Kyle nodded. "Supposed to."

They'd checked in and then promptly paid the maid an extra fifty to let them in a different room and keep quiet about it. On the very slim chance someone else showed up and checked into that same room, they'd plead confusion and ignorance. If someone showed up looking for them, they'd at least have a little warning and a chance to escape. A cheap burglar alarm.

"He's putting the bag in his trunk," Max said.

"Of course."

Max watched a black Lincoln town car pull in behind the police SUV and felt his stomach drop. The suspension rocked to one side and Little John climbed out. He took in the scene, and Max took an involuntary step back as his gaze swept over the closed curtains of their actual room.

"More company." Max stepped back to let Kyle look.

"The big guy."

"Not that we needed confirmation that Carter was involved."

Kyle stepped back and started throwing his few things in the room into his bag. He disappeared into the bathroom. Max stayed at the window. When Kyle came back out, they switched places. Max quickly packed and placed his bag near the door. He also stood and removed the rest of the money from its hiding place in the room's vent. They'd lose the bait money, but it had more than served its purpose. Waking up without a corrupt cop or Little John looming over him was a price definitely worth paying.

Max came back to the window. The two men were arguing outside the broken door. Still nothing and no one moving outside.

"I don't think we can wait them out. Once they finish bickering, they'll likely get to the desk guy and start checking the remaining rooms. We dodged the first bullet, but if we don't move we're sitting ducks for the next one."

"Car is toast."

"Agreed. We aren't driving out of here. Not in that car. There's a bus stop I saw down the street, but I have no idea if it runs regularly. Not like we can sit around and wait."

"Office park."

"I think that's the best bet. We head around the fence, get into those trees, and either get a ride or borrow a ride from there."

They waited another five minutes. Little John kept going in and out of the room. Max knew he wasn't a stupid man. He'd seen too many people make that mistake just based on the man's massive size. Insanely large people can also be very smart. He was grinding through the variables. His problem was numbers. He couldn't watch all the exits. Finally, he jabbed the cop, not gently, in the chest and sent him back to the SUV. They watched the SUV back up and disappear out of sight in front of the motel.

"You were right."

Max nodded. "No way to watch all the entrances. He's still hoping we're here and will panic. Maybe make a run for it. Next, he's going to get the keys from the clerk. With the cop out front, that's our chance."

On cue, Little John went down the stairs. He left his own

car blocking their damaged Taurus and walked around the front of the motel toward the office. Max waited for a beat, then picked up his bag and the bag with the money and opened the door. He didn't wait for Kyle. He knew he would follow.

They went down the opposite stairwell, actually closer to the office where Little John was probably terrorizing the poor clerk, and stopped at the end of the building. Max jumped back when someone moved at the corner, but it was only the maid. She was smoking a cigarette and talking on the phone. She gave them a look when Max came around the corner and then nodded.

"Gracias," Max whispered and then threw the bags over the short fence. He followed, careful not to snag his legs or arms on the rusty fence top.

A quick ten-yard run and they were in the small grove of trees that surrounded the manmade lake at the entrance to the office park. They worked their way through the trees and came out onto a crushed gravel path, likely meant for employees to sometimes escape from their cubes. It was empty. They were completely screened now from the motel and the main road. They weren't safe, but the immediate danger from Little John appeared to be over.

Max had underestimated Carter. He didn't think he'd get on top of them this quickly. Max had to make his move and he realized now he probably couldn't do it alone.

CHAPTER FIFTEEN

Colleen glanced at the time on her computer. Almost five. She was feeling antsy and restless. For the last three days, she'd felt at loose ends. She knew it was Sullivan. She just didn't know what to do about it. She had no jurisdiction. No way into the case. Not that there was a case. As far as she, or Foxx knew, no one was trying to find him. Foxx had kept his word and sent over a package of reports. She'd read through them twice but hadn't found any ready answers. Bobby Briggs and his pals weren't pressing charges, and there was no evidence tying Sullivan to the fires. Presumably someone from Boston PD was chasing down some leads, but she doubted Carter or anyone else was pushing them very hard for answers.

She could ask Foxx to get her some access to the files but what would that get her? What would she do? She glanced down at the file on her desk. She had actual cases assigned to her to solve. She had already written up and delivered a report on the Min's Hair Salon case, but the lack of a motive was still eating at her. She thought about the third fire in

Southie, also at a hair salon, and that odd trapdoor space. What was that about?

As far as she knew, Min's had no connection with Carter. The Chelsea guys had never mentioned anything in that direction. They were treating it like a straight up murder case, even if the motive remained murky. And she didn't blame them. If you heard hoofbeats, you thought horses, not zebras. But they'd gotten nowhere with the straight ahead approach. The backgrounds on the victims had come back clean. But how hard had they really looked? Maybe it was time to look for those zebras. Chelsea was probably only five or six miles from Southie. Foxx had said Carter's influence was waning, but was it such a stretch to think he still might have some ties in Chelsea?

She picked up the phone and dialed a four-digit extension.

"Rabalais."

"Hey Rabies. It's Adams. I need a favor."

"What's up? I need a distraction. I'm going blind reading this cyber-security report from the Feds."

"Can't promise anything better than that, but I need some help digging into ownership details of a business. Can you do that?"

"Forensic accounting would be better."

"But I don't know anyone in accounting and I'm hoping to get some answers fast. If I have to run through official channels, it might be a week or more before someone talks to me, let alone is willing to help me."

"Ok. You have an address?"

"Min's Hair Salon, 135 Broadway in Chelsea."

She could hear him typing. "Ok, I see it. What am I looking for?"

"I'm helping the locals with a double murder. The owner and an employee were the victims. They did all the usual background checks. I want to go a level deeper. No one knows why these two were killed. At least not that they're telling us. I want to see if everything with the salon is on the up and up."

"What are you thinking? Organized crime?"

"Gangs. OC. I'm not sure. Anything that looks a little off or throws up a red flag. I don't like random killings. There's got to be a reason. We just haven't found it. If you get ambitious, maybe you can poke around in the owner's background. Min Lee. Just like it sounds." She spelled it out for him anyway. "She was 42."

"Alright. This is definitely more interesting than this report. Give me some time."

She hung up, feeling a little better for doing something. She picked up the three-ring binder that held her copy of the Min file. It remained a depressingly slim account of the murder of two people. She flipped open the cover and scanned the list of contacts and numbers on the first page until she found the number she wanted.

She glanced at the time again down in the corner of her monitor. It was creeping up on five-thirty. It was fifty/fifty whether anyone was still around. She dialed and it rang through to voicemail. She didn't leave a message. Instead she Googled the front desk number for the Chelsea precinct and eventually got transferred to the general number for the homicide desk. It rang through to voicemail. Either a shift change or a busy day. She was bounced back to the station duty officer.

"This is Adams with the state police. I'm looking for Detective Petrie or Goinns. I'm working the Min murders with them. They around?"

"I can't see 'em and this ain't a big room. You tried their phones?"

Great, an obnoxious smartass. Why did every male cop think he was a comedian when talking to a female colleague?

She bit back her own response. "I've only got their hard
lines and emails. You have a mobile number for either of
them?"

"Who'd you say you were? State?"

"Colleen Adams. I'm a detective from the state police
over at the DA's office. You want to call over there and check
me out?"

"You related to Bud Adams?"

"He's my father."

"I worked with him for a few years at the A15."

Her dad had spent a lot of years chasing down bank heists
and rackets in Charlestown. She wasn't going to look a gift
horse in the mouth. "Then you know bullshit doesn't run in
the family. Can you help me out?"

That got a genuine laugh. "It definitely doesn't. Hold on a
minute, let me see if they're on the radio or if they signed out
for the day."

There was a pause. She could hear the officer trying to
raise Petrie on the radio. He was the senior detective in the
partnership. She heard a response. A moment later he was
back in her ear. "Give me your number. He's out on something but he's going to call."

She gave him both her office and mobile numbers, then
disconnected, and sat back to wait. If they'd been called out
to a fresh scene, she couldn't expect a call anytime soon.
Maybe not even until tomorrow. She picked up the file.
When she was stuck on something, her habit was to read the
file obsessively until something clicked. She could still quote
whole witness statements from tough or worse, still open,
cases three or four years old.

Solving a murder was like lining up puzzle pieces. Often,
you didn't have all the right pieces at the same time. So, you
constantly had to keep going back to the beginning and try to
fit things together. She didn't necessarily have any new pieces

to add to the Min file yet, but she didn't have anything else to try.

Thirty minutes later, the office had completely emptied out. She was contemplating calling it an early night when her desk phone rang.

"Adams."

"Shit. Don't you have a life Adams?"

She heard someone laugh in the background.

"Petrie?"

"I had a bet with Goinns that you weren't still tethered to your desk and would pick up your cell. Now I owe him a six-pack."

"Tell Goinns he owes me at least one of those beers."

"Will do. Hey, thanks for the quick turnaround on Min. Sometimes we're waiting weeks for anything from you guys."

She ignored the dig knowing it was probably mostly true. "Wish I could have been more helpful. Maybe I can actually. It's why I was calling."

"How's that?"

"It might be nothing. Just chasing a hunch. Don't want to get your hopes up, but I was wondering if the scene was still sealed?"

"Yeah, it was as of this morning. It's been processed and cleared, of course, but my understanding is that no one's stepped forward to claim it."

"No family or relatives in the country. I remember that."

"Right, no will either. It'll eventually end up in court, but right now we're sort of stuck with it. It might eventually end up with property or go up for auction. Not sure. Can't say I've had one where the home or business ended up like that."

"It is unusual. Reason I'm asking is that I was wondering if I could get one more look at the scene."

"Sure, shouldn't be a problem. One sec." She heard him talking to someone. She assumed it was his partner. "Goinns still has the key here in his bag. When do you want to take a look?"

"Could I do it now?"

"Now? We just got called out to this thing. We're waiting on prints and blood."

"I can meet you. I don't think it will take long. Need to scratch an itch."

"Alright. That works. If you promise to share whatever this itch is."

"If it pans out, you'll be the first to know."

"You know Summit Avenue? By Malone Park?"

"Sure."

"We're on the north side, near the entrance, up by Warren. Look for the circus."

CHAPTER SIXTEEN

Max knew the knife was sharp. He knew it because he could barely feel it. But he could sense it. It glided across his skin like a soft and dangerous whisper. He kept his eyes closed and tried to remain still. The man appeared to know what he was doing, but Max felt it was always better to be cautious in these types of situations. He swallowed extra slowly.

The barber shop looked like the neighborhood type of place that a politician would visit while on the campaign trail. Rotating red, white, and blue striped pole outside, gold leaf hand script spelling out the name in the front window under a weathered blue awning. Inside were three black cutting chairs in front of a long counter filled with scissors, trimmers, combs, pomades, and disinfectants. The floor was black and white tile laid out in a diamond pattern. Sports photos in various sizes and shapes dotted the walls. Wooden chairs ran down the wall opposite the cutting chairs for people waiting.

When Max walked in, seven of the twelve chairs lining the wall were taken, along with three people getting cuts. Not bad for a late Thursday afternoon. Either it was a popular place, the only place, the best place, or they were giving it away. Knowing Lawrence, it wasn't the last one.

The rowdy conversation paused as they all got a look at Max. Roxbury was now primarily a Hispanic and black neighborhood. Max wasn't surprised to find he was the only white guy in the room.

The barber manning the middle chair turned, maybe caught by the hiccup in the vibe. He was tall, a couple inches over six feet, with some gray and white sprinkled into his classic short and sharp afro. Rimless bifocals were perched on the end of his nose. He looked at Max and indicated the chairs with his scissors. "Have a seat. Be a little bit of a wait, as you can see."

"Not in any hurry."

Max found a seat and settled in to wait. The conversation slowly built back up around him. The talk was mostly about basketball and football, pro and high school. Boston was a pro sports town. College sports barely registered. Max let it wash over him. When he was younger, his sport was hockey. He guessed bringing up hockey in here would stop the conversation just as quickly as he did walking in the door.

The three barbers kept up the patter. It seemed to Max that it was all a long running and repeating script, but they were also quick and efficient with their tools. Less than a half-hour after walking in, Max was settling into the middle chair.

"Monte," the tall barber said extending his hand.

"Max."

"Looking for anything in particular?"

"Not really. Just a shave and a general cleanup. I'll leave the details up to you."

"Gotta tell you, I don't have much experience with white boys' hair."

"It's all just hair."

"True enough."

The man picked up a comb and a spray bottle and set to work. It wouldn't be easy. Max typically liked to keep his hair very short, one less thing to worry about, but with all the recent trouble in Chicago and then cross-country travel, personal grooming had been low on his list of priorities.

"You from around here?"

"Grew up here, but moved away when I was a kid."

"What brings you back?"

"Visiting an old friend."

Max closed his eyes and the barber went back to trading barbs with his neighbors and arguing about whether the Celtics had enough to get to the finals this year.

As Monte used the small clippers to square off his neck, Max asked, "Is Lawrence around?"

"Lawrence?"

Max met the man's eyes in the mirror. "Yes, Lawrence. Heard he might be found here."

"Never heard of him and I've been running this shop for nearly twenty years now. Who told you that?"

"Just heard it around."

Monte laid a hot towel over Max's face and neck in preparation for the shave. "Must have heard that wrong. No Lawrence working here."

"Didn't say he was working here."

"No? Guess you didn't. Still the same answer."

Max listened to the soft whirr of the shaving cream dispenser, then inhaled the wood shavings and powder smell of the sandalwood cream as Monte spread it across his stubble. He noticed the chatter in the shop had again gone silent. He was quite the conversation killer today. He took that as a good sign. He wasn't actually sure Lawrence was still around. It had been twenty years, a lifetime on the streets, but Max still remembered all the stories and characters, including

Monte, that Lawrence had talked about back in RFK, the juvie center where they'd first met. He took the sudden change to be a sign he was on the right track. Lawrence's name got a reaction. Lawrence was either dead or very much alive.

The razor worked its way carefully around his ears and then slid down the sides of his neck. The haircut and shave had left him feeling clean and fresh. It felt good after all the time he spent cooped up in the van.

Monte wiped the remaining cream off with a clean towel and then lifted the hot towel from Max's eyes. Max blinked in the glare of the bright fluorescent overheads and went to sit up. He felt the razor dig into his neck. He eased back down in the chair.

It wasn't Monte holding the straight razor.

Monte was sitting in one of the waiting chairs. The rest of the shop was empty. The man holding the razor was slim, almost slight, but even looking at him upside down, Max could feel the coiled energy and fierce intelligence in his brown eyes. His head was shaved, but there was a rough patch of facial hair running along his jawline and around his chin.

"I don't know you."

"You don't know this face, not exactly, but you know me, Lawrence."

"What's that supposed to mean?"

"It means I had some trouble with Carter a few years back, maybe you heard about it, had my face altered a bit as part of the deal."

Lawrence studied him more intently but kept the knife at his throat. It was clear the man wasn't convinced, and you didn't last this long by being sloppy or careless. "Gonna have to do better than that," he eventually said.

"Alright. I know you always cried when you got to the end

of 'Where the Red Fern Grows.' I know you can't go left when you drive the lane. I know your dad started this shop after he got back from his second tour of Vietnam. I know that scar you're hiding with that sad excuse for a beard came from a cafeteria fight with Lonnie Baxter. You want more? I can keep going. You never did keep your mouth shut for long."

There was a moment of silence and then Monte slapped his leg and laughed. "Damn, Lawrence you better hope that boy is who he says, otherwise someone really got your number."

Lawrence let the knife drop and stepped back. "Pretty sure I recall you getting a little teary when Old Dan died, too."

Max stood. "It *is* a sad book."

There was no hug or handshake. They'd been close back in juvie, as close as white and black guys could get, but that was almost twenty years in the past and there was no shared history since.

"Not as sad as that nappy head of hair you sporting now."

"Hey now," Monte spoke up. "Don't insult a man's work."

"I think it was less an indictment of your work and more an indictment of my character. Or lack thereof," Max said. "You always did have a thing for personal grooming."

"If a man can't take the time and attention to care for his own body, what does that say about his character?"

"You make a good point. Had a bit of a rough patch lately."

Lawrence dropped the banter and turned more serious. "I did hear about that thing with Carter. I'm sorry about your wife and daughter. Things we do, world we live in, it shouldn't cross over into family. Not right. We made a choice, they didn't."

"Part of the reason I'm here."

"Go on and tell it then."

Max glanced at Monte.

"My business is his business. He can hear anything you got to say."

"Alright then. I'm going after Carter. I tried to get clear of him and do it with the cops the first time and that didn't work. I lost everything. Now, I want him to lose everything."

"You the one behind the fires over there a few weeks back. Heard those were his places."

"That was me."

"So, what's your plan? Death by a thousand cuts?"

"Maybe not a thousand but something like that. I want to harass and annoy him and piss him off enough that he does something stupid. He makes a mistake and I step on his neck. I think the rest will take care of itself."

"Meaning there are plenty of predators out there ready to pounce on a weak rival."

"Exactly. Boston is just as screwed up as when I left. There's no big heavy holding everyone in line. Most groups have carved out a niche and fight tooth and nail to keep it. Carter's got Southie and the fringes. You got this pocket here. The Hispanic gangs are chewing Eastie and Chelsea. It's dog eat dog. Carter looks weak or that he can't put down a threat and he won't last long."

"And you want my help?"

"No, I got an offer. Carter's got a truck coming down from Canada twice a week. Dropping off at one of his places in the dry dock. You know anything about that?"

"Probably pills. Fake Oxy. I heard he's been dealing around the hospitals and clinics."

"How'd you feel about taking that over?"

Lawrence ran his hand over his stubble and glanced over at Monte before looking back at Max. "Gotta be honest, not our typical thing. You're right, we got our patch here, but we're not a big outfit. We're more strategic, you might say. If we do this with you and you take your swing and miss, it couldn't come back on us. He can't know we were involved. You might be able to move on but we gotta live here."

"I understand. It might cost you a percentage, but I can get you help on the initial takeover. Keep you mostly out of it."

"Alright, set it up."

"Good. I'll do that." Max hesitated.

"Spit it out. I could always tell when you were lying or holding back."

"I need another favor. You got anyplace we can stay. Somewhere off the grid."

"We?"

"I've got a partner in this."

"And you guys can't afford a couple rooms? I know there are some cheap-ass motels over in your old neighborhood."

"There are, sure, but that's also the problem." Max filled him in on the cop and Little John breaking down the motel room door.

"Gotta be honest, didn't think Carter still had that kind of pull. Sort of impressed."

"He's still got influence but it's shrinking."

Lawrence walked over to a short shelf and wiped both sides of the straight razor on a white towel before placing the metal in a cup of blue Barbicide disinfectant. "Yeah, I think I got someplace you can hole up."

They agreed to meet up again in a few hours, when the shop was closed. This time, the pair did shake and Max walked outside with a fresh haircut and the first part of a plan to start seriously putting the screws to Carter.

CHAPTER SEVENTEEN

Carter was sitting in his small office at Clover, looking at his spreadsheets on his laptop. Something still wasn't right. It had been four days since he'd dealt with Barboza in the basement and a week since he'd originally traced the leak to him. He clicked and changed to a different tab. The numbers had definitely bounced back but maybe not enough. He pulled his notes closer and started going over them for the third time.

He was halfway done when the phone on his desk rang. It stopped after one ring. Ten seconds later, it rang again, this time for two rings. Carter took a cell phone out of the top drawer and then walked into the back room where two large commercial washers and dryers worked most of the day and the employees finished the garments with press machines. If he had to talk sensitive business at the cleaners, he liked to do it in here where the noise and commotion would make it difficult to eavesdrop. He had his home, the warehouse, and the cleaners swept for electronic bugs each week, but you could never be too careful.

He punched a number from memory into the phone. It

only rang once before Little John's voice was in his ear. "There was a problem."

Carter's grip on the phone tightened. "What happened?"

"Our guy got a little anxious. I think he wanted to be a hero. He went in before I got here. Room was empty."

He could feel the rage rising and tried to keep his voice calm. "We're sure it was the right room?"

"Yes, I spoke to the desk clerk. The car was outside and there were a couple of personal articles, as well. It was likely Sullivan."

"No way to sit on the room. See if they come back?"

"Our guy made quite an entrance. The room's door was busted up. He said he'd been across the street for over two hours and didn't see any movement in or out, so it's unlikely they just went out for food or something quick or he would have seen them."

So close to ending this thing for good and the guy gets impatient. He kicked the side of a washing machine and left a dent. "Goddammit. What is this idiot's name?"

"Anson."

"Alright. Stay put for a bit, just in case. You're probably right, but you never know. I have another call to make and then we'll remind Anson who he works for."

He disconnected and looked around the room. He was alone. The two employees who worked the straight side of the business had been around long enough to recognize Carter's moods. He felt a little calmer. He was frustrated at missing the chance but knew letting the rage out now would do little but cloud his judgment. He'd save it for later when he could put it to good use.

He stood still for a moment and listened to the watery swooshing of the big washing machine until his fingers stopped twitching and he felt the tension in his back release and his shoulders drop. Only then did he put a new number into the phone and then hung up after it connected.

Five minutes later, he was still waiting and he could feel the anger coming back like an incoming tide. He knew it sometimes took time to find a place to call back and that he was being unreasonable, but he was not always a reasonable man. He was bringing the phone up to redial the number when it rang.

"You know I don't like talking during the day. During business hours," the man whispered.

"Special circumstances, but you don't get to tell me when I can or can't call."

Carter knew the man wasn't used to being reprimanded or reminded of their relationship in that way but sometimes you had to put the bit in the horse's mouth. "Tell me about Anson."

"What do you want to know?"

"You approached him, right?"

"Yes."

"What's he like then? Why'd you pick him?"

"He's mostly a big lug. Likely spend his career in uniform. Got a chip on his shoulder. Bit of a bully. Likes his guns. Will stay in line with the proper incentives. That enough?"

"Yes, that's good. I need his home address. I assume you can get that."

The man remained silent.

"Relax," Carter continued, "he's not in trouble. Not that type of trouble anyway."

"I don't know. That type of information, home address, personal phone, is kept pretty close."

"Find it and get it to me. You have half an hour."

Carter was finishing his dinner at a small table in the kitchen, when he ate at home it was most often alone, when Little John and Anson walked in. Little John looked impassive and stolid as always and stood just inside the doorway. Anson was a big man on his own, but standing in Little John's shadow he looked like a child. Right now, he looked like a very nervous child. One that hasn't done his homework and is desperately trying to avoid the teacher's eye. He shuffled his feet and kept his eyes down then looking up, then back down again. Carter let him sweat for a minute before he pushed his plate back.

"Caprese chicken," Carter said. "My housekeeper, Maria, is Italian. Or mostly Italian, I think. Either way, she's not Irish and she can definitely cook. I ate too many bland and boiled dinners as a kid. Then, I just ate absolute shit in prison for a while. Now, I don't waste a meal on crappy food. She can be a chink, a spic, or a wop; as long as she can cook, she can work for me. Anson. Where are your people from?"

"Mostly English, I think."

"You just think? You should find out. It's important to know where you come from. If you're English, then you're in the same boat as me. Terrible food. Last time I was over there, it was all curry and chip shops. Can't take pride in that. The English know their beer, though, right?" Carter stood and carried his plate to the sink where Maria would deal with it in the morning. He moved toward the refrigerator. "You want a drink? A beer?"

"No, thank you."

"No? How about a coffee or something?" He moved down the counter to the stainless steel espresso machine. "I like to have a little after dinner shot of caffeine. Not a lot. Just a little to perk me up. Especially when I know I'm going to be working, you know? I'm not as young as I used to be." He took out two thick white mugs and started prepping the machine. "Hey, do you know the difference between a latte and a cappuccino?"

"No, sorry."

"Eh, don't be sorry. Most Americans probably don't know the difference. And, to be fair, on the surface they are very similar. They are both Italian, of course, and use a mix of espresso, steamed milk, and foam. It's their structure that differentiates the drinks. A cappuccino is a true test of a barista's skills. It's split evenly into thirds and you can almost feel the quality of a cappuccino by its weight. Done correctly, it should be a third espresso, followed by a third steamed milk, and topped with a third airy foamed milk.

"Now, a latte in the evening is more my speed. I like the control of it. If I want more caffeine, no problem. Compared to the cappuccino, it's served in a slightly larger cup and is a mix of one to two shots of espresso and five or six ounces of steamed milk. That mixture is topped with a thin layer of foam on top."

Carter picked up one of the mugs and turned to Anson. He held it out and, when Anson stepped forward and raised his hands to take the mug, he flicked the boiling milk and espresso into the man's face and then swung the stout mug and hit him in the side of the head. Anson screamed and stumbled sideways into the counter and went to his knees, trying to wipe the burning liquid from his face with his shirt sleeve.

"Take Trooper Anson to the basement."

Little John moved from the doorway and took hold of Anson's collar, dragged him into the hallway, and disappeared.

Carter put the empty mug into the sink and left it, and the small puddle on the floor, for Maria. He picked up the full mug, stepped around the mess, and sat back down at the table and drank his coffee. He sipped and replayed the image of swinging the mug into Anson's ear. It made him smile. He thought about popping a pill but knew he had to show some restraint. He loved the rush of the pills but also knew he could sometimes get carried away in the rush. Killing a cop, even one as lowly and stupid as Anson, would bring heat he didn't need right now. He took another scalding sip. He'd have to make do with the espresso and get creative. He could do that.

When Carter came down the basement steps, Anson was on his knees, sniffling and mumbling under his breath. Little John stood at the bottom of the stairs.

"What's he doing?" Carter asked.

"Saying the Our Father, I think."

"Didn't take him for a religious man."

"They all find something at the end."

"Stand up, Anson."

The man struggled to stand on shaky legs. His face was a wash of angry red splotches. To his credit, this time, he looked Carter in the eye. Maybe he did have a little backbone after all, Carter thought.

He walked over to the construction supplies and found an old sheet. He shook it out and looked at it. "This will work." He heard Anson whimper. He dug around some more in the crew's supplies and found a black marker and some duct tape. He drew a circle in the middle of the sheet. He thought about adding more but left it at one. "Let's keep this simple."

He handed the tape and the sheet to Little John. "Go hang this up on the far wall, will you?"

He pulled a semiautomatic pistol out of the back of his pants and held it out to Anson, grip first. "It's the mid-size so not exactly like your service weapon but pretty close. I'm told you're a man that likes his guns, so I thought I'd give you a chance. I apologize for upstairs, but I was pretty upset that you screwed up. You do admit you screwed up, right?"

Anson nodded. "Y-y-yess."

"You should have done as you were asked and waited for Little John. Maybe you still would have missed our guy, but it wouldn't have been your fault." Carter waved the gun slightly.

Little John came back. If he was surprised to see Carter offering Anson a gun, he didn't show it. He stopped within an arm's reach of both of them.

"Go ahead, take it," Carter said. "You get one shot. Put it inside the circle and we're done. Miss and, well, we'll have to figure something else out."

Anson took the gun and looked at Carter, then turned and looked at the target. The basement was narrow and deep. The target was taped fifty feet away against the far wall. Not an impossible shot. Not even an especially difficult shot.

Anson raised the gun and they could all see his arm shake. He lowered it and looked back at Carter. "Ricochet?"

Carter gave him a thin smile. "Guess that's a risk we're all going to have to take."

Anson raised the gun again and fired.

The noise was loud in the small space but there was no ricochet. Just a small hole in the sheet but not inside the circle.

"Guess you need to get to the range more," Carter said. He held his hand out for the gun. Anson gave it to him. Carter stuck it in his belt and walked back to the construction supplies one more time. He'd seen something earlier that might work. First, he carried two five-gallon buckets full of primer over to Anson. Next, he grabbed the rubber mallet and came back. "Put your hand on top of the bucket."

Anson's face went pale, the burned skin now standing out starkly around his nose and eyes.

"Tell you what, you're still relatively new, I'll even cut you a break. Make it your left hand."

Anson's eyes were like dinner plates, but his arms didn't move.

"LJ, I think we might need some help here."

Little John grabbed Anson's left arm and moved it up on to the bucket. Anson tried to resist but it was useless. Little John was far too strong.

"That's good. Now just stay still."

Carter lifted the mallet and swung it down.

CHAPTER EIGHTEEN

She got her car out of the employee garage. Feeling better now that she was on the move. It was past peak rush hour but traffic was still heavy. She crawled through the traffic lights and congestion of downtown, dodging the tourists shopping in Quincy Market or those heading to the North End for an Italian dinner. Eventually, she made it to the Northeast Expressway and picked up some speed as she passed the Navy Yard and crossed the Mystic River on the creaking span of the Tobin Bridge.

Ten minutes later, she took the Webster Avenue exit, looped around, and picked up Summit and followed the flashing lights to the scene. Two patrol cars were angled to the curb along with what she assumed was Petrie and Goinns's ride. The criminalists' van was parked farther down by a hydrant. An ambulance was pulling out and leaving as she drove up. She pulled into the vacated spot.

It was a perfect rectangle of a box, wrapped in beige vinyl siding and faded green shutters. There was a tiny yard enclosed in a chain link fence. Crumbling brick steps led up to a plain white door. An old window air conditioner was rattling away, balanced precariously in the window right above the door. She guessed the box was divided up into separate apartments inside.

She had to wait fifteen minutes before Goinns exited the front door. She pushed off the side of her car and met him on the sidewalk.

"Nice ride," Goinns said, taking in her Mini Cooper.

"Thanks."

"Fun to drive in the city?"

"You bet. Handles like it's on rails."

"I know some people don't like the trend toward smaller cars, but I grew up racing mini sprints up on dirt tracks in New Hampshire. I love the little guys."

They walked the short distance down the sidewalk to the unmarked. Colleen couldn't really picture the clean-cut, polite, and organized Goinns as a dirt track rat up in New Hampshire but, as she constantly learned on this job, people were full of surprises. Both good and bad.

Goinns opened the rear passenger side door and pulled a large black bag out and put it on the trunk. It was the kind with wheels and a retractable handle. It was not small or subtle. It was almost as big as a suitcase and she idly wondered, as Goinns flipped through folders, if it would even qualify as a carry-on or if it would be too big.

"Thanks for the beer by the way."

"I'm not sure that was a compliment."

"Take it any way you want," Goinns said, as he straightened up, holding a set of keys. "Front door." He handed the keys to her. "You remember where it is?"

"Yeah, it's on Broadway. I'll retrace my steps to Webster. That intersects with Broadway, right?"

"Yeah, two blocks east."

"Address is in the file. But I'll remember it when I see it. I was there with Petrie a few days after for a walk through."

"Right, I had court."

The conversation petered out. Goinns glanced back toward the door. Adams took the hint.

"I'll bring the keys back in a bit. You gonna be here for a while?"

"Couple hours probably. If it's longer, don't sweat it. We can get them tomorrow."

"Sounds good."

Goinns put his mobile office back in the car and locked it up. She watched his brown leather oxfords take the steps back up into the apartment house and thought again that she couldn't imagine any mud sticking to Detective Goinns.

Min's Hair Salon was located in a commercial strip anchored by a large Home Depot. The Home Depot had the prime real estate and access points near the road. You had to drive through or around it to get to the smaller strip of stores on the left. Min's was between a Subway sandwich franchise on the left and a Chinese buffet on the right. Colleen could only imagine the mix of smells during lunch. A dollar store and an auto parts shop filled out the rest of the strip.

The Chinese buffet was open but appeared empty except for a waitress and a hostess talking near the welcome station by the door. Maybe they did a good takeout business? A quick glance showed the rest of the shops were dark and closed.

She knew from the reports and witness statements that this section was a well-established commercial strip with plenty of traffic. By all accounts, Min's was a successful business. Each of the businesses surrounding the salon had also been tenants for more than four years. Pretty good for retail. Better than good.

She wondered if the murders had tainted it somehow.

She'd seen it before. A place or a house just never recovered, as if the violence had seeped into the fabric of the place.

Or maybe it was just the late hour.

She parked in front of Min's and got out. Then stopped and reopened the door and took a pair of latex gloves from the box she kept in the door pocket. Goinns and Petrie had told her the processing was done but why risk it.

She paused at the stain on the sidewalk a few feet to the left of the door. It had been cleaned, but it was still clearly visible even weeks later. Heng, the employee. It wasn't clear if she had been leaving when the killer showed up or had tried to flee. Either way, she'd died violently, and the killer was still out there.

She pulled the tape off the door and used the key to open the front door.

The bodies had been found quickly so the air inside smelled stale but mostly like a nail and hair salon. The overly sweet smell of shampoo mixed with the sharp tang of acetone and artificial nails. She walked around the high welcome counter with the computer, credit card reader, and a large vase. A bunch of what might have once been lilies were wilted over the side of the vase.

The interior of the shop was made up of five manicure and pedicure stations along the left wall. Big black chairs set up high so the employees could sit on the small roller chairs and have access to the clients' feet and hands. The right side of the shop had three stations set up for hairdressers to do cuts and colors. Each station was neat and orderly, ready for the next business day that would likely never arrive.

She walked slowly through the place. Fingerprint dust coated most of the surfaces and the light-colored laminate floor. It swirled in her footsteps.

At the back, a small restroom was in one corner with a separate office, Min's she would assume, on the opposite side.

There was another computer in the office, along with a file cabinet and a safe. The safe had been closed and locked when the officers had responded. There had been just under two thousand dollars in it when the locksmith had gotten it open. She used a finger to push open the door. Nothing in it now.

She pulled open the file cabinet and riffled through the neat labels. Taxes, receipts, order forms, suppliers, licenses, employee files. Everything in its place.

At the back of the shop, there was a single door in the middle of the wall. It opened onto a small vestibule with two doors. One directly ahead. One to the left. She pushed the one in front of her open and looked out onto a narrow alley of sorts with employee parking spots and dumpsters up against a worn wooden fence. She let the door close and opened the second one.

There was a staircase leading down to a basement. She flipped the light switch just inside the door. Milky light showed the stairs ended in a concrete floor. Her hand went to the small holster on her waist as horror movie clichés flashed through her head.

"Get a grip, Adams."

She went down the stairs into a small, cramped basement space. It did not extend all the way back to the front of the store. Even at her size, she could feel the ceiling was lower than normal. Different sized cardboard boxes were stacked up haphazardly around the walls. She glanced in the nearest one. Shampoo. A couple older, presumably broken chairs were also squeezed into the space along with a rinse sink and some rusting length of pipe. She could make out decorative lamps or sconces, maybe, for the workstations. Plus, old cabinetry in a different style and color than what she saw upstairs. It looked like a salon junkyard. She could only take a few steps in any direction before hitting a virtual wall. She checked a few more boxes, nail polish and conditioner, before going back up the stairs.

She was walking through the main room heading for her car and thinking about a late dinner when she stopped. She looked at the salon stations on the right and the mani/pedi stations on the left. Everything neat as a button. She went back and looked in Min's office. Nothing out of place. No clutter on the desk. All those file folders labeled.

No one who ran a business like this would have a basement like that.

She went back down the stairs. It was too messy. Now that she was looking at it with a different perspective, it looked staged. Why keep rusting pipe or old out-of-date furnishings?

But what did it mean?

She took out her phone and turned on the flashlight to get more light. The boxes were stacked up to the low ceiling all the way around. She looked down and noticed it. The little bit of floor she could see showed patches of wear and tear as if things had been moved regularly.

She started moving and shifting boxes, trying to make a space toward the wall space under the stairs.

Twenty minutes later, she was sweating but she'd cleared a space.

She was staring at a very solid-looking steel security door.

She picked up her phone from where she'd leaned it against some boxes to provide the most light. She dialed Petrie.

"Was about to give up on you for the night, Adams."

"Petrie, what's behind this door in the basement?"

"What door?"

CHAPTER NINETEEN

The lock was shiny and new. None of the keys on the ring from Petrie worked.

"We're almost done here, Adams. We'll bring a tech with us and come and meet you. I'll also get a locksmith sent out. He might beat us there. If he does, have him wait until we arrive."

"Alright." She hung up. She knew "almost done" could be anywhere from thirty minutes to two hours. She got a weird vibe being down in the basement alone and went back upstairs, but couldn't think of anything else to do that hadn't already been done. She went outside and decided to risk the Chinese place.

Forty-five minutes later, after polishing off a surprisingly good Kung Pao chicken that she might regret later but tasted good going down, the locksmith pulled up in a white van with Chelsea Locksmith stenciled on the side in red with a phone number inside a key-shaped logo.

A short, trim man, probably near sixty, with an old-style brush mustache, hopped out of the van. He seemed remarkably awake and alert for the time of day. Maybe you needed that personality to be on-call twenty-four seven. She put the white tray aside, wiped her mouth, and got out to meet him.

"Michael Francis."

"Colleen Adams, State Police."

"State? Was expecting the local guys."

"They're on their way. Afraid we've got to wait."

Francis shrugged. "No skin off my nose. Contract with the city says I get paid by the hour once I arrive. As long as you'll vouch, I'll wait as long as it takes."

"I'll vouch."

"They said they needed a door opened?"

"Steel security door in the basement. None of the keys we have are a match."

"Mind if I take a look? Make sure I have the right tools."

"Sure, that'd be fine. Bring a light if you got it. It's a little dark down there."

She led him through the salon and down the basement to the door. If he knew it was a murder scene, he never let on. Maybe not his first time being called out to help the police.

"Don't touch it. We're going to need to process it before you get your shot."

"Okay. No problem."

He ran his flashlight over the door and then took a closer look at the handle, lock, and hinges. "Really solid piece of security here. Wouldn't expect to find this down here."

"Sort of what I was thinking, too."

"You want to keep the door intact?"

"I just want to see what's behind the door but, yes, the first option would be to preserve the property as best we can. Not illegal to have good security."

"Okay, not sure I can drill this anyway. I might be able to pick it. Otherwise, you might just consider going through the wall. It might be faster. This door is a beast."

"Can you do it?"

"I can try. I can honestly tell you no one else you can pull in on short notice is going to tell you any different."

"Good enough," Colleen said.

They headed back upstairs, and Francis started pulling things out of his truck. Colleen went back to her car and checked her email on her phone and resisted calling Petrie and telling him to hurry up. They had a fresh body, and nothing was changing here. Twenty minutes later and karma rewarded her patience as Petrie and Goinns pulled their city ride in next to her and a crime scene van pulled in next to the locksmith. The once empty parking lot was filling up.

It took the tech, a middle-aged mousy woman with steel gray hair named Hudgins, Colleen never did get her first name, just over a half-hour to photograph and process the basement and door before the locksmith was able to start on the security door itself. Just over an hour later, after some cursing, his task probably not made any easier by three cops peering over his shoulder, Francis stood up. "It's open. Keep the tab under the handle there turned to the left, at nine o'clock, to keep it that way."

Petrie signed the work order, keeping a copy for his own rolling file cabinet, and then walked Francis out. They waited for him to return before opening the door.

It was all anticlimactic. The room was empty. Completely empty. It extended to the front of the store. Goinns found a light switch to the left of the door, and four sixty-watt bulbs gave the place a dim yellowish glow, like a mining tunnel.

"I'm sort of relieved," Goinns said. "Would have been embarrassing to find some key evidence now just because we missed the door two weeks ago."

"You smell that?" Colleen asked.

"What? I smell mildew and concrete," Petrie said.

"No, under that."

"Bleach," Goinns said. He sniffed again. "Something vegetal."

"Body odor," Colleen said.

"Shit," Petrie said.

"Yeah, there might not be anything here now, but this might still be evidence of something," Colleen said.

"Of what?" Petrie asked.

"Nefarious shit," Goinns said. "Why buy that door and pile up all that crap around it unless you were up to some sneaky shit?"

"Might give you a motive, too, for popping Lee and Heng like that," Adams said.

"It might also just be an empty room," Petrie said.

"Not with that door," Goinns countered.

They went around like that for a bit but, in the end, the room was still empty. If it was a motive, they weren't going to learn it tonight. Petrie and Goinns said they'd get a full team back in the morning to scour the floor and walls and see what they could pull out of the room. Colleen handed the keys back and said goodnight. She was caught in-between the feeling of almost breaking the case and coming up short. At least for now.

By the time she got back to her apartment, it was almost midnight. Her father was asleep. She made a cup of peppermint tea and sipped it while watching but not really hearing the news. Her thoughts were still back on that empty room and how it might have killed Min and her employee. When the news ended, she dumped the cold tea in the sink and went to bed.

CHAPTER TWENTY

Max called the number and left his name and a different number. He pulled the SIM card from the phone, cracked it in half, and dropped it out the window. Five minutes later, Smith called back.

"Didn't expect to hear from you again, Mr. Strong."

"I didn't expect to be calling."

"Have you reconsidered my offer?"

Smith once worked as the right hand of Alexei Yushkin, a man who had risen to be the local pakhan, or boss, of the Netsev Bratva based out of Chicago. Yushkin and Max had crossed paths in Essex. Yushkin held a grudge against Max and tried hard to track him down and kill him in the aftermath. Yushkin was no longer the boss and no longer alive. Smith was more pragmatic. He just wanted power and money.

"No. That hasn't changed. I'll be content if we never lay eyes on each other again."

"Pity. I'm finding it difficult to find good people."

"I'm not a good person."

Smith gave a dry laugh. "Exactly. That type of self-aware-ness is sorely lacking in our field."

"I can imagine."

"As much as I like repartee, I am a busy man. Why are you calling?"

"I have an offer of my own. I figure by this point you've settled into the top spot and are looking to prove your worth to the big boys down in Chicago. You aren't the typical boss."

Smith was silent a beat. "Go on. What are you offering?"

"A profit share. Low risk. Not huge dollars but no ongoing commitment of resources. Think of it as a steady source of cash. Like treasury bills. Low risk, low return, but still useful for a man who knows what he's doing."

"I'll admit I'm interested. And how would one go about purchasing these T bills?"

"What do you know about the scene in Boston?"

"Not a lot, but enough to know it's not worth a lot of time. We don't go much further north than New York."

"Doesn't mean there isn't money up here if you know where to look."

"True. There are always opportunities on the margins."

"I've got some history up here."

"I'm aware."

"Good. I won't waste your time rehashing it. I'm going after a guy. I've got a few things working to put some holes in his armor. He's got some drugs coming in regularly from Canada. Guessing pills. I've got a local guy to step in, but he doesn't want to expose his involvement too soon. He's afraid this guy will come back on him if he knows who did it. He'll help and he's willing to cut in a partner for an ongoing percentage in exchange for some upfront muscle to take over the route."

"And why would I stick my neck out when he won't?"

"I said it was low risk. Not no risk. I know you wouldn't

mind having an alternative revenue stream to work with. Ambition doesn't come cheap."

Smith gave another dry laugh. "Ambition is cheap. Power isn't." There was a pause, but Max knew the hook was sunk. Smith was already spending the money. "How many bodies do you need?"

"I don't think more than four."

"I'll send six."

It turned out Lawrence owned more than just the barber shop. Probably a lot more but he didn't elaborate. Just said he had a well-diversified portfolio. As agreed, they'd met up with him as he was closing the shop. Max introduced Kyle and the two men shook hands. Max watched them sizing each other up.

"You serve?" Lawrence asked.

"Yes."

"Army? Special Forces?"

Max had rarely seen Kyle surprised, but the way Lawrence quickly pegged him did it. "Yes."

"Got the look. Met a few in my line of work."

"As a barber?"

"Something like that." Lawrence gave them both a grin. "Everyone needs their hair cut, right?"

He drove them ten minutes away and eventually pulled into a painted brick five-story apartment complex. "Got lucky. Had to evict a guy last week. Just turned the place over. Guy was both a deadbeat and a slob. That'll teach me to do anyone favors. I had a feeling but let my generous nature win out. Anyway, just finished turning it over. New paint, new rug."

They got out of Lawrence's Escalade and entered a small lobby. Dead ahead were the closed doors of the elevator. To the left were rows of tenant mailboxes. A cork bulletin board was on the right with a few multicolored notices tacked up about moving sales, ride shares, and community events. The black and white checkerboard floor was clean and waxed. A light smell of lemon lingered in the air. "One other thing. Don't take the elevator," Lawrence said without any other follow-up. Max and Kyle followed him through a door to the right of the elevators.

They walked up three flights and exited into a carpeted hallway. Lawrence led them down to the last door. He pulled a key from his pocket and opened the door. "Your new and temporary safe house," he said and waved them inside. The smell of fresh paint lingered. They walked down a short entryway, to the right was a kitchenette with a cutdown stove and fridge. There was a slim table against the wall that might fit two if you didn't mind bumping elbows. Further in, the hallway ended and opened up to a living room. There were two windows that faced the back of the property and looked at another apartment complex. The living room held an old green couch, a chipped coffee table, and a mismatched easy chair. Two doors were to the left behind the couch. Max could see the edge of a box spring and mattress sitting on the floor through the open door of one.

"Bathroom and bedroom through there. One of you will have to sleep on the couch. Unless ..." That grin again.

"We're good," Max said.

"The super, guy by the name of Derek, is going to bring up some basics later today. Sheets, towels. Shit like that."

"Thanks, Lawrence. We can pay you. For all of it."

Lawrence waved it off. "Don't worry about it. It'll even out."

CHAPTER TWENTY-ONE

Twelve hours later, Max watched out the passenger window as tall spires on the edge of the Financial District gave way to the shorter retail buildings and restaurants of Summer Street. They cut through Dewey Square and passed South Station. He wondered briefly where the little street gang was now. He hadn't hurt them too badly. Maybe they'd think twice about trying to jump strangers in the train station. Even if it was for a bounty. He shook his head. Probably not. They'd lick their wounds. They'd rationalize it. They'd wonder what other choices they really had. In their minds, it was mug people or go hungry. Not a hard choice when framed that way.

The 2012 Chevy Express van rumbled over the Reserved Channel bridge and into Southie. Despite all that happened, and might still happen, this was home. Max felt his shoulders relax just a fraction. It was hard to scrub the feeling of home out of your bones. There were a lot of memories. Not all of them bad. Max rolled the window down a fraction and let the salt and petroleum smell of the place wash over him.

They'd picked up the work van that morning. Rizolli's

Pre-Owned was a small used car and truck lot on the edge of West Roxbury near where Lawrence had put them up. He'd suggested it. He'd been right. Max could almost see the desperation and hopelessness slicked across the windshields of the motley assortment of vehicles displayed in the front lot. By putting down all cash on the asking price, they side-stepped some awkward questions about paperwork and ID. They let the salesman, Max wasn't sure if he was a Rizolli or not, put down whatever name he wanted on the paperwork. Max didn't expect to use the van for long. If someone had enough time to dig into the proper ownership, they had bigger problems.

The guy only asked one question. "You're not going to load this thing up with fertilizer and McVeigh anything are you?"

"No," Max said. "Just a man that values his privacy."

The guy wore a gray golf shirt with the Rizolli logo printed on the chest. Max noticed the dribble of a coffee stain running below the red logo. He looked at Max as if expecting more. Max just looked back. "I can respect that," the guy eventually said. "Many people will pay a premium for privacy."

"Five hundred."

"That works." He put the paperwork aside. Fifteen minutes after they pulled into the lot, they pulled back out again with a work van that Max knew would blend in well in Southie.

"Turn right here," Max said.

With the empty apartment across from Carter's dry cleaners used up, they decided to try Carter's house to get more intel. Max already had a few ideas on the strings they could pull to goad the man, but any additional information would be helpful. There wasn't a lot they could do during daylight, most of Carter's businesses got up and running after dark, so sitting on his house rather than the cleaners again or watching bad daytime TV at the apartment seemed like a better use of their time.

They followed East 1st Street to the west, took a left on D into the narrow warren of streets that ran behind Broadway. Carter lived in his mother's old house. Carter had lived with her, too, until she died, right around the time that Max had all his trouble with Carter. Max sometimes wondered if her death had somehow played a hand in his own family's death. Maybe her death had thrown Carter off-kilter enough to justify his eventual actions.

They drove down a tight city street full of various walk-ups on either side. Some were done in brick though most were wrapped up in different shades of vinyl siding. All of them were stuffed in next to each other cheek-to-jowl, with slim alleys separating the spaces. Sneeze in one room and someone could pass you a tissue from the other.

Mature oaks and elms were planted at intervals on the sidewalk. Cars were parked along the right side making the road barely sufficient for two-way traffic. Further complicating things was the construction, or more likely, renovation, of a home halfway down the block. Scaffolding clung to the brick face and blocked the sidewalk while an extra-long dumpster jutted into the street. As they passed, Max watched two guys carry out a rolled up carpet and heave it inside.

It was nice enough, nicer than a lot of the city, solidly middle-class, but you'd never guess that a man like Carter lived here. Max wondered what some of the neighbors thought. He guessed some of them quite enjoyed the notoriety. He knew many viewed Carter as a modern Robin Hood figure, despite the ample evidence, not to mention bodies, to the contrary.

"It's the yellow one on the right. He actually owns all four.

The ones on either side and the green one at the end of the block."

Kyle didn't slow, but Max could see him studying the homes as they passed.

"That's actually the house he grew up in. His mother lived next door until she was too old to live on her own. Then, he moved her in with him. I'm not sure what he does with the other houses now. He could easily rent them out, but I presume they're empty."

"Soundproofing," Kyle said.

"Maybe. Perfect buffer against anyone trying to get eyes and ears close."

Kyle made the turn at the end of the block.

"What do you think?" Max asked.

"We get a spot, it could work."

"Three other similar vans. Blending in shouldn't be a problem."

"We could use the reno house at night," Kyle said.

"Good idea. Not the best angle but good enough. Less conspicuous than sitting in the van at midnight."

"Need to be careful with the neighbors."

"True. I'm sure some of them are probably happy to be Carter's little spies on the street."

They circled for forty minutes until the right spot opened up with a decent view of Carter's front door. They parked the van and settled in to watch.

It took three days. The van, which didn't smell like pine needles and fresh laundry to start with, now smelled strongly of fast food, burnt coffee, and body odor. During the day, they would mostly stick to the front seats of the van. With all the construction on the street, there was plenty of traffic and turnover; no one appeared to be giving them a second look.

When another spot opened up, they would occasionally move the van if it still offered a decent view.

In the evenings, they would move the van to a nearby public parking garage on Broadway and walk back. Both the front and rear of the house being renovated across from Carter had new doors and substantial locks, but the windows had yet to be replaced. They easily slipped the simple latch lock on a ground floor window in the rear and were inside. From the second floor, they continued to watch Carter's house at night. They would leave around four a.m. when the whole neighborhood was quiet and return to the apartment for a quick shower, change of clothes, and maybe a few hours of sleep, before repeating the whole process.

They watched and noted the comings and goings. Carter was a man of routine. Max was surprised. This hadn't been the case when Max was involved with him. Maybe being at the top of the heap had made him sloppy or complacent. Max was surprised, but he could use this. Routines could be predicted and planned for. A short, older woman would arrive by seven a.m. and let herself in. Max assumed she was a housekeeper. Little John would arrive by eight, park the car in the slim driveway, and go inside. Twenty minutes later, the two men would exit together via a side door, get into the car, and leave, presumably heading for the dry cleaners.

Carter also appeared to be having work done on his house. A regular work crew of three showed up in the morning after Carter left and were gone before he returned. Max assumed this was by design. Occasionally, other service workers would arrive and be let in by the housekeeper. Carter would be driven back around six p.m. Two nights, he went back out with Little John but returned again by midnight. The other night he remained inside. The curtains facing the street remained drawn and it was difficult to tell any more about what was going on inside. Max had been inside on multiple occasions in the past but couldn't be sure things hadn't changed in ten years.

The only curious things were the nurses and the second floor. At regular eight-hour intervals, a different nurse, so far they'd seen four different women and one man over the three days, entered the house. They wore the typical light scrubs, and each carried a large bag or backpack. They could sometimes see the flicker of movement in a second-floor window through the thin gaps in the curtains. One day was unseasonably warm and they'd seen the housekeeper appear in the window to open it a crack. What was going on in that room? Who was up there?

So far, only Little John and the housekeeper, and presumably Carter, had a key to the house. All of the nurses knocked and waited for the housekeeper to let them in. They'd seen three other guys that Max could comfortably say worked for Carter, and not at the dry cleaners front desk, come by the house. They didn't have keys either. The sporadic visitors, delivery people, mail carrier, handymen obviously didn't have keys. Access to Carter's house was tightly controlled.

"Want to take a closer look?" Max had asked on the second night of their watch. Kyle had gotten up without a word, taken the camera, and disappeared. Even watching the property and knowing that Kyle was out there, Max never saw him. When he returned an hour later, he handed the camera to Max. "Decent security."

Max flipped through the photos, looking at them on the camera's viewfinder. Kyle had taken pictures of the doors, windows, locks, and surrounding properties. The windows were wired. There were multiple outside security cameras, floodlights with motion detection, and serious deadbolts on the door.

"Could we get in if we had to?"

"Sure, but it would take time and be noisy."

"Not ideal."

"No."

Max flipped back through the pictures and stopped on a shot showing a window. A small security company sticker was in the lower pane of the window. That could be useful.

Max thought all of this might be useful at some point but none of it felt actionable right now. And he didn't think they had a lot more time to waste on setup and planning. They needed to put things in motion. Max was beginning to think he'd have to try to use the truck they'd tailed to the border, and the few other pieces he knew from his time in the organization, to move forward with his attack on Carter when the cop showed up.

It was late, near eleven p.m., and they were in the house. Max was lying on the floor trying to sleep when Kyle said, "Guy approaching."

Max stood up and went to the room's other window. The curtains had been removed so he stood a few feet back and to the side so he wouldn't be seen. A man in a suit was walking up the sidewalk on Carter's side of the street. He was looking around every few strides, trying to casually check if he was being watched.

"Car?" Max asked.

"Didn't park on this street."

Kyle handed over the binoculars. "Anyone you know?"

Max focused in on the guy and tracked him until he passed under a streetlight. He'd guess late forties. Full head of dark hair though graying at the temple. Trim and in decent shape given the way the suit fit. The suit wasn't expensive or tailored, but it didn't look straight off the rack either. Max didn't have to look long or hard to know what he was. He knew Kyle had probably come to the same conclusion.

"Cop."

Kyle grunted in agreement.

The suit turned into the driveway and knocked on the side door and was quickly let in. It was clear it was not an unexpected visit.

"Weird time for a meeting," Max said.

The man exited the same door almost thirty minutes later. Kyle took pictures. The low light and cheap camera weren't ideal. There wasn't a lot of detail, but they did get one shot as he passed back under the same streetlight that gave a full view of his face. The series of shots clearly showed the man exiting Carter's house. Max now had two questions. Who was this man and why was he here?

"Follow?"

"You tail him if you can. I'll stay and we'll see if there's any fallout."

Kyle slipped out of the room without another word. Max was sure a shadow would make more noise.

CHAPTER TWENTY-TWO

The house was dark and quiet. Little John had left, and he'd sent the nurse on duty home, too. This part of his business he kept completely to himself. He was a smart and ruthless man. He hadn't risen and stayed on top without help, but it came with a price that even he didn't like to admit to himself. But if it wasn't him, it would be someone else and he'd be long dead and buried. Put that way ...

There was a light knock and he went to the side door and let Creeger in. They went to the kitchen. Carter poured two glasses of Jameson over ice.

"We got a problem," Creeger said.

"What kind of problem? I got plenty of my own problems. I don't need you bringing me new ones in the middle of the night."

"It's McGinnley. He's bound and determined to take a bite out of you guys. The indictments are coming, and I don't think I can stop it."

Carter felt a flash of panic stab him in the gut. "I'm named?"

"Yeah, you're on the list right now. It's not final though."

"For what?"

"RICO. What else? They got someone saying you rigged the bids on the trash pickup from the convention center. Said competitive bids would have been half a million less."

"Bullshit."

"Maybe. I'll admit it's not the strongest case on the list, but McGinnley and the DA are hellbent on getting some ink out of this. Not sure they care much about convictions. They want to look like they're doing something."

"You can't use my CI status to keep me clear?"

Creeger took a sip and had the decency to look mildly embarrassed before he said, "You haven't had much lately. Getting complaints from Florence that maybe you're a dry well."

"Screw that guy. I've given you both plenty over the years. You're both looking pretty healthy. You're a lieutenant and he's a fuckin' captain."

"Relax. I know. I told him that."

"Relax? I can't relax when you're telling me my name is on this RICO list. Even if it's bullshit. It's expensive bullshit."

"You got anything I can use? Maybe there's still time to use your informant status to get your name scrubbed."

"Fuck. This is not what I needed right now." Carter crunched an ice cube between his molars. "You guys still got the Roache killing open?"

"You know we do. No one cares much about Roache but that bullet that clipped the seventy-nine-year-old woman walking home from the grocery store? People care about that. You know who did it?"

"Will it get me off the list?"

"Shit, probably."

"I've heard something. If I give it to you, you gotta get my name off the list."

"I gotta talk to Florence, but I think we can do that."

"You know Steve Barboza?"

"The accountant? Doesn't he work for you?"

"Yeah, he had. It's why I didn't give it to you right away. And I had nothing to do with this. I heard this was more a personal deal. They got sideways on some piddly shit land deal. It got out of hand."

"And Barboza shot the guy?"

"Way it got told to me was that Barboza was the brains and the money. Roache was handling the stuff on the ground. Getting the sellers to actually sell. Getting the permits. They hit a snag. Roache blamed Barboza and vice versa. It got heated."

"Apparently. Shit. Barboza. I met him a few times. Never figured him for a killer."

"Push anyone far enough."

Creeger finished his whiskey. "Alright. I'll talk to Florence and write this up." He stood. "Sit tight."

As Creeger went to leave, Carter said, "Marty, get my name off that list." He didn't have to say anything else. The relationship had benefited them both over the years, but they also both knew any divorce would likely get very public and very messy. Creeger and Florence had just as much and probably much more to lose than Carter. Even if this ploy with Barboza didn't get him free of the RICO indictments, he'd been prepping for this day. He had stockpiled some leverage and wouldn't be shy about using it.

CHAPTER TWENTY-THREE

An hour later, Max heard footsteps coming up the stairs. He was sure Kyle wanted him to hear. Max kept watching the window. There'd been no change other than the lights going off on the first floor since Kyle left to follow the cop. No one else showed up. No one else left. Whatever had brought the cop out to Carter's place didn't appear to be an emergency. Or, not the kind that needed to be handled in the middle of the night.

Maybe it was nothing. Maybe the cop was trying to intimidate or handle Carter. Good luck with that, thought Max. Carter had been dealing with cops of all kinds since he was fourteen years old. Max doubted they'd come up with any new tricks that Carter hadn't seen already. No, the late night visit was risky for the cop. Even from his perch on the second floor, Max could tell the guy was nervous. The visit was not business as usual.

Max felt, rather than saw, Kyle's presence in the room. He turned and found Kyle leaning against the doorjamb. Despite his eyes looking sleepy and relaxed, Max could see the coiled tension and balance in his posture. Always watching. Always ready.

"Anything on our mystery man?" Max asked.

"Followed him back into the city. Got a plate, but it looks like a cop car."

"No help there. Unlikely to be registered to him and unlikely we'll be able to pull who signed it out."

"He didn't go to a station. He went to a house. Or an apartment. Got an address."

"Now that should be helpful."

They lapsed into silence after that and resumed watching the house. At one point, Max thought he saw the curtains flutter in the second-floor window and he had that prickling sensation of being watched. He stared hard into the darkness, but he never saw anything and figured he was jumping at shadows. Wanting something to happen when the whole house was actually sleeping. He looked over at Kyle, but the man was impassive. If there were any ghosts over there, they were only for Max.

Ten minutes later, he was ready to pull the plug. "I think they're done for the night. Head back?"

Kyle nodded and pushed off the wall.

The next morning, the knock at the door came early and unexpected. It felt like he'd just laid down. Max sat up quickly and instantly regretted it, as his body reminded him of all the various injuries it was trying to heal. He really needed a week of uninterrupted sleep. Wasn't going to happen. He went to the doorway. Kyle was at the window, looking out. He shrugged at Max's glance. Nothing out there to tell them who might be at the door. Max walked to the door, keeping to the side of the hallway in case someone decided to shoot through the door. If Carter had found them here ... If Lawrence had sold them out. He didn't want to go there.

There was no peephole. Max was getting ready to pull the door open when the knock came again. "Up and at 'em boys."

Max relaxed and opened the door. Lawrence stood waiting, holding a tray of coffees and a brown bag that smelled like sugar and frosting. "Just checking on my favorite new tenants."

"You know what time it is?" Max said, walking back toward the living room.

"I thought you boys were the industrious types. I *know* the Ranger wasn't sleeping," Lawrence said, handing the coffees around and dropping the bag on the table before sitting in the easy chair. "Couple donuts, couple bagels."

Max took a coffee. "What brings you over?"

"You make that call?"

"Yes. He's going to call you but he's in."

"Ok, good. Caught another bit of news, might be a rumor, could be bullshit but thought you'd want to know. Word is that there's a whole lot of arrests coming down soon."

"Carter?"

"Yup. He's still a name and the new chief wants to make a splash. They're going after a bunch of the OG that's still around. You might not have to lift a finger to get rid of Carter."

"Not exactly the end I had in mind. Where'd you hear this?"

"It's out there. Carter's not the only one with inside sources."

"That might explain something else." Max got up and retrieved the digital camera from the bedroom. He flipped through the photos until he found the one showing the mystery man, the presumed cop, under the streetlight. He handed the camera to Lawrence. "You recognize that guy?"

Lawrence took his time and studied the picture. "No, don't think so. Smells like a cop, though, right?"

"Yes, we both had the same thought. Couldn't figure out why he would be going to Carter's place at that time of night."

"But now you might." Lawrence handed the camera back.

"Makes sense, right? That guy is not a detective or some low-level cop walking a beat."

"He's management."

"Exactly. He'd be plugged in. He would know about indictments. You hear anything about timing?"

"No, nothing specific but I don't think it'll be long. Got the impression they were dotting I's and crossing T's. A day? Two at the most."

"Could still make it work. Could even help us. The plan was always to annoy and disrupt, get under his skin, and force him to make a mistake. Give us an opening. Any police pressure could be a bonus."

"Could be," Lawrence agreed, "but you're not controlling this pressure. Puts a lot of variables in play."

They thought about this. Lawrence and Max batted around ideas of how they might use it but, without more information, it was difficult to make any definitive plans. Kyle drank his coffee, passed on the pastry, and stayed by the window at the ready. Always ready. In the end, they agreed Lawrence would try to get more specifics and Max would push ahead as quickly as possible.

"There is one more thing," Max said. "At some point, we might want to get inside Carter's house. It's all wired up for security. You have anyone good with computers?"

Lawrence smiled. "Funny you should ask. That was my next stop. Follow me."

They followed Lawrence down the hallway, past the closed elevator, and took the stairs up two more flights to the top floor. After exiting the stairs, they turned in the opposite direction and walked to the other end of the hall. Lawrence stopped at the last door and pulled out his key ring. Max could hear a low buzzing behind the door. He looked at Kyle and then at Lawrence.

"I'd try to explain but it's easier if you just see it for yourself," Lawrence said and opened the door.

The apartment was set up the same as the other one, but faced the street, so everything was reversed. Kitchenette on the left, central living room, bedrooms and bathroom on the right. But that is where the similarities ended. The hum Max heard from the hall was coming from the racks of computers, electronics, A/C units, and other hardware crammed into just about every available space in the living room. Max was surprised not to find them in the kitchen, too. He was afraid of what he might find in the bedroom if he looked.

"Eddie! You in here?" Lawrence called.

"I'm here. Who are the other two?"

"Friends."

"Okay."

Max still couldn't locate the source of the voice.

"How did he know anyone was with you?"

"Cameras," said a voice coming from a speaker on a table near a forty-inch monitor. The monitor rippled a fluorescent pattern to match the sound wave of the voice coming from the speaker.

"Eddie, cut the crap. Got a question for you. A challenge," Lawrence said.

"Why didn't you say so?" This time the voice came from a skinny kid standing in the bedroom's doorway. Except for the glasses, it was like looking at Lawrence back in reform school.

"Michael and Kyle, meet my half-brother, Eddie."

"Half-brother, but full-on genius, right?"

Max could see Lawrence roll his eyes but could also see the pride in his face.

"Something like that. If Eddie can't get it done, then it is likely impossible," Lawrence said.

"That's right, big brother. So, what do you guys need help with?"

Max pushed a button on the digital camera's display and cycled through the photos until he found the shot showing the security sticker on the window. "Can you override or disable this house's security? This shot shows the security they're using."

Eddie took the camera and walked over to the laptop that was sitting on a table. He sat down and then his hands started flying over the keyboard. "You have the address?"

"Sure." Max gave him the address. Five more minutes passed. "Listen, if you can't do it, it's not a problem."

Eddie looked insulted. "I've been inside their system for the last four minutes. I can definitely disable the house alarm and turn off the call to the police. I was just checking to see if I could jump from the security system to the home's wi-fi remotely. That is proving a little more challenging. This is not your routine homeowner's setup. It's been hardened pretty good by someone that knew what he was doing. Not like me, of course, but pretty good. Who's house is this?"

"You don't want to know," Lawrence said.

"This would be a lot easier if I was near the house. It might give me more options. Might find more holes."

"Not gonna happen," Lawrence said.

"Just knowing that the alarms are vulnerable is good," Max said.

That was a chink in the armor he fully planned to exploit.

CHAPTER TWENTY-FOUR

Colleen often felt like she was playing an endless game of tag with sleep. And she was always losing. She dozed off and on, but swirling dreams of her sister, Michael Sullivan, and locked doors kept any of it from feeling restful. When she woke up for the third time, at four a.m., she gave up. She put on an old academy sweatshirt and black leggings and went for a run. Five hard miles in the dark calmed her racing mind, but she knew she wouldn't get back to sleep. She showered, left her dad a note in case he woke up early and wondered where she was, and drove into the office.

The floor was quiet and empty, just the hum and glow of sleeping machines at six a.m. It didn't feel much different from her usual nighttime hours. She made a fresh pot of coffee and took a large cup back to her cube. She spent a half-hour clearing her email inbox, voicemail messages, and other administrative tasks. It was still too early to return any requested phone calls. Free of immediate and official work obligations, she allowed her thoughts to turn again to Michael Sullivan.

She stood, stretching her shoulders and arching her back,

then walked across the floor to the narrow office windows and looked out over the vast concrete expanse of Boston's city hall complex. It was a hideously ugly artifact of the 1970s brutalist architecture movement. She didn't know anyone that liked it. It was all the more incongruous in a city filled with historical landmarks and preserved colonial buildings. She looked past the hard, gray edges to the more pleasing pitched roof and gold cupola of Faneuil Hall, then past that, just a strip on the horizon, the dark water of the harbor.

"Why now, Sullivan? What brought you back?"

Unlike Foxx, she didn't think it was blind revenge. Sullivan had never struck her as a person driven by emotion. He was a planner. If anything, he was good at bottling his emotions. Her sister had always insisted there was another side to him, but Colleen mostly saw a polite, careful, and calculating man who appeared to be hiding some part of himself. At the time, she guessed it was likely due to the fact that her father was a cop and Sullivan was ... sometimes on the opposite side. It wasn't something they discussed, but it was something they were all aware of. When Cindy agreed to marry Sullivan, it was on the condition that he go straight. Totally straight. He had agreed but there had been no fairy tale ending. Colleen's hand gripped the mug tighter; she could feel the pressure building behind her eyes. She shut it down. Revisiting how it all came undone wouldn't help her now.

She refocused on Sullivan and what she knew. After disappearing from the bloody events of Essex a year ago, he had shown back up in Boston and was deliberately provoking Carter into some kind of showdown. Why? What did he have to gain from taking on an entrenched power like Carter on his home turf? What would motivate him to risk everything and why now? Despite herself, her mind went back to her sister and she found an answer that made more sense. He would do it for family. Family mattered to Sullivan.

She sat back down at her desk and pulled up the file that police intelligence had on Danny Sullivan. He'd been arrested a few times on low-level charges but nothing serious. All the incidents had been in the last few years when Michael Sullivan would have been out of the picture.

The police contact appeared to be getting more frequent. She continued to read through the notes and built up a fuller picture. Danny was a volatile guy, relaxed one day, hyper and on the edge of violence the next, likely manic depressive, but unlikely to have ever received treatment. At the time, she guessed everyone had just chalked it up to environment, loose parenting, and a wild streak. Once Michael, and perhaps his steadying hand, was removed, the volatility picked up speed. Danny was a train without brakes.

If something had happened to Danny it could be a tipping point. Colleen knew Sullivan already blamed himself in part for Cindy. Himself and Carter. Taking out Carter was revenge, but it might also be about making amends. Sullivan felt guilty. Maybe for all of it—her sister, her niece, Danny— and the only way he saw of putting it right was coming back and taking Carter down.

She leaned back and rubbed her eyes. Did knowing why Sullivan was back matter? Did it change things? Maybe not, but it might help her understand just how far he'd go to carry out his plan.

She switched over to the aggregated police blotter database and scrolled back to the day Sullivan had shown up at Kelly's Tap. If something had happened to Danny to pull Sullivan back here, it had happened prior to that night, at least a few days, maybe more depending on how long word took to reach Sullivan. She started reading.

Occasionally, she would click from the summary to the arrest report for more detail but most she was able to rule out almost immediately. It was boring and monotonous work. In short, it was typical cop work. She'd learned fast that the flashy cases that made the papers were few and far between in a cop's life. Most cases, successful ones anyway, were just simple, nose-to-the-grindstone affairs. You piled up witnesses, you went through statements, you gathered enough facts that eventually whatever happened began to make sense.

She went back six weeks and had read her fill of drunk and disorderlies, domestic disputes, drug possession, and overdoses. Her eyes were starting to glaze over, but she'd found nothing about Danny Sullivan or anything that sounded like it might be him. He was in the system. If something happened locally, it would have popped, she was sure of it. Since 9/11, the quilt-like network of domestic law enforcement was sharing more information, sometimes grudgingly, but sharing nonetheless, but now everyone had the opposite problem. It was too much sharing. Instead of a trickle of information, it was a roaring river with little in the way of tools to help anyone make sense of it.

She took one last shot. She plugged in the same timeframe and did a simple keyword search, the only kind allowed, really, on Danny, Dan, and Daniel Sullivan. No results. She searched on John Doe in case fingerprints had gotten screwed up. Fourteen results. She read those summaries, but none of them jumped out at her. Most appeared to be homeless drug overdoses.

She expanded her search through New Hampshire, Rhode Island, New York, Connecticut, New Jersey, and Pennsylvania databases. In for a penny, in for a pound. The results came back with two hits, it was a common enough name, but neither one was her Danny Sullivan. One was seventy-nine years old, veered out of his lane on the Schuylkill Expressway and ran head-on into a SEPTA bus near Philadelphia. The other was fifty-four and arrested on the Atlantic City boardwalk for indecent exposure. Colleen inferred that the guy was probably taking a leak off the pier after a long (likely losing) night of blackjack and poker.

At the end of two hours, she had nothing and needed a break. She felt like she had splinters in her eyes from staring at the fuzzy type on her old computer monitor. She stood up and took her mug back to the kitchen. It was close to nine a.m. and, while she'd been reading, the warren of cubes and conference rooms had been transformed into a hive of bustling activity.

She passed the big conference room with the ugly panoramic view of City Hall. It was full of suits, mostly men, mostly middle-aged. They were milling around picking danishes off a tray and preparing for a meeting. She didn't recognize many and chalked it up to some interagency bullshit.

She was surprised to find Lieutenant Creeger in the kitchen area. She'd assumed her boss would be in the conference room with the rest of the suits. He was hovering near the machine waiting for the last of the coffee to stream into the pot. He glanced over his shoulder when he heard her enter.

"Morning, Adams."

"Morning, sir. What's going on in the conference room?"

"Task force meeting."

"Task force? For what?"

"Organized crime. New city chief is hot to trot to make a mark."

"With OC?" She remembered a similar remark Foxx had made in the car while they toured the fires. "Surprised he didn't go after terrorism."

"I'm sure he'll get there."

He said it plainly. She couldn't tell exactly what he thought of the new chief. As a state guy, he wouldn't have much direct contact with the man, but they were all stationed in the same city and his influence would be felt one way or another.

"OC used to be your beat, right?"

He finished prepping his coffee and raised an eyebrow. "That's right. Fifteen years ago, I spent a lot of time listening to muffled tapes and watching guys eat cannolis. Never did make much of a dent. To be honest, there just wasn't much to dent after the Feds finally got their act together and blew through town in the early '90s. A lot of time and manpower but very few cases. Couple low-level guys we never got to flip. Eventually, they pulled the plug."

She didn't know what to make of her boss and it made her a little uneasy. She was used to getting a good read on people. He'd transferred in only six months ago from the gang unit. They'd spoken passing hellos in the hallways and had been in the same meetings, but this was by far their longest conversation. Marty Creeger had a reputation of being tough but fair, letting his people do their work. He took a swallow from the steaming mug. She winced but he didn't seem to mind. His throat must be made of Teflon.

"I know you've been putting in time with the Chelsea guys on the hair salon, anything there?"

"Nothing new, sir." She didn't want to mention the door or the empty room. Not yet. It might still just be an empty room.

"You got anything else going on?" He gave her a steady look over the top of his mug.

For a moment, Colleen wondered if they monitored agents' computers. She might get a mild rebuke for pursuing Sullivan, but it wasn't totally *not* state police business. Despite being cleared in Essex, at least partially, he was still a fugitive. There were active warrants out for him. As long as she stayed on top of her other cases, she didn't expect much blowback if her work on Sullivan came to light.

Still, she thought it best to keep her unofficial work quiet. "No, that's it."

"Alright then." He nodded, refilled his cup, and left.

Her phone was ringing as she made it back to her desk. She spilled some of the coffee on her desk as she reached for the receiver. "Shit."

"Not the standard greeting, but okay, I should probably expect it from you," Ted Rabalais laughed.

"What's that supposed to mean, Rabies?" Colleen replied.

"Just that you are unconventional, Adams. In the best ways, of course. Look, sorry it's taken so long but wanted to get back to you about Min Lee and the hair salon. You still need that?"

Colleen had almost forgotten she'd asked Rabies to do a deep, deep on the hair salon's owner and employee. "Yes, I could still use it. What did you find out?"

"Well, the locals weren't wrong. Min Lee appears pretty clean. Immigrated from South Korea in '98. Opened the salon on Broadway a year later. The salon has done okay. Makes her a good living, judging by both the business and her tax returns, but she's not buying private islands. Personally, she's squeaky clean. Not so much as a parking ticket or late credit card payment in her history."

Colleen listened and thought about it. "A year is pretty fast for a new immigrant to open a salon. That's a decent location. Rent can't be cheap. Even if she bought an existing place, there must have been start-up costs. Any way we can pull some information about her from before she came here?"

"No, no can do there. Beyond a mere state cop like myself. But you didn't let me finish. There is one bit of information you might find interesting."

Colleen felt the tug in her gut. "C'mon, spill it. I can hear you smiling through the phone."

"Don't get too excited. I'm sure the Chelsea guys found it,

too, and ran into the same problem. She's not the owner of the salon. Or, to be more precise, not the sole owner."

"What! Who is the other owner?"

"That's the problem and that's what took me so long. The short answer is that I don't know. It's a company incorporated in Nevis."

"Where's Nevis?"

"It's a small island in the Caribbean that is very friendly for incorporating offshore companies. If you don't incorporate in the Caymans, you're probably doing it in Nevis. They've got strong asset protection provisions, low costs and high standards. No one is likely to steal your money. Plus, there are flexible operational structures and very few statutory requirements. Oh, and no additional taxes or regulations."

"Sounds illegal," Colleen grumbled.

Rabalais laughed. "Blame capitalism. It makes the world go 'round."

"So, this other company is a dead end."

"Pretty much. Without a subpoena from Uncle Sam, the island nation of Nevis is free to ignore us."

"Unlikely to get that with what we've currently got."

"You're limited then to the public filing information. And even that is pretty opaque. The only name on it is a law firm that handled the incorporation. Holden, Hart, and Taylor. They have an office in Manhattan. I called and left a message. I'm not holding my breath on a call back."

Holden, Hart, and Taylor. Something about that name pinged in Colleen's brain, but she couldn't place it. "Okay, thanks, Rabies. I owe you one. Could you email me all of this?"

"Sure, no problem. You can pay me back with a beer sometime."

"Deal." She hung up and spent a minute thinking about a

cold beer, then Rabalais's broad shoulders before she tried to figure out why Holden, Hart, and Taylor sounded familiar. She turned it over and looked at it sideways and upside down but came up with nothing. She went and refilled her coffee cup and tried to figure it out by *not* thinking about it. That didn't work either.

CHAPTER TWENTY-FIVE

I t didn't occur to him until they were standing on the porch that Rory and his mother might have moved. He checked the dented mailbox next to the door, but there was no name and no mail inside. He knocked. If they'd moved, maybe the current residents had a forwarding address. But deep down, he knew that people like Rory didn't move. They were anchored to this neighborhood for better or worse.

A moment later, he heard heavy footsteps approaching the front door. Rory answered, somehow a few pounds heavier, some gray now flecking his temples, but the same man he'd counted on in the past and needed again now.

He stared out at the two of them through the screen door, then focused his gaze on Max who stood a step in front of Kyle. "Help you?" It didn't sound welcoming.

"Hey, Rory. Remember me?"

"Should I?"

"Maybe."

Rory glanced over his shoulder and then stepped fully outside. He squinted at Max. "Sully?"

Max nodded. "Slightly new face, but still me."

Rory stepped forward and enveloped Max in a crushing bear hug. Rory was shorter than Max by a couple of inches but seemed to loom over him. He was a large man who took up space. You knew when he was in a room. His stomach stretched the black Bruins sweatshirt he wore and spilled over the top of his jeans, but Michael could still feel the steel in his grip.

Rory released him and stepped back.

"Jesus H. Christ, Sully. Never thought I'd set eyes on you again."

"Never thought I'd be back. Rory, meet Kyle, a friend."

They shook.

Rory looked up and down the street. "Danny with you? Haven't seen him in a couple of weeks."

Max glanced at Kyle. "Mind if we talk inside?" Max asked.

"Sure, c'mon in." Rory led them inside and down a long shotgun hallway with peeling wallpaper. "Let's talk out back. More private. My mother and aunt are inside and would love nothing more than to eavesdrop."

They passed through a kitchen that smelled of grease, cats, and cigarette smoke. Rory's mother was sitting at a small round table across from a woman who looked remarkably similar, despite the ravages of wrinkles and age. They both even had matching oxygen tubes running under their noses. A game of mahjong was spread out over the yellow tabletop. Neither woman looked up as they passed nor gave an indication that they even noticed the three men.

They walked outside and pulled some old beach chairs that had probably never seen sand into a rough circle beside a rusting gas grill that leaned to the left. An empty dog chain was staked into the middle of a small plot of crabgrass and dirt.

"Don't let those two fool you." He said in a low voice.

"They only pretend they're old and invalid. They noticed the brand of belt you're wearing. I'll get the third degree later, I guarantee. They only care about appearing polite in front of others. So, what's up? A job?"

"Sort of. First, let me tell you about Danny." Max ran through an abbreviated version of Danny getting on the wrong side of Carter and how it all went sideways in Chicago.

"Shit. I'm really sorry to hear that. Danny could be impulsive and frustrating as all get out. But he'd have your back at the end of the day. He didn't deserve to go out like that."

"All true. And you know what Carter did to me and my family."

"Sure, I remember. Been awhile, but I'd guess most everyone around here still remembers. I gotta tell you, not everyone was on your side, Sully."

"I know. That's why I'm here. You know me. How did you feel? How do you feel now?"

Rory rubbed a large hand over his face and leaned back. "Here's the thing. I don't know you. Not now. Not even much back then. I think you'd agree we weren't friends. But I know your work and was always happy to join your crew when you'd have me. You were a pro and always treated me fair. That's enough for me. You know I never mixed with Carter. I don't go in for that mobster bullshit. Despite what he wants you to think, he's a cancer in this neighborhood. He's a psychopath, plain and simple. Always has been. That envelope you sent after the last job when I was laid up helped me and my mom a lot. I owe you for that. Always felt bad I didn't get to settle up. Whatever you need, sign me up."

"I'm glad to hear it helped someone. Here's what we want to do."

CHAPTER TWENTY-SIX

"It's so ... empty up here," Lawrence said.

"It's so green." Monte replied from the passenger seat.

They were somewhere north of Burlington, deep in the state of Vermont, a first for both men. Lawrence did nothing half-assed. He'd agreed to help Max, but he wasn't going to just accept that version of events. He'd run his own research and reconnaissance. If it didn't work out, it was better to know now and not in the middle of the job. Right now, it would only cost him fuel and time. He could afford to spend that.

Max had sent them the photos and the times and places they'd previously seen the truck. So far, the information had checked out. They'd parked outside of the old dock ware-house and had seen the truck enter on the same day and at the approximate same time. Twenty minutes later, they followed it out of the Seaport District and onto the express-way. Four hours later, they'd turned around near the border while the truck continued on to customs and into Canada.

Three days later, they did it all again. Monte was behind

the wheel this time as they idled down the street from the warehouse doors. They'd switched cars. They watched the same truck pull out again. Lawrence recognized the dent in the driver's door as it made the turn and rumbled past them. Same crew in the cab, too.

They took route 93 North into New Hampshire. They stopped at a rest stop just west of Concord, New Hampshire, before picking up Route 89 into Vermont. They stopped twice. Again, the same places. Once for food and gas and once for the restrooms. Both times, one guy stayed in the truck. They ate their bags of food in the truck as they drove.

"These guys sure like their routine."

"Simple minds require only simple things," Lawrence replied.

"If they're in a rut like that they've probably been doing it awhile. You notice they even parked in the same spot at that rest stop?"

"If they're comfortable, it's gonna make any takedown that much easier."

They were now passing a dot of a town called Swanton Junction. The roadside sign said it was less than 15 miles to the Canadian border.

They passed another large farm, the grass and hay fields divided by low fencing. A large herd of brown and white cows was scattered throughout the small rolling hills.

"I'm always bitching about the traffic at home but never thought I'd miss all the cars. It's so ... open up here. Makes me nervous."

They drove another mile in silence. Lawrence stayed well back, sometimes letting the truck disappear from view.

"I wonder why they use a refrigerated truck?" Monte said.

"Good question. You don't need to really keep pills or drugs cold. Not within reason. Maybe it's just part of the setup. Makes it look more realistic."

"Could be."

They lapsed back into silence.

"It all looks like it checks out," Monte said eventually.

"Agreed. I didn't doubt my boy, but I always feel better when I check it out with my own two eyes. You know what? We've gone through a couple tolls. I bet I can get Eddie to run that truck's plate and see how many times it's made this run. I doubt that old beater has a GPS, that wouldn't be convenient if it ever came to a trial, but it can't dodge the plate readers. Could get us one more piece of information and let us know how long this has been going on. Might be useful when we meet our new partners."

"So, it's on?"

"Yeah, it's on."

"What are you thinking?"

"The rest stop. Less people and they park away from the building. Gives us a little more room to maneuver."

They turned around at the last exit before the customs stop and double backed on Route 7 before hooking up with 89 and retracing their route south to Boston.

For Lawrence, one time could be a fluke, two times was a pattern, three times was a pipeline. You didn't set up a pipeline making this kind of run every three days unless there was going to be profit. Lawrence was always interested in profit.

Hijacking isn't hard. It requires two things. Speed and intimidation. It has to be done fast, and it has to be overwhelming. That's it. Again, not difficult but it can go wrong very quickly. Lawrence wasn't going to let that happen.

Once he was confident that Max's information on the truck and its route was solid, he'd talked to Smith and they'd worked out a percentage that they both felt was fair. Smith's guys had shown up the following day. Smith had insisted on six. Given the setup and what he was thinking it would take to get inside the cab and get control of the truck, Lawrence didn't think he'd need six. He might not even need four, but Smith had insisted and Lawrence accepted. No reason to get the new partnership off to a rocky start. Plan for the worst, hope for the best.

The six guys were all Eastern European and all looked sort of like ex-military: medium height, short hair, small scars, and tattoos poking out from sleeves and collars. He'd talked to Smith and the man had said he could send more ... variety. Lawrence had an odd vision of the man on the other end of the line pursuing a mail order gun-for-hire catalog but, in the end, Lawrence decided to go with the Russian look. The Russians didn't have a big presence in Boston. If the plan went south, and Carter got word it was Russians behind the move, then it would muddy the waters and help Lawrence.

They'd taken two cars. Monte and Lawrence up front in one with two of the Russians in back and another car, a generic gray Toyota, carrying the other four. Lawrence had laid it out for them in the barber shop before they all left.

"We go in hard and fast and get control. Guns are a last resort. We don't want the attention. That old truck isn't going to outrun anybody. We need the truck to make this profitable. Get it?"

He didn't know these guys and he worried they had itchy trigger fingers, but they all nodded. Smith had assured them that each man was a veteran of this sort of activity and would keep his cool, but you never knew how someone would react until they were in the thick of it.

"These guys typically park the truck at the edge of the lot, usually away from other cars. This stop is just outside a city and is usually pretty empty. They've been hitting it right about dark so that should help, too. You guys know each other, I'll let you work out who does what but here's how I want to run it."

The rest stop was built behind a screen of trees and up on a slight rise from the interstate below. The building and small picnic area were in the center, with the road wrapping around on both sides and offering plenty of parking.

Lawrence, Monte, and the six men were parked in the rest stop lot on the east side of the building. Lawrence was marking time and staring out the window at the various travelers going in and out of the weathered stone and wood building when his phone beeped. He picked it up. "We good?"

"You're good," Trevon said. "They passed through the tolls twenty minutes ago. ETA to the rest stop is about ten minutes."

Lawrence disconnected. He picked up the small radio from the dash. "Ten minutes. Let's go."

The two men in the back of the car got out without another word and headed into the building with the bathrooms and vending machines. Lawrence watched the other car back up and swing around behind the building before emerging a moment later on the other side. He was impressed. In the short time the car was out of sight behind the building, two of the men had jumped out and disappeared into the trees. It wasn't full dark yet, but Lawrence couldn't make them out. The car continued on and parked near the exit before the service road re-merged with the interstate. They would be the backstop, if things went sideways and the truck got free.

Monte was right. The drivers were comfortable, they didn't expect trouble, and in the end, it all went very quietly, which is how Lawrence always hoped all his jobs went down.

He didn't do it for the drama or the high of the violence. He did it for the money. Of course, the machetes helped.

The truck pulled in twelve minutes later, just about on schedule, and parked in the first slot, farthest from the building. The driver hopped out and headed for the facilities building. Given how he was limping and jogging at the same time, it looked urgent.

Monte brought the car around the building and circled back to the entrance and parked the car two spots away from the truck. Lawrence glanced over but couldn't completely make out the remaining man in the truck's passenger seat, just the top of his head, which appeared bent over. He was probably looking at his phone.

"Good luck. Be safe." Lawrence said and bumped fists with Monte.

Monte looked the part. He was older. His hair dusted with gray and white. He had the right wrinkles around his eyes. At first glance, he looked like a benign and harmless old man. Take a closer look and you'd likely see something else, but they only needed that first glance.

Monte hopped out of the car, put the hood up, and stood standing and staring down at the engine for a minute. Then he walked over and hopped up on the step for the truck's driver side and rapped on the window. Startled, Lawrence saw the man's head snap up. He saw Monte and waved him away. Monte rapped again. This time, the guy slid over and rolled down the window.

"Get the fuck out of here," the man said in French-accented English.

"No need to be rude. I just wanted to see—"

"Now."

Lawrence watched the guy flash something, probably a gun, and for a moment he thought things might get messy. Monte raised his hands and stepped back down. At the same time, one Russian stepped up and snapped a punch through the open window into the guy's nose. The guy fell back into the cab with a yell. The Russian reached in and opened the door and climbed in. He opened the passenger door and the other Russian climbed in. The man had recovered enough to start yelling. He must have dropped his gun. The Russian hit him again and then lifted his other arm to show the man the very sharp, very large machete he was carrying. The guy pushed back against the dash and then turned around to see the second guy. And the second machete. The guy shut up. They bound his hand with zip ties and put a hood over his head.

Lawrence smiled. He liked using machetes. There was something visceral about the fear they instilled. A big, gleaming, sharp blade made people think of blood and missing limbs. He liked them more than guns for intimidation.

Lawrence was beginning to regret calling in the Russians as insurance, but you couldn't regret insurance. That was the whole point. Better to be prepared and not get greedy. The percentage was worth the regret.

The driver was even less trouble. He came out of the restroom carrying a can of Diet Coke and looking much more relaxed. The two Russians from Lawrence's car shadowed him at twenty feet, but he was oblivious. He climbed in the cab and met the machetes. He didn't even try to yell just held up his hands.

Things didn't get strange until the cargo in the back started moving.

Lawrence didn't like surprises. He worked most of his life to avoid dumb decisions and surprises. His philosophy was that if you made more good decisions than bad decisions, you'd be okay in the long run. Simple, sure, but it had worked out well so far.

The rest stop wasn't crowded, but cars were pulling in at regular intervals. No one appeared to be paying them much attention. Most people tried to park near the restrooms and get in and out as quickly as possible. But it only took one person or, God forbid, if they had really shitty luck, one highway cop or trooper, whatever they used up here in Vermont, to take an interest and really push things sideways.

The first thump from the back could have been written off as the merchandise shifting around, given all the activity up in the cab. The second time made Lawrence take notice. The third time gave him a sinking feeling that made him briefly consider pulling the plug on the whole thing and walking away.

He didn't. He put four of the Russians back in the car and left one in the cab with the drivers and had the last one come with him to check the back of the truck.

He asked the driver, the one with the Diet Coke, "Where are the keys for the back?"

"On the ring with the truck keys." It was muffled through the hood but clear enough.

Lawrence grabbed the key ring from the ignition. There were six keys, two with the truck's logo, leaving four he'd need to try. Faster to just try it than get the guy's hood off and have him eyeball the correct one. He climbed down.

"Monte, close up the hood and get the car ready."

"What're you thinking?" He hadn't heard the bumping from outside by the cars.

"Nothing good is in the back of this truck. We might need to get out quick."

Monte didn't ask anything else. He went around the driver's side and climbed in. It was one reason Lawrence liked him. He'd question things, but also knew when to just act.

There was a lock built into the lever and spring system holding the roll top door closed. Only one of the keys was small enough to fit. He unlocked it, took a second to figure out the lever system, then pushed the door up. It was quiet now.

"Gimme some light," he said to the Russian.

The guy shone his light into the back. It was stacked high and tight to the ceiling with various cardboard boxes. Lawrence climbed up on the tailgate and removed a few boxes from one side. He opened one. It was filled with various electrical parts. At least he thought it was. They looked like circuits, chips, capacitors. They were definitely not pills of any kind.

He moved a few more boxes aside and found a second row. He started making an aisle along one side. He hit a third row. That was the last one. There was an open space in the back portion of the truck. The Russian's powerful flashlight gave him just enough light to see.

"Shit," Lawrence said. He took out his phone and dialed the number Max had given him. Max picked up on the third ring.

"Yeah."

"It's your favorite barber." He didn't want to use names.

"I figured. What happened?"

"We made a big assumption in this whole deal and we were wrong. Really wrong."

"What?"

"The merchandise we thought would be here. It's not."

"It's empty?"

"It's definitely not empty. I'm looking at ten very scared people."

"Oh shit."

"Exactly. This is fucked up and not something I want to get tangled up with."

"I get that."

"What do you want to do?"

"I want to walk away and forget you ever walked into my shop."

"You can do that."

"Yes, I could but I am not that cold. Not with something like this. We all got a line we won't cross and mine is several miles before this. This right here pisses me off."

"You think they can take a few more hours in that truck?"

"Yeah, they look scared and confused mostly but not in rough shape."

"Ok, keep driving south like we planned. I think I might be able to get some help."

CHAPTER TWENTY-SEVEN

The rare times his aunt had dragged the three of them to church as kids, they'd gone to St. Peter's just off Dot Avenue on the west side. It wasn't as big as Holy Cross Cathedral across the expressway, but it was big enough to get the point across. He and Danny would shift and fidget throughout Mass, enduring the intonations, incense, and sermon with barely suppressed impatience. Mary would sit on the other side and quietly read the hymnal.

He wondered why Joyce had bothered. They never went on Christmas and probably only went a handful of times, maybe five, that he could really remember. Maybe she'd been looking for something. Max hadn't found religion exactly in prison, but he'd found something in reading the Bible. Some sense of connection and spirituality had crept in despite the brutality of that place. It had faded a bit now that he was back out in the world, but he still thought about God often as he was falling asleep.

He thought about him now as he walked up the steps of St. Monica's Parish off Columbia Road near Old Harbor. What kind of God creates a world steeped in pain and suffering? What kind of God allows people seeking a better life to be kidnapped and used by others? And the most personal one for Max, what kind of God allows a man's wife and child to be killed? As usual, no easy or immediate answers came to mind. He pulled open the church door. Maybe he'd find some inside.

The church was dark and cool inside. He stood in the small foyer and looked through the inner doors into the church proper. The lights were off, and the stained glass diffused the sunshine from outside into a weak and watery light. He walked toward the altar. The church was narrow, longer than it was wide. The roof sloped down at a sharp angle with rough wooden beams crisscrossing the eaves. Max was reminded more of a chalet or European beer hall than a Catholic church. Wooden pews lined each side of the central aisle. There were two more narrow aisles against each wall. Older box confessionals were near the altar to the right. A statue of what Max assumed was Mary stood to the left with a lectern. The altar itself was simple, a large wooden structure stripped bare now. A large crucifix hung on the back wall and oversaw the sanctuary.

Max paused in front of the altar, unsure of what to do next, but was saved from committing some unknown blasphemy when a man appeared from some unseen door behind the Mary statue. He was short and thin with a soft, round face and small oval-shaped glasses framing his eyes. His dark hair was clipped short, and he wore a clerical collar with his black shirt and black pants.

"Father," Max said.

If he looked startled to find Max standing in front the altar, he didn't show it.

"Can I help you?" The man's voice was surprising, lightly tinged with a Spanish accent.

"Uh, yes." Max had been expecting to find the priest in a

rectory or office, not in the front of the church, and was suddenly unsure about how to continue.

The man appeared to pick up on this or was quite used to this type of reaction. "I'm Father Tomas. Perhaps you'd like to talk in my office?"

"Yes, that would be good," Max replied.

The priest led the way to an exit on the right, just behind the confessionals. They stepped out onto a stone path and the church's parking lot. They stayed on the path, their feet softly crunching the stones in the growing twilight.

"Are you the only priest here?"

"Yes, I am the only full-time priest. We have a few visiting priests and a deacon on the weekends to help out with Mass."

Tomas turned left and led Max around the back of the church to a small brick and cinder building. An equally small but well-maintained house also shared the property.

"Can't beat the commute," Tomas said in a flat tone that said he realized the joke was worn to the nub already. "There's a hall in the basement that we use for functions, but they built this small building about twenty years ago and moved the offices for myself and the religious education folks up here."

He opened the door and let Max step in first. There was a short hallway with a couple narrow tables covered in different piles of pamphlets. Two doors, now closed, were on the right. Max could hear a woman on the phone behind one of the doors.

There were matching doors on the left, both were open. Max could see the door farther down the hall led to a bathroom. The nearest door showed a desk. There was a laptop closed on the desk. Filing cabinets, two bookshelves, and two mismatched chairs faced the desk.

Tomas indicated the open door. Max stepped in. The room was probably ten-by-ten and felt smaller with all the furniture. It reminded him of the tight fit of his prison cell and he had a brief, uncomfortable moment of déjà vu as he took his seat. He refocused on the priest. Tomas edged between the desk and the bookshelves and continued. "Now, we could probably really fit back down in the basement but I'm not complaining about the natural light." He settled into his own chair. "So, what's on your mind ..."

"Max."

He spread his hands. "How can I help, Max?"

"This isn't exactly why I came here. I'll get to that in a moment, but it's sort of related. I found myself thinking about this back in the church. Why does God allow all the pain and suffering in this world?"

"Ah, the why question. You're going right for the greatest hits, huh?"

"Been asked that one before?"

"Personally? A couple times. I'm guessing every priest, rabbi, or clergy has. There was a national survey a few years ago and it asked people what question they'd ask if they could only ask God one thing. The number one response was: 'Why is there suffering in the world?'"

"I didn't really think it was a new or unique question. I've read Job. And, given all the slaughter we've seen in the last hundred years alone, hell, the last twenty years, I'm sure it's been asked by better people than me, but what's the answer? Why do you still believe, Father?"

"The most honest answer I can give you is that I don't know. I don't share God's mind or His perspective. But the fact that suffering exists should not come as a surprise. Jesus told us to expect it. You *will* have suffering in this world. But why?" He shrugged. "In Corinthians, we're told, 'Now we see things imperfectly, like puzzling reflections in a mirror, but then we will see everything with perfect clarity.' But what kind of priest would I be if I didn't at least have some ideas?"

Max smiled. He found himself liking Father Tomas and could imagine him preaching very effectively to a full church from the pulpit.

"I think it's important to understand that God did not create the pain and suffering you ask about. God actually created a world that was good and pure. Think on one of the first lines of the Bible from Genesis: 'God saw all that He had made, and it was very good.' And then God decided to create human beings and He wanted us to experience love. Love is the highest value in the universe. The bond that holds the Father, Son, and Holy Spirit together. But to give us the ability to love, God had to give us free will to decide whether to love or not to love. Why? Because real love always involves a choice. But, unfortunately, we have abused that free will by rejecting God and walking away from Him. And that has resulted in the introduction of evil into the world."

"But God knew this would happen? He must have known, right?" Max asked.

"Do you have children, Max?"

The question caught him off guard and unprepared and, for a moment, he didn't know what to say. He felt a wall of emotion rushing at him and he had to blink back sudden tears and look away. "No," he finally managed.

Father Tomas was too involved in his theology to notice or perhaps too polite to comment further. He continued, "Many parents, even before they had children, could foresee that there was the very real possibility they may suffer disappointment or pain or heartache in life from their children, but they still had children. Why? Because there was also the potential for tremendous joy and deep love and great meaning.

"Yes, God knew we'd rebel against Him, but He also knew many people would choose to follow Him and have a relationship with Him and spend eternity in heaven with Him.

And it was all worth it for that, even though it would cost His son great pain and suffering to achieve our redemption."

"That's a pretty good answer, Father. Gives me a lot to think about."

"Thank you, but that's not why you're here."

"No. A woman was dropped off outside a few days ago. I need to speak to her."

Max watched Tomas's face closely and saw something shift. The man's eyes twitched to the door. Fear? Sadness? He couldn't tell. It was there and gone again, replaced by the placid calm of the preacher in the pulpit. "We have many people that come through these doors seeking help." A non-answer, Max noticed. He was stalling or probing for more information.

"Not like this, Father. It was late. Very late. If she found help here, she woke someone up to do it."

"And why would you need to speak to this woman now?"

"Perhaps she is now in a position to help others. To repay the help she was given. There might be others in a similar situation."

Father Tomas looked at him, and Max felt the man studying more than just his face. He was weighing a heaver decision and wouldn't be rushed. Finally, he pushed back from the small desk and stood up. "I'm afraid I can't help you. If you'll excuse me, I need to prepare some remarks for a funeral tomorrow."

Max stood, unclear on what to do next. The meeting had come to an abrupt end. He followed the priest out into the hallway. Tomas picked up a tri-fold pamphlet off the table. He paused, considered the closed door where they could hear the woman now typing but no longer on the phone, and pushed through the main door and stepped back onto the stone path.

"You seem more like an Old Testament type of guy."

"I do find Him a little more relatable."

"Touche." Tomas smiled. "I have a favorite passage from the New Testament you might bear in mind. It's from Matthew. 'And in the fourth watch of the night He came to them, walking on the sea.'" He handed the pamphlet to Max. "I've heard these people are doing God's work."

CHAPTER TWENTY-EIGHT

Carter read the story again. It was on the front page, not above the fold, but prominently in the lower half. You weren't going to miss it. The new chief would be happy, no doubt. Creeger had come through. Carter's name was not in the story. His ploy to pin the Roache murder on Barboza had worked. He'd have to follow-up with Creeger soon to let him know that he'd heard Barboza had split town. Better yet, maybe he could figure out a way to convince him Barboza had been killed. That would put a nice bow on things.

He flipped to the inside pages where the story continued and read the rest of the names. Even if they all eventually slipped the indictment's noose, it was going to be a distraction. And expensive. Fighting and lawyers were always expensive. Maybe Carter could find an opportunity in there somewhere. He folded the paper and set it aside. He'd have to think about it.

He was about to pull up the spreadsheets and update them with today's numbers when there was a knock at the door. Jimmy stuck his head around the jamb. He looked uncomfortable with interrupting and Carter braced himself for more bad news. It had been mostly raining bad news lately.

"Uh, boss, there's a, uh—"

"You tell James that Mrs. Regan wants to speak to him." Carter could hear the woman's voice from the hallway. He knew she wouldn't bother waiting back by the register as she was probably asked. The voice continued, "I've known him since he was running around L Street in short pants. He'll talk to me. You go on and tell him."

"There's a woman here that would like to speak to you."

Carter smiled. "She's not lying. I know her." Raising his voice, he continued, "Come on in, Mrs. Regan." He stood and came around his desk to stoop and buss the elderly woman on the cheek. "We're okay, Jimmy. Please, sit down, Mrs. Regan." He put a hand on the chair in front of his desk. "What can I do for you?"

Mrs. Regan was somewhere north of eighty with a round face and wavy white hair. Today, she had on dark red lipstick and a pearl choker necklace above her gray-patterned cardigan. She might look frail but, as Jimmy just discovered, her mind was still sharp. Carter recognized the spark of challenge in her blue eyes.

"You still handle the dumpster and trash pickup in the neighborhood?"

"The city handles the trash and recycling in Southie."

"Pssh," she said and rolled her eyes. "Don't play games with me. Do you have the contract or am I wasting my time?"

"I don't think you're wasting your time. I can probably help."

"Good. I thought so. For the last week, the dumpsters at the end of the street, behind Mullaney's. You know the ones?"

"I know them, yes."

"Well, some genius thought it would be a good idea to

pick them up after midnight and they weren't quiet about it either. Not just the infernal truck noise but they had their music going and were shouting to each other. Decent people are in bed at that hour. Now, I can understand this happening once in a while. Schedules get screwed up. You need to catch up. But this is beginning to feel like a regular thing and it's not right. It's a nice neighborhood with hard-working people. People that need to sleep so they can get up and go to work."

"I understand, Mrs. Regan. I'll make sure some changes are made. Thank you for letting me know."

She smiled at him. "I knew you'd understand, James. Thank you."

She stood with some effort, and he walked her to the office door. "Say hello to your sister for me." Jimmy was standing discreetly down the hall. "Jimmy, please see Mrs. Regan out and then come back to the office."

"Sure thing, boss."

He took the old woman's arm who smiled in appreciation of the old-time manners and chivalry and walked her back toward the front of the store. He returned to the doorway a minute later. "You need anything else?"

"Yes, call over to Lamberti's and order fruit baskets for each house on Silver Street. Have a card in each that says, 'Sorry for the recent disturbances.' Something like that. Then get me O'Connell on the phone."

Jimmy left, and Carter spent a half-hour updating the spreadsheets with the latest numbers. He flipped through them and tried to see if they made sense. Was the operation making all the money it was supposed to? Was it leaking somewhere? Was someone stealing from him? With the salon, flower shop, and bar offline because of Sullivan and the fires, it was difficult to tell. Money was down a little with no revenue from those sources, but was it down more than it should be? He went over each input again, tying the numbers out. Then, did it again. The numbers made sense based on what he put in, but were people reporting the right numbers? He was thinking about that when his desk phone rang.

He picked it up expecting O'Connell, the man who ran his sanitation and trash hauling business, but instead heard Little John's voice.

"There's a problem down at the warehouse."

Jesus Christ, trouble was all he had lately. If he hadn't dodged the indictments, he would have thought he had picked up a curse. "What now?"

"This week's shipment didn't arrive."

Carter glanced at the clock. "Are you sure they're just not running late?"

"Not one hundred percent, not yet, but there's no accidents or incidents being reported and, more importantly, we can't get them on the phone."

"Sullivan?"

"Or a coincidence. Not sure how Sullivan would have gotten onto this."

"It's Sullivan. The man is like a bad penny. This has to stop."

He hung up and then started pacing his office. His blood was up. Sullivan. He'd let this go on too long. It had to stop. He was just one man and he was starting to become a big nuisance, making a fool of Carter. He felt beads of sweat break out along his hairline. He paced more, then abruptly pulled open the door and went outside into the back alley.

The late day sun was too sharp. It was an assault. The fumes from the cleaners' vented exhaust mixed with the alley trash to twist Carter's stomach. He felt like the low buildings were hovering too close. Carter's vision blurred at the edges. Was he having a stroke? A heart attack? He needed to get to the end of the street. There was a small park. He would feel better there. He stumbled down the alley. A homeless man or a vagrant was picking through the dumpster from the convenience store next door to Clovers. He didn't see Carter coming, absorbed in the bag he'd just pulled. He bumped into Carter as he passed, spilling the warm bottle of Pepsi on Carter's pants. Carter lashed out a fist and hit the man in the face. The crunching of his nose felt just and satisfying. He did it again. The man made a muffled sound, but Carter kept hitting him in the face, head, body.

Eventually, he felt hands pulling him off. He turned, ready to hit someone else and found Jimmy backing away, hands raised. Carter stumbled out of the alley and across the street to the small park. He found a bench and sat down under the trees. He wiped the blood from his hands on his pants and watched the neighborhood kids go down the slide or play on the swings. His breathing slowed. He felt his chest open. He'd been right, sitting here in the open space of the park did make him feel better.

CHAPTER TWENTY-NINE

Max wasn't surprised when Father Tomas opened the rear door to the Catholic Charities building. "I was hoping you'd understand."

"I wasn't sure on the exact time, but I got the gist of it."

"Thank you. I wanted to be more direct, but there are ears everywhere. Binh's appearance the other night, even though I tried to keep it quiet, has caused some whispers."

"I appreciate it. I do. It might be like putting a finger in a dam, but I hope we can put a stop to this. Is she here?"

"Yes, she is here. Her English is very basic, but the woman she's staying with is also here and can translate."

"That's great. I'm also afraid I need to impose on you even more. Follow me, Father." He led Tomas outside to the rear of the truck. Lawrence stood next to it. They'd dropped the Russians off earlier. Max wasn't sure what he was going to tell Smith. Lawrence thought they might still be able to work out some other business arrangements. If Max was ultimately successful, there would be other pieces of the pie to divvy up. Max nodded and Lawrence unclipped the latch and pushed the door up.

They'd cleared out the boxes behind Lawrence's shop, but they didn't have any other way of transporting the group quickly so, after feeding them and letting them use the bathroom, they got them back in the truck. Max tried to explain as best he could that it would be a short trip. One guy in the group was able to speak rudimentary English, which he appeared to have learned from YouTube, but it was just enough to get the basic point across.

They sat, now huddled in small clumps in the back of the truck. Max didn't know if they were related or maybe they had just found solace in each other during the trip. There were nine women and three men. Almost all appeared to be from parts of southeast Asia and ranged in age from late teens to mid-twenties. They might have been younger. It was difficult to tell. They blinked and held up their arms in the dim light from the parking lot lampposts.

"Dios mio," Tomas said. "Where did they come from?"

Max glanced at Lawrence. They had talked about this on the way over. They would keep it vague but mostly true. "From Canada is the short answer. We were expecting a different type of shipment. Very different. When we found these people, we called off the deal and tried to figure out a way to help. That led us to you."

"You don't think they were being smuggled just over the border? And then let go?"

"I don't have proof one way or another. But I know one of the parties involved and, no, I don't think that's what was happening. Look at them. I think you can guess where they were headed. Most likely. It's also why we need to speak to the other woman. Try to get more details. Get more proof."

Tomas shook his head. "The wickedness in this world, it never ceases to surprise me." Max watched the priest make an effort to take in and assimilate the burden of what he'd just learned and how he might help. Max could see the resolution harden on the man's features and realized he was lucky to have stumbled across Father Tomas. "Yes, of course. First, let's get these children out of the truck and cleaned up." He stepped up to the tailgate. "Come on, climb out. Come inside." Maybe it was Father Tomas's natural warmth or the sight of his clerical collar, but they all quickly climbed down and followed the man inside.

Max found Lawrence in the driver's seat. "That's one problem taken care of."

"Glad you accomplished something tonight."

"No one could have seen that coming."

Lawrence flashed a quick smile. "I know. I'm just giving you a hard time."

"You got a truck out of the deal."

"You kidding? I'm taking this down to the Mystic and burning it. Bad karma. What I got was a couple dozen boxes of cheap Chinese electronics and a headache from listening to those Russians."

"They didn't strike me as a talkative bunch."

"No, you're right about that. They were quiet and creepy. Very effective. Your man could be a good contact. He's just got to tell his guys to lay off the Axe body spray. That's probably what gave me the headache."

Max laughed despite himself. "Get out of here. Do what you want with the truck. I'm going to talk to this woman. Maybe get some details that I can hang on Carter. I'll catch up with you later."

"Sounds good."

Max stepped back and banged the side of the truck. Lawrence pulled a tight U-turn in the parking lot and then disappeared around the building. Max listened to the engine disappear into the night and then went inside.

He went down a half flight of stairs into a basement and followed the soft susurration of conversation to a large room at the end of a hallway filled with closed doors. It was an open space set up with two rows of fold-up cots. Plastic storage tubs sat on metal shelves that lined one side of the room. Just to Max's right, inside the door, was a sink set into a Formica counter that ran the length of the short wall to the corner where it met the shelves. An old upright coffee perco-lator sat unplugged on the counter. It was clean and tidy, but Max had the sense that it wasn't used often.

Tomas was laying out sheets and thin blankets on the cots and getting people settled. Max stepped back and waited in the hallway, not wanting to interrupt or put the people more on edge. After five more minutes, Tomas stepped out in the hallway and gently closed the door.

"Okay?" Max asked.

"Hard to tell. I can't really talk to them. I'll have to see if Hanh can help later. Physically, I think they're fine. Tired and worn out by the ordeal but not needing medical attention. Mentally?" He shrugged. "I can't know. I'm sure there will be scars but only time will tell."

"It could have been worse."

"Yes, it certainly could have. We'll do our best to help them. At the very least, we can reunite them with their fami-lies in their home country. Perhaps not what they hoped for when they set out but, as you say, far better than where they were headed. Follow me, let's get this long night finished."

Max followed Tomas back down the hallway, up the half flight, past the back door, and down another hallway, this one carpeted in industrial tan, to an office near the front of the building. The office itself was also standard industrial. Metal desk, two tall mint filing cabinets, a bookshelf, a bland land-scape on the wall, and two visitor chairs. The only thing slightly different was the gold crucifix hanging on the rear wall.

Two women sat in the visitor chairs and stood up when

Tomas and Max walked in. Both had long dark hair, almond-shaped eyes, and a light caramel complexion. They might have been sisters. Max recognized the woman on the left as the one from the beauty salon. She hadn't looked up since the men entered and appeared to be taking her cues from the other woman.

The second woman stuck out her hand. "I'm Hahn."

"Max."

"You brought Bihn to Father Tomas?"

"Yes."

Hahn nodded. "And why are you back now?"

"I'd like to hear Bihn's story. I'd like to try to put a stop to the trafficking."

"Why?"

"Why?" Max was momentarily taken aback by the question.

"Obviously trafficking is horrible and any reasonable person would want to put a stop to it. I meant, why you? What makes you think you can actually do it?"

"I don't think I can stop all trafficking or really make a dent in it, but I do think I can put a stop to this particular setup."

"Really."

"Yes, really. I have a personal interest in stopping the man in charge on one side."

Hahn looked at him as if expecting more, but that's all Max was going to offer. She looked at him a moment longer, then looked at Tomas. Max wasn't sure what she found, if anything, but she sat back down. Bihn followed suit. "Okay then, ask your questions."

CHAPTER THIRTY

She'd gone down hard, falling into a deep and utter blackness, the kind of sleep that comes only from exhaustion, where the body pulls the emergency brake and puts you in a chokehold for your own safety. She never slept well but Sullivan's return and the hair salon case had put her in tilt. She couldn't seem to get her mind or her body to rest. Finally, she'd been overwhelmed and given no choice.

To rouse her, the phone must have been ringing for some time. She sat up, confused in the darkness. She was still dressed in her work clothes but lying perpendicular on her bed. Her shoes were off and a blanket from the living room was draped over her. She remembered getting home tonight and talking to her dad, telling him she would order some Thai food and then coming into the bedroom to change. That's where the tape cut off. She must have sat down to take off her shoes and passed out.

She reached for the ringing phone on her bureau next to the bed. She was used to getting calls at all hours. "Adams," she answered.

She expected it to be the duty sergeant or Creeger calling

her out to a scene. She was looking down, trying to find her shoes, when the man spoke.

"Do you ever smell that terrible French cheese and think of her?"

She swallowed. "Camembert. Yes."

"I was walking by some French bistro yesterday and that's all I could smell. It must have been some special. Baked Camembert was all you could smell within a hundred-foot radius. I almost gagged. She would have loved it."

Colleen left her shoes and dropped back onto her bed. She was tired. Tired of fighting it all the time. This was okay. These were older memories. Safer memories. "She used to hate when I wouldn't eat the white rind. She said it was rude."

"Oh, I know. She used to give me the same lecture. One time, in the early days, I made the mistake of buying Brie instead. It was a soft, white French cheese, what did I know?"

"Bet you got an earful."

"I did. I know all about the different regions of France that produce crappy cheese."

She smiled again at that. They lapsed into a silence that stretched out. She was beginning to drift back to sleep when he spoke again.

"You're a cop. Do you believe people are hardwired for revenge?"

"What do you mean?"

"When I was in prison, I had a lot of time to fill and I did a lot of reading. Do you know what some of the oldest stories are about? Revenge. Even Shakespeare thought it was totally normal. 'If you prick us, do we not bleed? If you tickle us, do we not laugh? If you poison us, do we not die? And if you wrong us, shall we not revenge?'"

"I don't know if that means humans are hardwired for it. It does mean we've been struggling with it for a long time," Colleen said.

"All those stories I read present it sort of as a form of establishing justice or a form of social cooperation. The mere threat of revenge was meant to entice people into cooperation."

"That seems like a dangerously simple and anachronistic view. What about law and order and civil society? I've mostly seen revenge as an act of anger. I've seen it destroy lives, innocent and guilty alike. It's incredibly self-destructive when it's allowed to run amok. 'An eye for an eye only ends up making the whole world blind.'"

"Gandhi. Touche. You might be right, but I can't help but think that revenge is one of the deepest and long-lasting instincts we have. I'm sure there are cave paintings somewhere depicting some ancient wrong and then the revenge. If it's in us that deep, don't you think it must serve a purpose?"

"You're asking big questions for the middle of the night. I think it mostly serves to keep me employed. We aren't living in prehistoric times."

"Hard to tell sometimes. The things I've seen, Colleen, not just back then, but here and now. This isn't something I'm doing in a hot-blooded rush. I'm doing it for me, no doubt, but I'm also doing it for other people. If my revenge ensures people can avoid pain in the future does that change the equation?"

"Not for you or me. It's not going to change our pain."

He let out a long breath. "I'm sorry. I'll let you go back to sleep now."

"I do know one thing, Michael. As a cop, I've never seen it make people feel better."

"I'm not looking to feel better."

CHAPTER THIRTY-ONE

They came off Route 93 and crossed over the Seaport Boulevard bridge and into Fort Point. The city was at their back, but the construction cranes, fencing, and skeletal foundations showed it was quickly spilling over its banks. Max glanced out the window at the Children's Museum and quirky Hood milk bottle and could barely believe it was the same barren space from his youth. What had once been landfill, broad empty lots, and old waterfront warehouses was quickly being transformed into craft breweries, glassy office towers, and boutique hotels.

He wondered if Pete was still there or if he'd been pushed out with the rest of the artists, weirdos, and other people who made their living on the fringes. Kyle drove on. They eventually left the cranes behind and things began to look a little more like Max remembered, but he didn't think it would last much longer. Those cranes were on the move. They might move slowly, but they rarely stopped.

They reached the end of Northern Avenue and took a left, getting closer to the water and the old industries. They drove past rotting wharves, fish mongers finishing up for the day, a couple of dive bars, unmarked businesses, and run-down warehouses pocked with broken windows.

"Slow down, it's been awhile. Not even sure he's still here."

Kyle braked, and they eased past another row of tired-looking bricks.

"Pull over here. That's it. On the left."

Kyle pulled the van to the curb. You had to squint, but there was a small hand-lettered sign in the corner of the first-floor window: Tide Street Pawn Shop. Max always wondered why Pete even bothered with a sign. It wasn't the type of business that advertised, and its clients weren't the type to walk in off the street.

"I'll go in by myself. On his good days, Pete is a paranoid nutcase surrounded by guns. We used to do plenty of business, but I'm not sure how he'll react to me."

Kyle nodded. Max got out and jogged across the street. He skipped the front door. He couldn't remember anyone ever using the front door. It was almost like a test. If you tried to enter that way, you didn't belong. He noticed the cameras on each corner and guessed there were four more he couldn't see. He went around the side. The warehouse was an old two-story pile made up of mismatched bricks and took up the entire narrow lot. It was longer on the sides than the front. On the right side, an iron staircase that was bolted to the bricks ran up to a steel door on the second story.

Max went under the stairs and around the back. He found the fire door propped open with a plastic milk crate. After all the changes he'd seen in the city over the last week, he felt a warm feeling of nostalgia at the sight of that milk crate. He pulled open the door and was unsurprised that nothing had changed inside the dilapidated shop. He immediately flashed back to his previous trips to Tide Street. He was sure some of the merchandise hadn't been touched since he last stepped foot in the place more than ten years ago. Most of it was just window dressing in case any cops or straights happened to walk in. The old glass-fronted display cases were still stuffed with cheap jewelry, counterfeit watches, and other two-bit trinkets. The floor-to-ceiling shelves were crammed with other dusty, discarded pieces of people's lives.

He carefully made his way between the shelves and found Slippery Pete in his corner office. The place was really just a couple of walls framed out of the larger space, and it was just as cramped and dirty as the rest of the place. Pete was sitting behind his desk working an adding machine and periodically writing tiny numbers into a black composition notebook. An adjustable neck lamp was pulled low over the table, almost burning the old man's papery skin.

"Hi, Pete."

Even though Max was sure Pete had spotted him on the cameras, he started slightly and squinted up at him through the gold-rimmed bifocals perched on the end of his twisting nose.

"Christ, I can't hear a thing anymore." He didn't show any signs of being surprised to see Max. All indications from Pete were that they had just met up last week. Max had a sudden thought about Pete's mental state. He might look like a guy you'd find at the neighborhood bar at two in the afternoon, but Max knew the shambling appearance hid a sharp mind.

"C'mon, c'mon. Have a seat," Pete said and motioned at a folding chair against the wall.

Max unfolded the chair and sat on the opposite side of the scarred desk.

"You know who I am?" Max asked.

"Don't give me that look. Or that tone. I haven't lost my marbles yet, Michael. I might be deaf, but I'm not senile."

Something pinged deep in Max's brain. Something wasn't

quite right here, but Max smiled. Pete was still the same. No nonsense. No bullshit. He cared about staying out of prison, his profit margin, and his Jameson. Mostly in that order. "Didn't mean any insult. Been awhile. That's all."

"People come and go. Appear and disappear. I don't forget a face. Especially not a regular."

"Not exactly the face I left with."

"Can't change the eyes."

"How's business?"

"Eh." He shrugged and tilted his head. "I'm glad I won't be around much longer."

"Where you going?"

"The Keys if I'm lucky, but anyplace will be warmer in January than this rat trap."

"No money left in it?"

"This game is changing. I'm too tired to keep up anymore. Cheap guns are everywhere. Any thirteen-year-old living in Charlesgate could get a plastic piece of crap like they were buying a bag of Doritos. The pros, like you, are either locked up or retired. No one left to appreciate quality."

The store was stage dressing, a prop. Pete sold a few things over the internet, but it was just to keep the IRS off his back. His real trade was guns, other weapons, and fencing stolen property.

"Sorry to hear that."

"Eh," he said again and waved a hand. "Nothing you didn't know and probably not why you're here."

"I need some things."

"What are we talking?"

"Four handguns. Ammo. Maybe something larger and longer. Depends on what you have. Some two-ways if you have 'em and some flashbangs."

Pete tapped the chewed pencil on his notepad and looked at him. "Why are you back, Michael?"

Max frowned. It wasn't like Pete to ask questions. It was better all-around if he didn't know the details.

The question was so out of the blue that Max was at a loss about to how to actually respond. "Business," he eventually said.

"Loose ends?"

There was that ping in the back of his brain again. This time, Max was paying more attention. "Just business." He stood. "You have the stuff, or should I go somewhere else?"

"I don't like being the spark for a war."

"I'm not interested in a war." Max was losing patience in this back and forth.

"Or an execution."

"Since when has morality entered your equation, Pete? You sell guns for Christ's sake. I have the cash. You wanna deal or not?"

"Alright, alright," he mumbled and pushed himself up from his chair and walked into the other room. Max stood in the doorway and watched as he shuffled around the room, sometimes disappearing from sight between the rows of shelving. Max could hear him opening and closing boxes but couldn't make out more than a shadow in the dim light. He knew Pete didn't have a problem seeing. He was like a bat in his cave. Latches and cases opened and closed. He came back into the tiny office two minutes later and put down two 9mm Glocks, a box of bullets, and two M84 stun grenades, or flash-bangs, on the desk.

"Take a look at these. Both guns are used, but there's nothing tied to them. No numbers. I thought I had the radios in here somewhere." He disappeared back into the shadows without waiting for an answer.

This was taking too long. Max stood and turned over one of the guns. It was well oiled and looked well maintained. He rubbed a finger over the acid mark where the serial number used to be engraved. No way to tell if Pete was lying about the past pedigree, but he hadn't known the man to lie before and Max didn't really have any other options short of trying to buy one cold off the street. He didn't want to do that.

He slipped both guns into the pocket of his coat. He put the flashbangs and bullets in the other pocket. His coat was now heavy and awkward, but he felt better that he was making progress. He was ready to move out. He'd give Pete two more minutes before he dropped some cash and split.

He walked around the desk. Three small black and white televisions sat on a low shelf behind to the left of the chair. They were invisible to the person in front of the desk but easily seen from behind. He bent and looked at the security screens. One wide view showed the street outside. Max could see the work van just inside the edge of the frame. The camera must be mounted high, maybe off a light pole or in one of the second- or third-story windows. He couldn't tell if Kyle was in the van or not.

Pete was still moving around in the other room and called out. "No dice on the radios, so I'll need a day, maybe two, for those. That gonna be a problem?"

"No. I can spare a day." Max wasn't sure he was coming back. This was starting to feel really hinky.

"That large caliber. What do you want? Something full auto? Short? MP5? Uzi?"

"No, I was thinking a shotgun. A pump. Something like a Mossberg."

"Ok, let me check one last place." Max heard him moving away down the aisles, his voice getting fainter and bouncing up off the ceiling. "Give me a little advance notice next time and I'll have it packaged and waiting."

Max went to the door but couldn't see the old man anywhere. "Uh-huh. Will do." He went back behind the desk.

The second camera view showed the front of the pawn-shop, the door, and the display cases. Empty and still at the moment. The third must have been mounted on the building's rear cornice and showed the rusted chain link fence and dumpsters in the back alley. Max watched the chrome grill of a Lincoln sedan inch into view, then the mountainous form of Little John step out and push a dumpster back against the fence so he could maneuver the Lincoln past it and up to the rear door.

He thought about the guns in his pocket but knew he'd never get the magazine loaded in time. Better to get out and meet Little John some other time.

He turned and started for the door and found Pete blocking his way. The old man had a .38 Special leveled at his chest.

"Sorry, Michael. Like I said, business isn't good. Little John came around last week and told me to keep an eye out for you." He waved the gun barrel a little. "That hatchet job on your face isn't half bad. I might not have tagged you right off if Little John hadn't clued me in. You've got quite a price on your head. Not enough to get me to Key West but enough to start thinking seriously about it."

The guns were useless, but the flashbangs in his other pocket might give him a chance. He pulled the circular primary pin with one hand and hooked a finger through the triangular secondary pin.

"Dead or alive?"

"He didn't specify."

Max flung the grenade forward, disengaging the secondary pin in the process, and dropped to his knees, rolling left.

The light was blinding even with his eyes squeezed shut, and the percussive wave made him dizzy as he tried to regain his feet. He crashed into the desk and then the shelf next to it. He felt a lance of pain down the back of his head and between his shoulder blades. He couldn't see or hear anything. He didn't know where Pete was and he didn't care. Feeling with his hands, he stumbled toward the door, eventually found the opening, and kept moving forward.

His vision was coming back slowly, in splotches. He was getting a stuttering picture full of black spots, like his brain was rebooting. He kept a hand out to the wall. It was like he was trying to stand up in a rowboat on choppy seas.

He tripped and went down once but, after what felt like an eternity, he pushed through the heavy curtain into the front of the shop. It was small and narrow and mostly covered in a skein of dust. He moved over to the gatefold dividing the display cases and customer areas and found he couldn't open it. He couldn't lift his left arm. He looked at it dumbly, but like a stubborn mule, it wouldn't obey. He ducked under the counter, fell to his knees, then couldn't get back up. He wretched up a puddle of bile and spit.

The hairs on the back of his neck stood on end. He could feel them coming.

Pete.

Little John.

Someone with a gun was at his back and he needed to keep moving.

He stayed down and crawled for the door.

More black spots. Getting bigger now, not smaller. The color was bleeding out of everything. He could see, literally see, the strength ebbing out of his body, a blue liquid, like deep ocean water, leaching from his pores into the dirty beige carpet.

His brain was seriously scrambled.

He reached for his pocket to pull one of the guns out, but it was empty. He'd lost them somewhere in the confusion.

The soft tinkling of bells made him look up at a body wreathed in light.

He felt himself being lifted up.

Damn, Little John is strong, he thought as he blacked out.

CHAPTER THIRTY-TWO

Rory thought he might have made a good carnival barker in another time and in another life. He had the voice, deep and warm with a little gravel. It whispered in your ear 'Trust me.' He could have seen the country. Talked to all sorts of different people. Get them to give up their money with a smile. It definitely would have beat a life mostly spent with a back bent, working the baggage belt at the airport.

It took a couple tries to get his sidewalk patter down but, after the third guy, he was able to smoothly talk each guy off the sidewalk and through the door of the vacant storefront without too much trouble. Not that any of these guys would give Rory or his crew much trouble. They were bookmakers. They were comfortable in the world of odds, lines, and handicaps. They would hire out the rough stuff. Hijacking and robbery wouldn't enter their orbit. Until it did.

Rory had been a little worried that he would have trouble recognizing the marks, even with the cleaners bags Max said they'd be using to carry the money. How would he tell a real customer from a guy coming to pay a tribute? Max had told him not to worry, it wouldn't be a problem, and he'd been right. The guys that allowed themselves to be pushed into protection by Carter all gave off a similar vibe. They were middle-aged, stooped, graying, slightly scared, and mostly ashamed. Rory could pick them out from two blocks away.

He glanced up now. The street was empty, save for an older woman pushing an upright folding cart down the side-walk, teetering with brown grocery bags, struggling each time the plastic wheels hit a seam in the concrete. They'd been at it almost two hours and he didn't want to stay much longer. He was starting to feel the risk like a band around his chest, squeezing tighter with each minute that ticked by.

With just three of them, they were getting close to maximum capacity in the room anyway. These guys were scared and skittish. Tommy and Sean had guns, but Rory didn't want to push it. It only took one to get brave enough for them to figure out they could band together and bum rush the guns and get control. Better to wrap it up a guy, or two, early rather than wind up with more than they could keep passive.

He glanced at the door, as if he could count them all and reassure himself but of course he couldn't see anything. They'd soaped all the glass so no one could see inside. If Sully were here, they could handle a couple more and it wouldn't be up to Rory to make any of these decisions, but he wasn't here. He pulled out his phone. No messages. Rory wasn't sure where he was.

They'd set it all up that first morning. Over the next week, Rory had recruited Sean and Tommy from the line to help. Rory had watched Clover for a few hours from the Chinese restaurant across the street to get a feel for it. Then, they'd all met up, Sully included, at a Dunkin' on Broadway and taken a table toward the back. Most customers used the pickup window that fronted the street and the employees were too bored to care what the four of them were discussing.

Like most of Sully's plans, it was daring but simple. If you had the stones, taking money off the street wasn't difficult, it just took confidence.

"Tuesdays and Thursdays, Carter gets his cut from the bookmakers he controls. They all walk in. You know the cleaners where he keeps an office, right?" Sully asked

"Clover, right where Dot meets Broadway," Rory said. The other two nodded.

"Right. These guys walk in from both directions. They carry their money in laundry bags. We set up on one side. Take half of them."

Sean interrupted. "Why not all of them?"

"Two reasons. First, not enough manpower. Second, in the big scheme of things, this is not going to hurt Carter. It's going to annoy him though and that suits my purposes. I want to be a mosquito in his ear. I want to piss him off. I want him rattled enough to make a mistake. One other reason. I want what is happening to sink in slow, so we have a chance to grab the money and get away clean. Sound good?"

"As long as we get enough to make it worth our time," Sean said.

Rory gave the man a look and started to say something, but Michael waved him off. "You'll get enough. They come in spread out by a few minutes. Five, sometimes ten. We set up shop down the street. There's a vacant storefront I'm thinking will work fine. We get them off the street and through the door and then we brace them. Nothing harsh. Just take the money, bind them up, keep them quiet."

"We muscling them off the street? Someone's bound to notice," Rory asked.

"No, I'm thinking we, more precisely you, can talk them through the door. We'll be close to the cleaners. We tell them a story they'll believe. Cops are watching Carter. We do the exchange this week in here. These guys don't want to tangle with the cops either. They'll bite. These guys are mostly pushovers, cattle. If we divert them from one chute to another, they won't be a problem."

The plan was working but Sully had ghosted. Rory was tempted to put it off. If something had happened to Sully and Rory was left holding the bag on this ... He felt something slither through his guts, but he pushed past it. They were doing this. He was doing this. If he was honest, the fear felt good. He felt alive being out on the edge again. He could get this done for Sully and for himself.

The plan was simple enough. Hell, it was almost done. He decided right there. One more and they were done. Collect the money and get gone. And the payday would help a lot. He bitched and complained about the airport job, but he knew he had it far better than some of his friends. Most months, if they were careful, he and his ma could make ends meet. Maybe have a little leftover for a dinner out or some scratch tickets. The health insurance covered her pills.

That was all good and he was thankful, but he also felt tired, as if he were treading water all day, every day. It was exhausting. Maybe with this little hustle, he could finally get his head above water a few inches. Catch his breath. Maybe do a few repairs around the house. They wouldn't know how much they took until later. If there was enough, he thought he might even take Ma down to Foxwoods for the weekend. Stay overnight. Let her have a good time. She'd like that. It could also provide a nice cover if anyone noticed his sudden influx of cash.

He heard the shuffling steps of someone approaching and

didn't have to even look up to know it was another one of their guys. They even sounded pathetic when they walked. One more, this was it. Rory blew out a breath, put on his carnival smile, and stepped out of the doorway into the middle of the sidewalk.

CHAPTER THIRTY-THREE

Jimmy put the Sports Illustrated magazine down and pushed the brim of his pork pie hat back slightly. This one was gray with a subtle plaid pattern with a solid navy band around the base. He watched the traffic slowly crawl by on the street. It felt like the afternoon was passing the same way. He looked up and down the street from his seat inside the door and near the window but didn't see anyone else approaching. He glanced back at the clock over the register. Jeannie was hunched over her phone. She was always hunched over her phone unless there was a customer. It was not yet four. Just one of those weird days, he thought. Everything feeling just a little bit off from normal, a little slow and syrupy.

He had a sudden and discomfiting thought. Maybe it wasn't the rest of the world that was off its axis today, maybe it was him. He rubbed gently at the back of his head. Maybe he'd gotten a concussion from falling and hitting his head in the alley and maybe it had scrambled his brains a bit. He didn't like that thought. He didn't like to think of that fight in the alley either. It had been stupid and impulsive. He hadn't mentioned it to anyone else. He'd woken up with one of the kitchen workers from the Chinese restaurant poking him with a broom handle. He'd stumbled out of the alley and managed to make it through the rest of the day. He'd been chewing aspirin like Tic Tacs for a week and the headaches finally appeared to be fading. Bright lights still bothered him, but otherwise he thought he was okay. Until today when that thought had popped into his head. He picked the magazine back up. Better not to think of it. Wasn't much you could do to fix your brain anyway.

Ten minutes later, he put the magazine back down. It was a month old and he'd already read it cover to cover multiple times. It did remind him that he owed Harry Spencer a few good insults. One of the problems with being a Philly boy but working up in Boston was that you had to deal with Boston fans. They were always bad before but, since they started winning, they were downright insufferable. Jimmy was a basketball and football guy so he'd gotten in a few licks with the Eagles, but it had a been a long fallow period with the Sixers. But maybe that was changing. They pasted the Celtics at the Garden last week, and Jimmy had made a nice little pile of cash off Harry. When that little weasel came in today, Jimmy would be sure to remind him.

Jimmy glanced again at the clock. In fact, he should have already been here.

"Jeannie, has Harry come in today? Did he sneak in when I was in the bathroom?" Maybe the little schmuck was trying to dodge his payoff. That would be like him.

Jeannie glanced up from her phone with blank, glassy eyes. "What?"

Harry liked to try to flirt with Jeannie. Jimmy didn't know why. The woman was short with blotchy skin and dyed hair that looked like thin shards of glass. In their limited interactions, he thought she might also be incapable of having her own thoughts beyond food and water. She lived inside her phone. Did what her phone told her.

Jimmy suppressed a sigh and said it again. "Harry Spencer? Has Harry come in yet today?"

She shrugged. "Don't think so." Her phone beeped and she looked back down.

Everyone had a small window of time to come by the store and see Carter. It kept things orderly and manageable. It also added a rhythm to the day. The guys, and it was all guys, came through the door in a certain order. You traded the same banal small talk and thin jokes. Jimmy now realized that's what was bothering him. It wasn't his head or time bending out of shape. It was the order. The routine. That's what was bothering him. Now that he'd spotted the hole, the rest of it snapped into focus. It wasn't just Harry. It was a bunch of guys missing their drops.

He stood up, went behind the register, and down the short hallway to Carter's office. He waited a moment, both to see if Carter was talking to someone on the phone, the man hated to be interrupted, but also to go over it one more time in his mind, get it all straight. He decided he was right. He heard no voices, just the occasional clack of keyboard keys. He knocked and was told to come in.

"Boss, I think we might have a problem."

Carter tapped his pen against his teeth and thought about what Jimmy had just told him. The local protection racket was one of his first and oldest gambits. It was mostly pocket change, but it came in handy as seed money for other ventures. And, more importantly, kept his name and reputation on people's minds out in the neighborhood.

He had been working on a different project, quickly handling the sad sack bookies when they came in but largely doing it on autopilot. Neither he nor the bookies wanted the interaction to last any longer than necessary. There was no sitting down, no small talk. They came in, handed their envelope to Carter. Carter counted it, compared it to the previous couple of weeks, maybe asked a few questions or made a few suggestions, and that was it. He marked the week's take on the spreadsheet and the bookie left, tail still tucked proverbially and firmly between his legs. He did it almost thirty times a day, twice a week. It was a reflex now, while he did other things. If he was from a different generation, he'd say he was able to multitask quite effectively.

He closed out of the construction proposal he had been reading and went back over to his spreadsheets. Jimmy was right. He should have noticed it himself much earlier. Almost half the guys had yet to show and it was getting late in the day. He pulled up a new browser window and loaded the cleaners' security camera footage. There were five camera setups. Three were inside the shop. One showed the register, another showed a reverse view from the customer's perspective. Those two covered most of the front of the shop. A third showed the hallway down to Carter's door all the way to the exit to the alley. He wasn't interested in those today. He pulled up the two outside views, one front and one rear. The drops always came through the front door. Carter clicked and enlarged that view to fill the monitor's screen. He scrubbed the video feed back to noon and then started watching on fast forward up to the present where the video snapped back to normal speed.

The camera was decent quality, full color. It gave an almost 180-degree fisheye view of the sidewalk in front of the cleaners. It also spilled over and picked up a few storefronts to the left and right of Clover.

He watched it through three times. Each time, he moved

a little closer to the screen. When it was finished playing the last time, he picked up his phone and called Little John.

He answered on the second ring. "Yes, boss?"

"Might have a situation down here at the cleaners. Half the drops are missing. Guys aren't showing up."

"You think it's Sullivan?"

"Cameras didn't pick up shit. Who else could it be?"

"You don't think it's the bookies themselves? Sort of ... I don't know ... unionizing?"

"Most of those guys can't stand up to their own mothers, you think they're going to suddenly find the backbone to take on me? They've been paying me for twenty years and now all of a sudden they grow a pair? Why?"

"Maybe Sullivan is helping them?"

"Eh," Carter shrugged that off. "Too complicated. It would take Sullivan too much time. If the objective is to piss me off and take my money, it's much easier to just stick a gun in their ribs and take the cash. Where are you?"

"Down on the South Shore putting out more feelers."

"Get back here and take a look. I was working on something else and didn't notice. Whatever is going on isn't going to last much longer."

"Give me twenty minutes. I'll call you back."

Carter could hear the squeal of the tires and the angry horn blasts in the background as Little John swung into action. He smiled despite himself. The big man was at his best when he had a clear objective. That was a scary thought.

As he cruised the block for the second time, Little John would have preferred to be on foot but knew his limitations. Most of the time, Little John's size was an asset in his line of work. It made things easier. He didn't need to threaten or cajole people into doing what was asked. He simply had to loom. Looking straight up into the blank face of a six-foot seven, three-hundred-plus pound man was enough to dissuade most arguments.

But it did make the sneaky work a little harder.

He'd spotted the fat man standing in doorway on his first pass. Little John knew that building. It used to have a small diner that served breakfast all day. Little John liked pancakes. He could eat them for every meal if he had to. The diner had lost its lease when the landlord jacked up the rents. The husband and wife were returning to Greece. The storefront had been vacant for the last three months. He now had to go across town, back toward his apartment if he wanted decent pancakes. He'd often looked through the front window at the cloth-covered booths and empty counter and thought about finding the landlord and having a brief word. A good diner shouldn't be wasted.

Today, he couldn't see through the windows to where he used to sit because the windows had been soaped up and were opaque. If he'd been driving by on another occasion, he might chalk this up to coincidence and hope a new diner owner was taking over. But that wasn't why he was driving past. And it wasn't why he thought the windows were soaped.

He finished his circuit of the block and looped around to a side street. He parked in front of a hydrant, close to the cross street, so he could still see the vacant storefront. He picked up his phone. "They're down the street to the east."

"You're sure? You see Sullivan?"

"I haven't seen Sullivan, but I'm pretty sure. You know the place where that diner used to be?"

"Sure."

"The windows are blocked and there's a guy hanging out in the doorway. Gotta be it. Nothing else is jumping out at me."

"You think you can get in and take them?"

"Hard to say. Risky. Can't see inside. I've only seen this one guy. Fat man but he has a certain look. He's been around. He wouldn't be a pushover. And if he has similar friends, or even Sullivan in there, it might get ugly."

"Okay, good point. Sit on it and call me back when you know more."

He sat in his car and ten minutes later confirmed his suspicions. He watched Lester Banks, a small-timer who mostly made his book on horse and dog racing, walk up the street. The fat man stepped out and spoke to Lester. Little John watched Lester stiffen and then relax. Whatever the guy was peddling, Lester was buying. Lester glanced around and then quickly disappeared inside the old diner.

Little John watched the fat man pull the trick twice more with the same results. He called Carter again. "Still don't know if it's Sullivan, but it's definitely where the money's going."

"Motherfucker. Has to be Sullivan. This has got his hand-prints all over it."

Little John could hear the hysteria and paranoia seeping into Cater's voice. It had been happening more and more since Sullivan's return. First, the whispers from the bar fight, then the fires, then the loss of the girls, now this. Whatever Sullivan's endgame, it was proving to be effective so far. They had to stop him soon or Little John knew Carter might implode on his own.

"Fat man looks like he's getting antsy. Keeps looking up and down the street. Can't stay still. I think they're gonna wrap it up soon. That, or he's gotta take a leak. You want me to go in? Maybe get Legs and Jimmy to help? Can't have more than three or four guys total. That might even things up."

He heard Carter tapping his pen against his front teeth. A tic that Little John knew meant he was thinking. He kept quiet. After half a minute, Carter responded. "No. You made a good point earlier. No reason to take unnecessary risks. Not right now. I don't need you getting shot. Hell, it might be part of the plan. Use this setup as a lure. Get you guys to bust through the door and then take you guys apart. Ambush you. That motherfucker was always good at planning. No, get the guys down there. Have them bring a car. Here's what I want you to do."

CHAPTER THIRTY-FOUR

Maybe if things hadn't gone so smoothly, Rory would have noticed the car sooner. But things had gone smoothly. Really smoothly. Sean and Tommy were still jacked up on adrenaline, almost vibrating in the seats next to him.

Hell, he was too. He could taste the bright, bitter taste of it back in his throat as if he were chewing on pennies. It used to happen all the time on the jobs he pulled with Sullivan. He knew he'd crash soon, and he wanted to be in the garage and off the road when he did. He wasn't twenty-two anymore, and he felt like his goddamn heart was doing the jitterbug in his chest.

"Jesus Christ, that was a rush," Sean said.

Tommy held out his hands. "No shit! Look at this. I can't keep from shaking."

"It's the adrenaline. Fight or flight," Rory said.

"Never felt it like this. You could get addicted to this," Tommy said.

"Some guys definitely do. It'll wear off soon. Get ready. Feels like your head got hollowed out with a rusty spoon."

"Always a downside."

Rory steered the van off the public road onto an access road that wound through the warren of service streets in the airport that linked up the rental car depots, the mechanic bays, the service huts, and the big storage bays.

"You see that one guy? Wet his pants?" Sean said.

"Didn't see it, definitely smelled it. Rory, you were lucky you were mostly outside." Tommy said.

"Lucky? Uh-huh. Anyone spotted us or anyone asks around, whose face are they gonna remember?"

"Fair enough. Still better than hanging out in the latrine, right? Smelled like the guy ate asparagus for lunch. Even the rest of the losers in there didn't want to be near him," Sean said.

Once they got the guys inside, Rory walked them around the counter, through a set of swinging doors to the kitchen area in back. There, they met Sean, Tommy, and a couple guns. Couple of the guys tried to back up, but Rory's bulk blocked the way. No one really resisted after that. Rory figured they'd all likely been robbed before at some point.

It was almost orderly. Tommy took the money in the laundry bag and dropped it on a steel prep table. Sean used some plastic zip ties on their hands and then led them back to the walk-in fridge, no longer on, where he had them sit and he repeated the zip ties on their ankles. They had duct tape for their mouths, but everyone kept quiet for the most part and they didn't need to use it. Once Rory decided enough was enough, they'd emptied the cash envelopes from the laundry bags into two backpacks they'd brought and left out the back-door where they'd parked a borrowed van. Rory figured at least one of the guys in the walk-in would work his way free before morning.

It had all gone smoothly. Except for Michael going missing. That still bothered Rory. He slipped his phone out of his pocket and checked the screen. No messages. They were driving an old Chevy Astro van that was at least fifteen years old, pulled to the left, and rattled like a maraca when pushed anywhere near fifty. But it was clean. If they ended up on any tape, it wasn't going to get traced back to them. Thousands of local guys worked at the airport, and this van had nothing to do with Rory or the airline he worked for. It was a dead end.

Most of the service vans around the airport had the keys in the ignition or under a floor mat. Convenience and efficiency were the rule of the day. Who was going to steal one? No one. Borrow maybe, but steal? Unlikely. After his overnight shift, Rory had walked across the tarmac, found an idling van, hopped in, checked that it was empty, and drove off.

Now, they were bringing it back less than twelve hours later. Rory doubted anyone was looking for it. Or had even missed it. They'd drop it off somewhere out of the way. Take the backpacks of cash and get the shuttle to the employee lot where Rory's car was still parked from his previous shift. With no word from Michael still, they planned to drive back to Tommy's, he lived alone, divvy up the cash, and then go their separate ways. They all agreed to keep their heads down for a couple of weeks until they were sure they were in the clear.

Rory slowed the van as it approached one of the rare four-way stops back here. The big airline sheds were to the right, shielding the roads that looped around the terminals a view into the maintenance bays and operational guts of the airport. To the left, were the crisscrossing runways of the airfield.

There was less than a mile to go now. He planned to leave the van outside the American Airlines shed. It was the largest maintenance operation at the airport, and he'd seen a number of similar vans parked around the entrance in the past.

There was a car stopped at the intersection. It wasn't moving. Maybe it was stalled or had engine trouble. He noticed another car now coming up behind him. Practically a traffic jam on roads that were usually deserted. Something deep and primal pinged in his brain. The taste of copper rose in his throat. Fight or flight.

The car inched forward and started through the intersection and Rory let a shaky breath out. Sean and Tommy were still jawing and didn't notice anything. *Getting too old to be playing cowboy like this*, Rory thought.

He brought the van to a rolling stop and then started through the intersection when he noticed the car had stopped again on the far side, the ass end of the sedan still sticking out in the intersection. Rory hit the horn, impatient and anxious to get the job done now that they were so close. He let the van roll into the intersection, crowding the first guy. He could see the guy's silhouette in the driver's seat. He wasn't moving. The car behind him was at the stop sign now, pinning Rory's van in place. *Like a bullseye,* he thought.

He felt the deep rumble through the van's tires before he actually heard it. Stuck in the middle of the intersection now, he could see around the end of the big maintenance shed. A heavy-duty tow truck was speeding in their direction. The big silver grill between the headlights looked like demented teeth.

"Oh shit," Sean said.

"Doesn't he see us," Tommy said. "He's not fucking slowing down."

He sees us, thought Rory. He slammed his foot down on the gas and rammed the car in front of him, but the van was old and used up. There was no real torque left. The big boxy sedan held its ground with ease. The truck kept coming. It lurched into another gear, like a lion gathering itself to pounce on its prey. The big wrecker ate up the last seconds of Rory's life in a flash of chrome and smoke. He saw a brief flash of blue sky and white clouds as the van flipped, then he didn't feel or see anything at all.

CHAPTER THIRTY-FIVE

He tried shaking him awake again. It was always better to keep them awake and talking, but Max's eyes remained closed and his face was pale, going to gray. Kyle put his eyes back on the road and pushed the old van harder.

The worst one looked to be high on the shoulder or neck. Or, Kyle thought it was. There was so much blood it was difficult to see. He'd seen a lot of wounds in combat and knew that the amount of blood didn't always make it better or worse. Sometimes it was the blood you couldn't see that pooled inside you that ultimately did you in.

This blood was bright red and Kyle didn't think any of the wounds had hit arteries. He just thought there were a lot of wounds. When he'd gotten Max to the car, he'd quickly ripped the man's T-shirt off his body and into strips for the wounds he could easily see. It hadn't helped all that much, each was already dripping and saturated, but it was the best he could do.

He pulled extra napkins from a fast food bag in the footwell and drove with one hand while trying to keep pressure on Max's neck wound. Max was very still, and his head lolled to the side and banged against the window whenever Kyle took the turns too fast. Kyle knew he needed to get to a hospital. This wasn't something he could handle on his own. The blood was pooling in the seat crevice. He needed to get to one fast.

When Kyle had returned from his first tour in Iraq, he had taken a bus down from Bangor to Boston and spent the weekend on leave before continuing on to New Jersey and reporting to, what was then, Fort Dix. He'd spent most of that weekend just walking around, stopping in bars, sometimes collecting a free drink, but never staying for more than one. He was always more comfortable on his own, on the move. It was summer, July or August, with the temperatures hovering in the nineties. The heat wave was all the newspapers or televisions talked about. To Kyle, after the kiln-like deserts of Basra, it had felt like heaven, a cool breeze after baking in hell.

During all that aimless walking, he remembered passing a vast hospital complex near the Charles River. But that was as much as he remembered. He couldn't stop and ask for directions with a guy bleeding out in the front seat. He aimed the van at the city skyline and floored it.

He got lucky. As he crossed the bridge and approached Atlantic Avenue, he saw a blue hospital sign on a lamppost. He blew through a red light, almost got sideswiped by a garbage truck, but kept following those blue signs until he found the hospital. He drove straight up to the ER doors and parked with two wheels up on the sidewalk. People scattered, then stopped to watch. He saw a security guard jump out of a parked cruiser and come running toward the van.

Kyle got out and went around to the passenger side.

The security guard, who looked like he might be able to shave twice a week, followed him. "Sir, you can't park here."

Kyle ignored him. He opened the door and pulled Max out. Unconscious and slick with blood, Max was heavy and awkward. Careful of his wounds, Kyle grabbed him under the arms and started dragging him toward the automatic entrance doors. He left a dripping, bloody trail on the concrete. "There was an accident. Help me."

The guard gaped for another second, then bent down and grabbed Max's ankles. "What happened to him?"

"Accident. Head wound."

Once inside, the emergency response and the machinery of the hospital took over. It was what Kyle was counting on. He handed Max off to a pair of orderlies who loaded him onto a gurney. Kyle then slipped out while everyone was swarming around Max. He was good at staying in the background, unnoticed. He caught a few looks bumping the van down off the curb, but no one did anything to stop him. He took a right, then another right and was on the highway in two minutes.

He'd come back later and find a way to check on Max. If he was dead, this little adventure was over, and he'd go back to Essex and finally finish packing up his dead sister's condo. If he was alive, well ... he'd signed on for the full hop. He'd see how bad it was and what Max wanted to do next.

Right now, his immediate priority was to get out of the area and avoid any further questions. He was sure it was all on camera. Multiple cameras. Hospital security would call in the Boston police and they'd get the videos and the guard's statement and be looking for him soon. You don't drop off a bloody gunshot victim and then not stick around. Not if you're innocent.

He'd also need to find a new ride. The van was done. He looked down at his blood-soaked shirt and jeans. So were his clothes.

. . .

He took turns indiscriminately out of the hospital complex. If he didn't know where he was going, they couldn't either. He eventually ended up just west of the city near Boston University. He pulled over and tried to get his bearings. He couldn't get out of the van to ask directions. Couldn't let anyone see inside, either. He'd been doing a lot of the driving, but Michael had been giving him directions. He'd be on autopilot. Turn here. Pull over here. He realized that was a mistake now.

He didn't have much choice and he didn't think he had much time, either. Still, he had a good general sense of direction. If he could get close, he thought he'd eventually find his way back to the apartment. He knew Lawrence's shop was close to the city but south, so that's the direction he went.

It took a handful of wrong turns and an extra half-hour, but he eventually found his way to the right neighborhood. Five minutes later, he was back in front of the apartment building. He pulled around the building to the back parking lot and squeezed the van into a tight space between the fence and a Chevy Yukon. You could see the van if you were looking, but you wouldn't stumble on it by accident. He sat and waited, watching the lot and the door, slouching low in his seat. It was early afternoon. Everything was quiet.

Blood caked his hands where he'd pressed the strips of T-shirt and napkins into Michael's wounds. Streaks and swipes ran down his face and splotched his T-shirt. He looked like a splattered extra in a horror movie. If anyone saw him, they'd scream or call the cops, or both. Kyle didn't want either to happen. He scrounged under the seats and found a few more discarded napkins and a quarter bottle of lukewarm Coke. He wet the napkins and cleaned as much blood off his face and hands as he could. If he moved quickly, the dark stains on his T-shirt could be anything. He couldn't put it off any longer. He exited the van and headed for the back door. There was no one in the entry vestibule. He made it to the stairs and heard a door slam farther up. He paused and listened. No one was coming down. They must have been going up. He sprinted up the three flights and then did a quick peek through the stairway door. Clear to his door. He didn't run but walked quickly and confidently, key ready, to the door and was inside.

He let out a long breath he didn't know he'd been holding, then headed directly to the shower. He cranked the water up as hot as he could stand and used half a bar of soap to scrub all the blood he could see off his body. Then, he did it again with the other half of the soap.

After he'd toweled off, he sat on the bed and thought about transportation. Before going back to the hospital, he needed a new ride. He didn't feel comfortable driving around the city in the van after the ER stop. He had no doubt an alert on the van and his description were circulating. He could dump the van somewhere and walk away clean. There was no documentation to come back on them. Maybe that's what he'd do, but he wanted to talk to Max first. There still might be a use for the van. In the meantime, he needed another ride. But first, he needed to clean his boots. He found paper towels under the sink in the kitchen and used them, along with some dish detergent, to wash his boots clean. He had another pair of jeans and more T-shirts. He did not have more boots. A good pair of boots was worth the effort.

Boots retied, he grabbed a clean towel, a bottle of water, a coat hanger, and a plastic bag he'd filled with his bloody clothes and went back outside to the van.

With the water and towel, he mopped up and cleaned off as much of Max's blood as he could and then added the towel to the bag of clothes and stuffed it all under some existing bags of trash in the apartment's dumpster.

Back in the van, he looked over at the passenger seat. The van was not pristine to start with, and the darker spots still left just looked like stains that had accumulated over time. It would have to do.

He started it up and then thought about the best place to get another car. The airport lots would be a good option, but he didn't want to drive that far. There would be a lot of cameras and security near the airport. He didn't want to hit up Lawrence again. The man was doing enough. More than enough. He needed something closer. He pulled out of the lot and drove three miles north to a train station on the edge of the neighborhood that they'd passed in their repeated trips back and forth from the city. The parking lot was almost full, with just a few isolated spots far from the train platform. He backed the van into the one farthest from the main entrance.

The Army had given him decent hotwiring skills. People were always leaving jeeps and trucks where they weren't supposed to, often without the keys, so racking the steering column and stripping some wires to get the ignition started was a useful skill. The problem was that it just didn't work on many cars anymore. The newer models relied on chips and computers to recognize the key, so he needed an older model, preferably domestic.

He studied the surrounding cars but didn't find the right one. He looked over the light poles and platform. He could see a camera up by the platform, but none pointed toward the parking area. He took the coat hanger off the seat and straightened it out, leaving a little hook on the end. He left the van, holding the hanger low by his leg, and walked over to the next row where he spotted an old maroon Chrysler Sebring with missing hubcaps and a cracked rear panel.

He quickly slid the hanger down between the window and the door and popped the lock up on the driver's side. He dropped into the driver's seat, the car smelled strongly of cigarettes, and used his pocketknife to pry off the plastic surrounding the steering column, found the battery wires, and sparked the starter wire. He was in the car and out of the parking lot in under a minute. Transportation taken care of, he turned his attention to the next thing he needed.

CHAPTER THIRTY-SIX

Colleen was still chasing the Sullivans. She wanted the reason. Maybe it was personal, maybe it was professional, but she wanted to know why Michael Sullivan was back. She'd tried chasing down Danny but had come up empty. She still thought he was the key, but she thought maybe she'd have more luck finding him through his big brother.

She decided she'd go back to Sullivan's last known whereabouts prior to popping up in Kelly's Tap: Essex, Iowa. She pulled the keyboard closer and opened the database back up. The black mark on his name had since had some of the mud washed off of it, thanks to some reporter breaking open the subsequent corruption and coverup story, but Sullivan had never resurfaced.

She let her mind ramble. Maybe he hadn't gone that far. Maybe he'd gotten comfortable up there and stayed relatively close rather than start all over a third time. Maybe Danny had run into trouble and needed help. Maybe Danny went to meet him. She didn't know how they'd stayed in touch but, if family was important to Sullivan, maybe he'd reached out.

She set up a search for all the Daniel Sullivans picked up within five hundred miles of Essex in the last month. The database chugged and then spit back zero results. She tried pushing the timeframe back to two months. Nothing. She tried a few variants on his name. Still nothing. Goddammit, nothing about this case was easy.

She opened up the results to include John Does. This time, her query returned one hundred and sixty-six unnamed victims. It was a start. She sent the whole list to the printer and then carried the thick stack back to her desk and started reading.

She hadn't made it through the first page of the first report when her desk phone rang. She was tempted to ignore it and plow through the paper, but then saw the Chelsea prefix on the display.

"Adams."

"Hi, it's Goinns."

"What's up?"

"Got the report back, the prelim, at least, on the salon basement. Since you found the door, thought you might want to know."

"By the tone of your voice, I'm guessing you didn't find the perp or the murder weapon hiding down there."

"No, unfortunately not. It was mostly exactly what it looked like, an empty room."

"So, there was nothing?"

"Just the opposite actually, but just as much of a problem. It had been cleaned up and tidied, but the techs tell me it wasn't cleaned in a way to suggest someone was trying to conceal or cover anything up. It was teeming with trace and even DNA. So much, that unless we get some kind of indication that something related to the murders happened down there, we are never going to get authorization to test it all. It would only confuse things."

"What do you think the DNA was about?"

"No idea. Techs said they could tell people had spent time down there, but that was about it. Your guess is as good as mine as to what happened down there, or didn't."

"Something was definitely happening down there. I can feel it."

"I think you're right. Petrie is more on the fence, but that door was no joke and they were hiding it. You don't go to that trouble for nothing."

"Hey, that reminds me, did you know that Min wasn't the only owner?"

"Yeah, we had that. Some offshore partner. Our guy figured it was some sort of tax thing. Why? You think it wasn't?"

"No, our guy sort of said the same thing. It's just another weird part of this thing. Like the door."

"I'd tell you to buck up, that we'll get them, but you know that's bullshit."

She could feel the same frustration in his tone that she was feeling. "I'm sorry, Goinns. I had my hopes up, too. I thought that room was going to tell us something. They must have been killed for a reason."

"Thanks, Adams. Stay in touch."

"Will do." She hung up and turned back to her stack of paper. After the conversation with Goinns, it was the last thing she wanted to do but it had to get done. She pulled the stack closer and made a deal with herself. Get through half and she could get anything she wanted from the vending machine.

Each John Doe had their vitals listed, approximate age range, and a synopsis of how or where they had been found. A few included a photo. It was slow going, but Colleen thrived on the methodical work of finding the needle in the haystack. She quickly sorted through the paper and eliminated the men whose age put them over forty-five. She didn't think anyone would mistake Danny for someone that old unless there were extenuating circumstances, like drowning or disfigurement. She put cases that might meet those criteria in a separate pile, regardless of age. That left her fifty-three unknown persons. Next, she eliminated any blacks, Hispanics, or Asians. That took her down to a manageable list of fourteen men. She read all of them closely, dividing them into different piles based on likelihood, and then selected four who died in circumstances that made her think Danny could be involved.

She would need to call each department to get the full reports, if they were willing to share, but all four cases were violent acts and likely had made the news in some form. She pulled up a web browser and started typing in the key details from the reports.

She eliminated one right away. He was no longer a John Doe. There was an update from a Detroit paper that a suspect had been taken in for the murder of Janus James in a public alley. According to the story, all the parties had known each other, and it was a disagreement over how to split the bill for the coke they had just bought in the bar's bathroom.

She moved on to the next one. A drive-by shooting in Memphis was termed a gang initiation, but that could be code for a lot of things. She couldn't rule it out. She put it to the side.

The last two were from Chicago. The first was from last Monday. A man was found beaten, stabbed, and tied to a chair in an abandoned riverfront warehouse. His teeth had been pulled and every finger cut off at the knuckle. While the victim was unidentified, the precinct report wrote it up as related to an escalating, and ongoing, turf war between ethnic Russian gangs. She didn't think that was Danny. She wasn't sure what kind of trouble he might have gotten into with

Carter, but a Russian turf dispute in Chicago seemed unlikely and the timing felt off. It was too recent.

The last one was almost three weeks old. She read the opening paragraph in the Chicago Tribune about a bank robbery gone awry and felt her pulse quicken. The sisters never talked about it, but she knew Sullivan had been involved in robberies in the past. Here, two men had ended up dead in the lobby. Two hostages, bank employees, were taken but left unharmed in a janitor's closet. Money was missing, but a comment in the story made it clear that a good amount had been left behind, too.

She clicked to another story and found an update in the following day's Metro section. Still no IDs on the deceased. The story did mention both were white males, one in his late twenties or early thirties, the other closer to fifty. No new leads or updates were provided about the recovery of the money or any suspects that had fled the scene. Whoever had pulled the heist had gotten away clean.

She stacked up the rest of her piles. None of the other leads were as promising. She had picked up the phone to start some follow-up calls when Rawls poked his head into her cube.

"You coming?"

"Shit. It's that time of the week again already?"

"Afraid so."

She thought about making up an excuse to skip the meeting, but couldn't come up with anything that sounded viable. For a cop, she was a terrible liar.

She put the phone down and followed him to a windowless conference room in the corner of the floor for the unit status briefing, a weekly death march through all the active cases and investigations. She glanced across the tops of the cube to the other side of the floor and could see the suits were back holding court in the other conference room.

"Rawls, you know anything about a new OC task force being set up by the new city chief?"

The big man glanced over his shoulder. "Nope."

"Seems like they've been busy bees lately, but I haven't seen or heard of any results."

Rawls didn't say anything. She wasn't surprised. She didn't think the man was holding out on her at all. Rawls was older and mostly counting the days until his pension. He wasn't interested in office politics, gossip, or extra work. He worked his cases and didn't go in for bullshit. In some ways, they were a lot alike. If he had heard of it, she likely would have, too. She pulled open the conference room door and found a chair.

As expected, the meeting dragged on into the early afternoon, then she was immediately pulled into a follow-up about community outreach tactics until two. By the time she made it back to the safety of her cube, her stomach was protesting. She eyed her phone and the stack of printouts but decided she needed the food more, even cafeteria food. She went down three floors and bought a turkey sandwich, chips, and a cookie and brought them back to her desk.

The message light on her phone was blinking. She put the phone on speaker and hit the message button while she started in on the sandwich.

"Adams, its Foxx. I'm at the station. Give me a call."

She finished chewing and swallowed. His voice hadn't sounded particularly urgent, but he also hadn't cracked any jokes. She called his mobile, but it rolled to voicemail after five rings. She looked up the number for the C-6 station house in Southie and dialed. The desk sergeant took her name and put her on hold. She was through the sandwich and eyeing the cookie when Foxx picked up the line.

"Detective Adams, I presume."

"What's up, Foxx? I haven't talked to you this much since my first communion."

"And I'm going to get a bad rep talking to the staties so much. Even a good looking, semi-competent detective."

"Aww. Now I'm blushing."

"I thought you might be interested in this. We just got called in to babysit a guy at Mass General. White male, mid-thirties, approximately six feet, two hundred pounds. GSW to the upper torso. He was in surgery last I heard. Pockets clean, no ID. Probably a robbery and the description is general enough to be just about any guy in Boston, but I thought I'd give you a heads up."

"Where was he shot?"

"All I know is upper torso. Could be the shoulder, back, ches—"

"No, I mean where in the city."

"We don't know. That's one reason we've got a uniform sitting outside his door until he wakes up. He was a dump and run. Word around here is a guy pulled up in a van, literally pulled up on the curb near the ER doors, pulled the guy out and got the security guard to help him carry the guy inside. Everything swung into action and no one saw the guy leave. Security guy didn't have much in the way of a description."

"Cameras?"

"Yes, MGH is a priority target and wired up pretty good. I'm sure it's on the record somewhere, but I haven't heard anything from the Ds assigned."

"So, he's got some help. No other bodies or walking wounded turned up today?"

"Nope, I checked. It's been a quiet morning. One domestic, the usual truancies and corner calls, but no other bodies. Two calls of shots fired down near the dry dock, but patrol couldn't find anything out of the ordinary."

"Doesn't sound like a robbery. Sounds like someone was desperate for a doctor and stripped the body. You got a room number?"

"No. Just ICU. Shouldn't be hard to find."

CHAPTER THIRTY-SEVEN

Kyle drove past the Tide Street Pawn Shop and saw the sign on the door flipped to 'Closed.' He frowned. The shopfront looked dark and uninhabited, but it hadn't looked all that inviting earlier in the day, either. He'd found an all-news station in the car, but didn't hear anything about any incidents at the hospital.

He drove the streets surrounding the pawn shop a couple of times, but saw no one who appeared to be waiting or watching. He pulled into the parking lot of a restaurant supply distributor that allowed him a good view of the front and side of the pawn shop's building. He waited thirty minutes. No cars or people approached the pawn shop building. Only three cars total passed by on the street in that time. No pedestrians. He spotted the cameras dotted around the building. He got out of the car, crossed the street, and approached the alley that ran behind the building. He did his best to stay clear of the cameras. When he couldn't avoid them, he tucked his chin low and turned his face away.

The rear door was closed. A scuffed blue milk crate lay on its side by the door. There was a dumpster against a fence that divided the property from the building behind it. Other than that, and a few bits of scattered trash, the alley was empty. He waited again, this time only fifteen minutes, but the results were the same. His presence triggered no response. He walked back around to the street.

The front door was locked. It wouldn't be that easy. He banged a fist on the glass, rattling the bars that covered the windows on either side of the door. No one answered. He double backed to the alley. The rear door was brown metal, pocked with flaking paint and flush against the dirty bricks. There was a heavy-duty lock cylinder but no handle.

He looked up. It was a two-story building in a row of mixed commercial lots. Two-, three-, and four-story buildings mixed in with long, unbroken blocks of warehouses. There were windows on the second floor that would be easier to get through, but they were easily twenty feet up and out of reach. The building was alone on the corner. The neighboring buildings to the right and behind were too far away to help with roof access. He wasn't sure that would help anyway. There might be an access door, there might not.

His last chance was the door at the top of the side stairs, but he didn't hold out much hope. He jogged up the steps, making them shudder slightly, tried the knob. Locked. He was higher but still ten feet short of the roofline. Dead end.

He went back down and started for the car when he spotted them. Two slim casement windows tucked low to the ground and under the stairs. The property wasn't well maintained. Weeds and trash had accumulated around the foundation. The space under the stairs was a natural catch point and had just about obscured the windows. He glanced around and, satisfied that he was still alone, ducked under the stairs and examined the windows on his knees.

The windows were each hinged from the bottom and opened outward, a space of maybe two feet in diameter. Each window was only three or four feet wide. It was going to be a tight fit even for a man with his slim build. He thought about breaking the glass and pulling off or unscrewing a window but decided it wouldn't be worth the time and effort. It would still leave the narrow frame.

He checked the glass for any wires indicating an alarm but found none. He took out his pocketknife and worked it into the top of the window until he could push the hinge lock to the side and open the window. It was dark inside. Too dark to make out anything beyond shadows.

He decided feetfirst was the best approach. He didn't want to go headfirst into the unknown. He'd rather break an ankle than his neck. He slid his legs through, holding onto the stair treads above to keep from breaking the glass. He dropped further, moving his hands to the side of the building for balance and then carefully shimmied one way, then another, until he fit his shoulders. He ducked his head and looked into the room. He was close to the ceiling and directly above a line of shelves that reached almost as high as the window. The shelves were made of thin aluminum and looked rickety. He could see two big eye bolts that were sunk into the wall to keep them from tipping over, but he wasn't sure they would support a man's full weight.

He took in the rest of the room. It appeared to be a storage space. He spotted an old piano on the far wall and some broken pieces of furniture, but the space was mostly filled up with rows of shelves and various sized boxes. There were stairs going up on the opposite side of the room. He slid further down and dropped to the shelf. It rocked and groaned but settled back and took his weight. He judged he was still close to twelve feet in the air. He jumped and rolled when he landed to distribute the shock. He felt a twinge run up his knee to his hip but otherwise was okay.

. . .

He made his way over to the stairs he'd seen from the top of the shelving unit and went up. He wondered briefly what he'd do if this door was locked, if he'd gone through all of that trouble just to trap himself in a basement, but the knob turned in his hand and he pushed the door open.

He was standing behind the glass display cases in the small customer area he'd seen when he'd grabbed a bleeding Max. He could still see the smears of the blood trail Max had left on the dirty carpet. There was a second door a few feet away. This one was unlocked too, and Kyle went through it, deeper into the building. It was darker back here, not pitch black, with the big windows up on the second floor providing some light into the big space, but it was still hard to see. He decided he would risk the light if it helped him get what he needed faster. He felt along one wall, but couldn't find a switch. He followed the wall to a corner of the building where a small office was rigged up.

He could make out the shape of a filing cabinet in one corner and the low profile of a desk. It was darker inside the office without the window's ambient light. He stepped inside and immediately banged his knee against the desk. He felt around on the desk with his hands until he found a lamp perched on one side. He turned the switch and saw the shape of a man in a chair. Kyle jumped back. The man didn't react.

He was older, with hooded eyes and short white hair showing patches of pink scalp. He looked peacefully asleep in the chair except for his dull, open eyes. Pinpricks of burst blood vessels showed in the milky whites. His pants showed a dark stain at the crotch. It still looked wet. He hadn't been killed that long ago. There were no obvious wounds. His neck looked odd. Strangled, maybe. Or suffocated.

Kyle looked away from the body and took in the rest of the tiny room. He found a flashlight with a magnet stuck to the side of a filing cabinet. He took it and went back out into the larger space. He moved the beam around. It was as cluttered as the front of the store and the basement. More shelves formed yet more rows out of the big space and, like most of the basement, most were filled with cardboard boxes and loose junk. He walked down one aisle and looked into some of the boxes at random. Old newspapers, magazines, and a box of broken watches. Some boxes were labeled with marker. He looked through a few more. More assorted junk. He walked another three aisles. Each box more of the same.

He went back to the office and leaned on the edge of the desk. "Where do you keep your secret stash, old man? No way you were supporting yourself with the crap out there."

He came around to the other side. He nudged the chair with the dead man to the side. He spotted three small televisions and an old recording system under the desk. He turned them on and found different views of the store and the surrounding streets. He punched the eject button for the mini cassette but found the machine empty. Someone had already taken the tape.

A ledger book sat open on the desk. There were two columns. One listing merchandise, the other a set of figures. He ran his hand down the column. Different brands of watches were listed. He went back out into the main room. He walked down a row until he found a box on a lower shelf labeled 'Omega.' He pulled it off the shelf. This one was taped on top. He cut the tape and opened the flaps. Omega watch boxes were stacked neatly inside. He pulled them out and found three black 9mm underneath.

Now he was getting somewhere.

He went back and grabbed the ledger and then walked the rows, pulling more watch boxes off the shelves. He found an old army surplus backpack on one shelf and filled it with a variety of handguns, boxes of ammo, some stun grenades, a vest, and a couple more knives.

He went back to the office and checked the monitors. The surrounding area was still clear. He left out the back door. He dropped his new arsenal in the passenger footwell, twisted the wires to get the car going again, and headed for the hospital.

CHAPTER THIRTY-EIGHT

The Massachusetts General Hospital complex was at the bottom of the hill, just down the street and less than a mile from her own office in the city's court complex. Colleen finished her cookie, no need for that to go to waste, and grabbed her coat. She'd walk down and take a look. Might be a waste of time, but exercise always had a way of ordering her thoughts.

She hadn't been outside since the sun came up and it was warmer than she expected. She could feel sweat breaking out on her lower back as she reached the bottom of Cambridge Street. She slowed her pace. She regretted the jacket but wanted it to cover her gun. She'd need a new shirt and a shower by the time she walked back up to the office. She turned right and entered the sprawling complex of hospital buildings through the ER entrance. She passed through the lobby and the welcome desk and continued down the hall, deeper into the building. She knew the way to the ICU.

They brought her father here when he'd had his stroke and collapsed in the squad room. At the time, the doctors had told her it was a blessing he worked so close to the hospital. If it had happened at home or if he'd lain somewhere undiscovered, he might have had much more extensive brain damage. She had just nodded. She had a hard time, even now, seeing anything about his accident, as he called it, a blessing.

She made her way to the stairs. The elevators were notoriously old and slow in the main building. The hum of the fluorescent lights made her squint. The bleach, antiseptic, and medicinal smells enveloped her. She felt her heart start to race as she climbed. Two people came out of a door somewhere above her, talking. A buzzing static started to fill her brain. She stopped at the next floor and ducked into the restroom. She leaned on the sink and splashed water on her face. She closed her eyes and made an effort to breathe steadily and relax her shoulders.

It was happening again.

Anytime she visited her father's room during his stay, first in ICU, then later in a private room on the general floor, the hotel-style trappings and the sense of stage dressing made her anxious, almost to the point of panic. Why wouldn't anyone admit what really went on inside these walls? People went to hospitals to die. Death stalked the halls. She was a cop. She knew death's scent. This was death's habitat.

A nurse in pink patterned scrubs came in. She gave Colleen a quick nod and smile in that brusque, efficient manner that they must teach at nursing school or hospital orientation. Colleen used a rough paper towel to dab her face dry and left.

She climbed one more floor, to the ICU, feeling a bit more steady, though she still jumped at a sharp, percussive bang that echoed down the stairwell. She stopped with her hand on the door. What was that? An explosion? It took her a second to place the sound because it was so out of context, but then she was moving, passing the ICU, and continuing up. The alarms in the stairwell started blinking and wailing. The screams were loudest two floors up. The plate next to the door said Oncology and Genetics. She placed a hand on the door. It was cool, despite the smoke leaking into the stairwell.

She pulled her gun, then opened the door. It was chaos. Swirling smoke filled the hallway. Her eyes started watering. Vague shapes passed in front of her yelling and coughing. She pulled her shirt up over her mouth and nose and walked toward what she judged was the center of the floor. People bumped into her and careened off in new directions. She re-holstered her weapon. She could barely see and didn't want to accidentally shoot someone. She couldn't see any flames. There was just an acrid chemical stench and heavy white smoke.

Her foot kicked something solid. She bent down and tried to pick it up and jerked her hand back. It was hot. Someone tripped and fell over her. She took a pen from her jacket pocket and nudged the object. She recognized it.

She stood up and retraced her steps to the stairwell. She went back down to the fourth floor. There was no smoke here, but there was still chaos. The noise and alarms had people panicked, some staff included. There was a wild-eyed energy in the air. Some people looking to get out. Some people looking to help. Everyone was scared and manic.

She fought against the flow of people trying to get to the stairs or elevators and searched the floor. She stopped outside room 413. The door was closed. There was a folding chair by the door, presumably for the officer to sit on. On the floor sat a takeout coffee cup and a Sports Illustrated magazine. There was no sign of the officer.

She opened the door.

A man in a light blue hospital gown was pulling the IV from his arm, as a second man in street clothes disconnected the heart and blood pressure monitors. The alarms were unlikely to be noticed in all the chaos.

"Hello, Michael," she said.

The man in the bed turned to look at her. His face was a little different, cheekbones, nose, and forehead reshaped, but the eyes, with their bright intensity, were the same. So was the wry, toothless smile.

"Bad timing, Colleen," he said.

The man in street clothes took a half step toward a black backpack on the visitor chair.

"Uh-uh," Colleen said, raising her gun.

The man was on the short side and his hands were empty, but Colleen could see the danger coiled below the surface. A wolf could look like the family pet at a glance, but you would never make the mistake of getting too close.

He slowed but kept moving almost imperceptibly in the direction of the bag and his weapons, no doubt.

She put a round into the chair.

The noise was deafening in the room but wouldn't carry too far. She didn't mind if it did. She had the feeling she was going to need some help.

He raised an eyebrow at her, then stopped. For the moment.

"Whoa," Max said. "Take it easy. Both of you."

"Tell your friend to step back and lean against the window in the corner there."

"Go ahead," Max said.

The man took a few steps back away from the bag. Colleen relaxed just a fraction. The man looked no less dangerous.

"What do you want, Colleen?"

She laughed. "What do you think, dummy? You. You're wanted in at least three states."

Max shook his head. "Not going to happen. Not today."

"You're not the one holding the gun."

"I don't have the gun, but I've got some leverage."

"Yeah? What's that?"

"Can I get something out of that bag?"

"Do you think I'm stupid?"

"Fine. You go into the bag. There's a digital camera. Can you hand it to me?"

She kept her eyes on the two them, approached the bag, and then carefully undid the top zipper. She quickly glanced down. "Interesting firepower in here."

"We can talk about that later if you want. After the camera."

She saw the lens peeking out near the bottom. She pulled it out and handed it to Max.

He turned it on and flipped through the images on the camera's LCD until he found the one he wanted, then turned the camera around so she could see it. "A friend of mine says you might recognize this guy."

She looked quickly at a grainy photo taken at night from some distance but one that obviously showed her boss, Marty Creeger. "Lieutenant Creeger, my direct boss. What of it?"

"Any reason he should be visiting Carter's house around midnight?"

She didn't say anything for a moment. "I've got no idea if that was taken outside James Carter's house."

"You might not but we do. My friend also told me the image's metadata has GPS coordinates that will confirm."

"You can fake those."

"You can, sure, but it's difficult. I'm sure you've got experts who could tell if the image has been tampered with.

But why would we do that? We couldn't know you'd bust in here. We were just scoping out Carter's place and this guy walked into the frame. We smelled a cop but had no idea who he was until a few days later."

"Lots of reasons Creeger could be there."

"Legitimate reasons?"

"Maybe." Colleen wasn't going to believe her boss was crooked on the basis of one grainy, questionable photo. She certainly wasn't going to let Sullivan walk out of here because of it.

"Not enough, huh? Okay, I like your loyalty. There's something else." He started flipping through the images again. "Funny, I noticed Carter's name wasn't in that big story the other day about the big organized crime takedown. Wonder how he managed to avoid that?" He stopped flipping and showed her the camera again. It was an overexposed shot of about a dozen Asian people squinting at the camera from the back of what appeared to be a van. "You think evidence of human trafficking is enough to put Carter behind bars or will your boss help him wriggle out of that, too?"

"Trafficking? Bullshit."

"No bullshit. The short story is that Carter and a syndicate up in Montreal are bringing in people from Southeast Asia, mostly by cargo ship to Vancouver and then overland to the east coast. He's then got people here, mostly nail salons and massage parlors, who farm out the people as prostitutes until they earn back their travel fees. As if that would ever happen."

"Salons?"

"Spas, salons, massage places. I can give you the photos and put you in touch with some of the victims. They're willing to talk."

Her head was suddenly spinning with different theories and connections. Min. The security door. The empty room.

"You give me the stuff and you'll back off Carter?"

He looked pained. "You let us out of here and we'll give you the stuff to nail Carter's ass to a cell in Walpole."

She lowered her gun. "Go."

She'd seen the DA cut worse deals.

CHAPTER THIRTY-NINE

They were back in the van. They'd stopped by a twenty-four-hour copy and business center and had some magnetic signs printed up to stick on the sides of the van to give it a different look. In theory, they were now AAA Temp, two guys with a heating and cooling business. They'd also driven through a downtown parking garage. Kyle had jumped out and done a quick plate swap with a similar make, model, and color work van. Max thought the second part was risky, but less risky than stealing or trying to purchase another van. How often did people notice or check their own licenses plates? Not often. It would buy them a couple of days, and Max thought that might be all they'd need.

"There he goes," Max said.

They watched Little John and Carter exit through the side door and climb into the Town Car. Little John maneuvered the car down the street in the opposite direction of their van. The street was still cluttered with construction and contractor's vehicles. It appeared another house had been inspired to start a renovation. The confusion and clutter on the street added to their cover. Max imagined the remaining neighbors were probably losing their shit. The thought of the neighbors getting mad and acting out against Carter over home renovations almost made him laugh. He stopped himself. It would hurt too much. His whole body now pulsed constantly with a low-frequency pain. He was only able to move because he was taking enough aspirin to mellow out an elephant. He needed a list to keep track of the various bruises, lacerations, and outright holes he'd picked up in the last week. None of it was serious on its own, even the bullet wound was less a puncture and more a deep groove, but it all added up. What he really needed to do was just stay in bed for three days and rest, but that wasn't going to happen. And with what he was planning, he fully expected it to get worse before it got better.

He watched Carter's car until it reached the end of the street, turned left, and disappeared. The street was noisy and active with the various construction projects, but the sidewalks were empty of what Max would consider neighborhood traffic. No one out on stoops or walking dogs. He figured most of the homeowners had fled the street and the construction noise if they could. Carter's house was still. They'd watched the housekeeper and a nurse arrive an hour ago but hadn't seen any movement since.

Max turned to Kyle and winced as one of his cracked ribs needled his side. "I think we need to get in the house. Specifically, I'd like to know if the basement has changed."

"You've seen it?"

"A long time ago. Not a pleasant memory. Carter's a psycho. You know that already. The basement is his psycho playground. He takes people down there and dismantles them for fun and profit. Mostly fun."

"Profit?"

Sometimes, Max thought, *having a conversation with Kyle was like playing racquetball*. No matter what you did, you got short, staccato bursts fired back at you.

"Sometimes for fun he takes out rivals or anyone stupid enough to try to steal from him. More money for him. Hence, more profit."

"Risky."

"I think that's part of it for him. Cops have been trying to get in there for years, but he's stonewalled all of them. He gets off on doing it right under their noses. They know he's doing it and he knows that they know."

"Messed up."

"No arguments from me. It gets worse though. Like a lot of psychos, Carter has a bit of a fascination with pain. He's got a chair down there. Or he did. Nothing special about it. Just an old wooden chair. Depending on his mood, he sometimes gives people a choice. They can be bound to the chair. Or they can choose to have a few teeth pulled out. Sometimes he'd change it up to losing a finger. People almost always choose the chair. Bad choice. The chair won't kill you, I mean, I guess, starvation and dehydration will get you eventually, but not being able to move at all becomes incredibly painful very quickly. I've seen hard men weeping for a bullet after six hours.

"The rumor is that the chair was the way his father used to punish Carter when he was a kid. He'd use these belts and secure Carter to a chair and make him sit overnight by himself down in the basement."

Kyle just shook his head.

"You need to be abused before you become the abuser. Same is probably true with crazy and he's plenty crazy. Smart and dangerous, no doubt, but also very crazy. In one sense, it's almost amazing he's not more screwed up than he is."

"So, the basement?"

"Carter has a couple of other ... quirks. I'm thinking we

might be able to use them for our own purposes. Let me tell you what I'm thinking."

Kyle thought the plan was crazy. That was his only response when Max was done explaining it. "That's crazy."

It was hard to argue his point. It really was a bit crazy, even Max would admit, but it was the only way Max could think of to get it done. "You have any other ideas?"

"Shoot him from half a mile away."

"This guy has been a parasite in my life for too long. He killed my wife, my daughter, my brother. A bullet out of the blue is too easy. He needs to know. I want him to know I'm coming, and I want him to know that I'm bringing death with me."

"Then let's get crazy."

First, they needed to go shopping.

Some of the items were a little unusual but, after stops at Walmart and Home Depot, they had everything they needed. It really was amazing what you could buy at the ubiquitous big box stores. They loaded the van and headed back toward Carter's house in South Boston.

As they were pulling out of the Walmart parking lot, Max said, "Did you know something like ninety percent of Americans live within 15 miles of a Walmart?"

"I'm not sure whether to laugh or cry."

They made good time in the early afternoon traffic and, after a stop for sandwiches and drinks from a mom and pop deli in Dorchester, they were parked back on the street outside Carter's house by three p.m. They ate their lunch and waited an hour until the crew renovating Carter's place started packing up for the day. By four fifteen, their van was packed and pulling out. They waited another fifteen minutes to make sure the crew hadn't forgotten anything and then Kyle climbed out and opened the back doors.

"Red stickers. Punch the holes," Max said.

"Got it."

Kyle pulled two five-gallon buckets with lids out of the back, then grabbed a second pair. The second pair of buckets were labeled and sloshed lightly as Kyle carried them up the steps to Carter's front door. He left them there and then came back for the other two.

Max watched from the passenger seat. The housekeeper came to the door. There was a brief back and forth as Kyle explained he had a delivery that the work crew was expecting. There was a little more back and forth and Max was starting to get nervous. They needed to get the buckets inside and in the basement for this to work. Finally, the housekeeper held the door open and stepped back. Kyle picked up the first two buckets and disappeared inside. Two minutes later, he was back and took the second two buckets inside. Two minutes after that he was back in the van.

"Any problems?" Max asked.

"Nope. Housekeeper had a few questions. I think she was bored."

"Any surprises down there?"

"No, it's how you described it. Narrow and deep. Mostly empty besides the reno supplies. The full buckets are along the wall to the right, near the stairs. Not a perfect match but they won't stand out. The other two are at the opposite end."

"Hopefully that gives me enough time. Doors?"

"Also like you said. One to the left and one to the right. Left is locked. Standard deadbolt. You're going right, first. No lock on that."

"Okay then."

"What next?"

"Before we end this, I need to visit my sister."

CHAPTER FORTY

J im Ryun sat on the stone bench between rows P and
Q, his favorite spot, the bench positioned on a little
rise between two white cedars. On a clear day, he
could just see the tops of the city's highest buildings.
They looked impossibly tall and majestic from this distance.
It was about as close as he wanted to get to the city. He knew
the reality was much different. Underneath that shiny skin of
metal glittering in the sun was a rotten core of graft, corruption, extortion, and patronage. He'd watched it grind his own
family to dust. It was a hollow city. He hoped one day he
would see it burn.

He took another pull from the bottle. He still had a little
more work to do before calling it a day. Traps needed to be
checked and the oil changed on the digger. But that could all
wait. No one was in a hurry. This time, he took a longer pull
from the bottle. He felt his toolbelt poking into his gut and
adjusted it.

Today, the clouds had remained heavy and dark, slowly
building throughout the afternoon. He couldn't see the top of

the Prudential Tower or the Hancock building today. Just thick roiling masses of ice and water, thousands of feet overhead. He watched them tumble across the sky.

The thing people didn't understand about working in a cemetery is that it didn't diminish death. Just the opposite. It amplified it. You become attuned to it on a heightened level. The cycles of it. The seasons of it. You notice the browning petals of a flower. The slow pollution of a lake. You go out of your way to step over a bug or a worm. You realize everything is connected.

Jim thought that might be the bourbon talking.

He'd almost forgotten about the big man, that was how Jim thought of him. The guy was the general size of a baby elephant, about as delicate, too. He'd asked his questions and tried to come off as affable, but it didn't work. Jim could see through the mask. Jim had witnessed a lot of funerals, hundreds of them, and had seen all kinds of emotions and reactions. He was good at reading people. The big man gave him the creeps. The man was faking it. He was lacking something. He wondered if he ever found the man from the photo.

He tipped the bottle back and was surprised to find it almost empty. Despite the clouds, the day had been warm. It still was. He felt the liquor working through his body. He didn't fight it. He'd locked the gates before walking to the bench. He didn't have to answer to a boss. Not today. He had a few more things on his list but they would keep. He looked up at the clouds and felt his eyes drift close. He'd take just a little rest to get through the tail end of the day.

He was dreaming of Martha and quiet picnics when they were both much younger. It was a nice dream. The kind that gives you a smile and the feeling of warm sun on your face. A hand pulled him out of the dream. He opened his eyes to a dark shape looming over him. A man? A demon? The dead? His mind was caught in that slim void between dreaming and being awake where anything felt possible. He slid sideways on the bench to try to get away. The shape followed. It was a man. Or at least man shaped. He slid off the end of the bench and landed in the grass. His hand found the gun on his belt. He pulled it free. The man shape moved closer. Another step. He was almost on top of Jim now. Jim didn't think. He couldn't think. He slapped at the trigger until he felt the safety click off. He pointed and pulled the trigger. The shape stopped, stumbled, and fell. Jim felt an overwhelming sense of relief. He let his head fall back in the soft grass.

He awoke the second time to deeper darkness. It was full dark now, the clouds still keeping vigil overhead and blotting out the stars. He listened to the low chirping buzz of the crickets and katydids. He turned his wrist and tried to look at his old watch, but it was too dark to make out the time. From where he lay, he could see down the hill to the adjacent street. There was a small convenience store on the corner. He could just make out the red neon open sign still glowing in the window. He knew they closed at nine p.m., so at least he hadn't slept that long.

He remembered his phone. He pulled it out of his pocket. The damn thing was usually more trouble than it was worth, but it did glow in the dark. He found the button to turn on the screen. Just past eight p.m.

He slowly got to his feet. His back and knees barked at him. His foot kicked something. He slowly leaned down, more protests, and picked up the empty bottle and dropped it in the trashcan. How had he drunk all of that? He felt his cheeks momentarily burn at the thought of what Martha would say if she saw him now. They'd never been teetotalers, but he knew she wouldn't approve. Hell, he didn't really approve either, but he also didn't seem to be able to stop. Most days were long and lonely.

He stepped carefully over to the man. He was lying on his side, a few feet in front of the bench, one arm crumpled awkwardly over his head. The other was clutching his shoulder. Jim gently rolled him over on his back and took a look at him. Everything was connected. He pulled the syringe from the guy's shoulder. The man didn't move or react. He was still deeply under.

He'd seen some coyotes around at dawn and dusk a few years back. They were most likely just passing through, but Jim had gotten a few pictures of them and used them to press the town to get him some more serious traps and bait. One of their solutions was the pneumatic air pistol with a few syringes of low-grade tranquilizers. If you didn't look close enough, it looked like the real thing. Like he told the big man, he mostly used it to scare kids and trespassers off the cemetery property. He'd never actually fired at anything before tonight. He'd read the manual, kept it clean, practiced it a few times, enough to remember about the safety, and that was it. Most days, he put it on like any other tool he carried around.

The man grunted and his left leg twitched. Jim pulled another syringe from the little pack that sat on the belt next to the holster. He loaded it into the gun and pumped it a few times. His mind now turned to what to do next. God his head hurt. It was hard to think. He'd just shot a guy with a tranq gun. Yes, the man had been trespassing, but he doubted that was enough to clear him. Especially if they made him take a breathalyzer. He could end up in prison. At the very least, he might lose his job. And then what? He had nowhere to go. No one left that could or would help him. He'd be out on his ass.

Thanks, but no thanks for fifty years of service. No, he had to make this go away.

He pulled his wallet out and found the card. He dialed the number. It was answered on the third ring.

"This is Jim at the cemetery. I think I shot your guy."

CHAPTER FORTY-ONE

Carter put the phone down and pushed the small filigreed pillbox around on the desk. Five minutes. It would all be over in five minutes. He knew the cemetery setup would work. Little John had called and told him he had Sullivan. They would come in the back through the tunnel and the other houses and be down in the basement in five minutes. Five minutes until things began to return to normal.

He pushed the pillbox around some more and then slid the box off the desk with his palm and into the open drawer. He wouldn't need them. It felt like he'd needed them more and more recently but not tonight. Tonight, he wanted to feel all of it. He wanted to remember all of it. The pills helped him amp up his emotions and energy when he needed it, but they also took their pound of flesh. He sometimes was left with gaps in his memory and a floating disconnected feeling, even in the moments that he did remember.

He smiled as he saved his spreadsheets and shut down his laptop before putting it in the small office safe. He wouldn't forget this. Sullivan had taken his shot and it had taken a toll, but once again Carter had risen to the challenge. He'd stay on top a little longer.

Max's eyes fluttered open. He saw damp, hardpacked earth and fieldstone walls. Someone had him under the arms. His heels were leaving a faint impression on the floor. Everything felt so heavy. His arms and legs were bags of sand. He closed his eyes again.

The next time he woke up was better. In some ways. His head felt clearer, and his arms and legs felt like they were attached to his body. He was seated in a chair, but quickly discovered his wrists and ankles were bound. He flexed his wrists. Not tape or rope. It felt like plastic zip ties. Probably grabbed from the contractor's supplies.

He tried to raise his head and look around, but stopped as alarm bells of pain rang through his body at the slight movement. He clenched his jaw and tried to breathe. He was beginning to think being unconscious was preferable. He slowly breathed in and out, concentrating on the movements of his chest and letting the pain recede.

After five minutes, the pain was still there, but he'd pushed it to the background. He lifted his head and looked around. He was seated in a chair in a basement. He didn't have to guess whose basement. If he had any doubts, the stacks and supplies of building materials against the wall dispelled them. There was no one visible from where he sat facing the stairs, but he felt the hulking presence behind him.

"Sorry about Frankie. He sort of brought it on himself, you know."

"Still didn't deserve to die," Little John said. "Not like that."

"Sort of like my wife and daughter?"

"You know that wasn't me."

"Guilt by association."

"Doesn't look like you're in any position to judge."

"What happened?"

There was a deep gurgling sound, like deep water flowing over jagged rocks, and it took Max a moment to realize that Little John was laughing. He wasn't sure if he'd ever heard the sound before or if he wanted to again. It wasn't natural.

"The cemetery caretaker shot you with a souped-up blow gun."

"I don't even know what that means."

"He has this gun with tranq darts for shooting coyotes and raccoons and things that get inside the cemetery fence. For humans, too, I guess."

"Feel like I've been stepped on by an elephant."

"Shot you a couple of times. I think he was drunk. You spooked him."

"You knew I'd visit my sister."

"Carter knew you'd go eventually. You always had a soft spot for family. Even if it could get you killed."

Max started to shrug and then stopped. It felt like someone was pushing a fireplace poker through his shoulder and into his neck. He hissed through gritted teeth.

"Worse reasons to die," he said eventually.

"I wouldn't know."

They both fell silent when the door at the top of the stairs opened.

Carter came down the steps and stopped a few feet in front of Max. There were times in the morning, when he looked in the mirror, that he was surprised at the old, wrinkled face staring back at him. He had that same momentary sense of displacement now. This man in front of him now looked like a stranger. In Carter's memory, the man tied to the chair would always be the boy he'd first met almost twenty years ago, robbing banks and trying to save his sister.

"Hello, Michael. The government hatchets did a decent job with your face."

Sullivan smiled. "Getting a little uglier would have been a bargain to see you go down."

There he is, Carter thought. That thin, wry smile that seemed to say you weren't in on the joke. That was the man he knew. That was pure Sullivan. That confidence, even trussed up like he was now, always used to bother Carter. And scared him a little, too. Carter was surprised to find it still did. He wiped at his brow. Was it hot in here? He felt the prickle of sweat on his lower back.

"You've made a real pest of yourself in the last couple weeks. Cost me money, too."

"Cops know about the kids you're bringing in?"

Carter waved a hand like swatting away a gnat. "I doubt it. If they did, they'd already be here. No, I think you stumbled on that one and have no idea what to do about it. Give it to the cops and they come in here all hot and bothered and arrest me. Where does that leave you? Are you willing to go back to prison just to get to me? I doubt that, too. So maybe you do know about my little sideline enterprise. So what? Are those kids really any worse off here than they were back in whatever upside country they came from? I didn't force them onto the boat."

"No, you just forced them into slavery once they made it over here."

"Slavery is a bit harsh. I incurred significant expenses to get them into this country. I'm just looking to make some of my investment back. That's how capitalism works in this country."

"Sounds like you're rationalizing away your soul."

"Do you think I really believe in something as hypothetical as the soul? I believe in dollars and cents. Supply and demand. This country was built from scratch on an economic system where trade and industry are controlled by private owners for profit. Profit, Michael. Never lose sight of the money. That's what I never understood about you. It was never about the money. Maybe I should have seen it from the start. Maybe we could have avoided all this."

"You would have just killed me sooner."

Carter shook his head. "You were so good. Planning, logistics, the job. It was easy money. I couldn't pass it up."

"Not everything in this world is about money. You need to stand for something beyond wealth and profit."

"It's worked for me so far."

"You must be a lonely man," Max said.

There was that smile again. God, he hated that smile. A bead of sweat ran down the back of his neck. His head felt like it was stuffed with cotton. He glanced up at Little John, but the big man was his usual dispassionate self. The rage and adrenaline momentarily cut through whatever was making him feel off, and he punched Sullivan in the face with a satisfying smack. A cut showed under Sullivan's eyes and a thin line of blood ran down his cheek.

"There you are. You've done a good job of impersonating a human over the years, but I always preferred to deal with the real you."

Carter hit him twice more as his anger overrode rational thought, then he stopped and decided he wouldn't give Sullivan the satisfaction of taking a beating, even if it might wipe that smile off his face.

"I think we're done talking," he said as he straightened and wiped the blood from his split knuckles on his pants. "You've been down here before, right?"

Max spit out a wad of blood. "Once was enough."

"Then you know how this goes." He pulled the stainless-steel cigar cutter from his pocket. Little John stepped around Max and the chair and handed Carter a fragrant Arturo Fuente cigar.

God, it is really hot down here, he thought. Maybe the smoke from the cigar would help clear his head. "I've been saving this one especially for you, ever since your imbecile of a brother gave you up." He was sweating freely now, and his hands were slick as he clipped the cigar's end.

"No Red stories?"

Carter dug in his other pocket for his stolen silver lighter. "I'm talked out and Red's dead. Just like you very soon."

He sparked the lighter and the room exploded.

CHAPTER FORTY-TWO

When you are trying to disappear and live in the margins you end up working a lot of odd jobs for cash. Max had mostly stuck to the steadier work of a short order line cook when he could find it. He enjoyed it and liked the way it constantly kept his mind busy. The pay was decent, and it left him tired enough to sleep mostly without dreaming. But those stretches of time where he could stick in one spot and get that type of work were unusual. Most of the jobs he took were daily or weekly jobs for cash under the table that relied mostly on strength and stamina: landscaping, loading trucks, construction.

Some were more dangerous, like installing concrete flooring. Max had done that for a week once in Ohio. It paid well and sounded innocuous when the contractor he met in the parking lot explained it to him, but Max quickly learned he was very, very wrong. Installing or refinishing concrete floors with lacquer and epoxy coatings was a deadly serious business. All the finishing products were extremely flammable liquids with flash points under one hundred degrees Fahrenheit. Some products were even well below that, closer to room temperature. The mixture of product vapor and air near the liquid could easily ignite and cause an explosion. Very easily.

Sparks became a serious life-threatening consideration.

The screams started almost immediately.

When Carter hit the lighter, Max pushed back with his heels and fell off the chair. He'd been afraid they would tie him to the chair which would have slowed him down even more and make escaping the fire unscathed even more of a risk. He still had no time to waste. He scrambled to the side, away from the initial source of the combustion, and managed to push himself to a standing position against the wall.

He took a quick glance toward the stairs. Carter was screaming and covered in splotches of flames. His hair was on fire and his face was stark white. His eyes appeared to be closed, but then Max realized that wasn't the case. The fibrous white sclerae were dripping down his face. Little John was also on fire. As Max watched, he stopped batting his hands against his boss in an effort to muffle the flames and dropped to his knees. His mouth opened but no sound came out.

Max pulled his gaze away. His wrists and ankles were still bound with zip ties. He lifted his arms over his head, gritting his teeth and trying to ignore the pain, and then brought them down hard against his stomach. The ties bit into his wrists but held. He did it again. Same result. He took a shaky breath. The heat was intense. He brought his arms up and then down again, clenching his stomach, and pushing his elbows out for more torque on his wrists. The bindings snapped. His wrists were raw and sore but free.

He turned his attention to his ankles. He put his hands together like he was praying and shoved them down between his legs toward his ankles. He pushed his feet and ankles outward to provide more tension. This time, the bindings broke on the first try.

Prison teaches you so many things.

The fire was eating all the oxygen in the room and Max could see it climbing the stairs, looking for more fuel. The heat was almost overpowering. He could no longer see Carter or Little John. He could also no longer hear their screaming. For that, he was thankful. Thick, black smoke was filling the room as the fire found the paint, drop cloths, and other contractor supplies. He didn't have much time.

He went to the floor and crawled toward the corner. He could feel the fire licking at his arms and legs and singeing his hair. His fire-resistant clothes handled the fire. He would deal with any hair loss. He made it to the corner and found the buckets Kyle had placed earlier. He grabbed both and went back in the opposite direction. He had to keep his eyes closed more now and got momentarily turned around in the smoke, but eventually found the cold room's door. He stood, feeling the fire on his shoulders even through his fire-resistant shirt, quickly opened the door and swung it closed again, then tried the handle on the inside, the door moved outward. He wasn't going to be trapped.

The fire hadn't made it inside yet, but Max had doubts about how long the door would hold up. He put the thought aside, he couldn't control that, and just had to hope Kyle had already made the call.

He moved away from the door and opened the two buckets.

The cold room was just that, cold. It wasn't as cold as a freezer, but it was sealed and below ground and much cooler than even the basement room just outside. He wouldn't get frostbite or hypothermia but a few more layers would keep him more comfortable. The first bucket was filled with an insulated hooded jacket. He pulled that on and followed it up with a wool hat and gloves.

If everything went down as they planned, he was far more concerned with suffocating. The cold room was twenty by ten by eight. That gave him approximately 1600 cubic feet of air to breathe. A person needs about 2800 cubic feet of air per day and can probably get by for a time with a little less. He had a little cushion there, but the room was sealed. He also had to worry about not just breathing in but breathing out. If the concentration of carbon dioxide got too high in the room, it would be a bigger problem than too little oxygen.

The second bucket held a small supplemental oxygen tank wrapped in extra fire-resistant clothes as a precaution. The tank was warm but there was little risk in it exploding unless it was opened and tossed into the flames. It would allow Max to breathe for two extra hours if necessary. He hoped it didn't come to that.

He pushed the bucket aside and made a space on the bottom shelf among the old jars, supplies, and various pieces of junk that had migrated into the cold room over the years. He pulled the buckets in front of him. It would never stand up to much scrutiny, but if someone hurriedly opened the door and glanced inside he hoped it was enough.

He settled in to wait.

CHAPTER FORTY-THREE

The Red Sox were finishing a long west coast trip with the last of four against Oakland. It was near midnight on the east coast. The sun was just going down out west. The Sox were up two to one in the fourth. It was the last game and they were looking for a split. She was sitting in her father's room, drinking a beer, legs hanging off the bed. Her father's papers were stacked next to his chair. His own beer sat half empty, sweating on the coaster by his elbow.

"Even if you're right, this could do serious damage to your career."

She hadn't told her dad about the deal she'd cut with Max, not all of it. She'd spent most of the afternoon digging on the trafficking angle. If that was bullshit, the whole deal was off, but she didn't think it was. She'd already connected one big piece. Holden, Hart, and Taylor, the big law firm tied to the part ownership of Min's Hair Salon, also had at least one other prominent client in the Boston area. They were the attorney of record in the last two depositions for James Carter in varying civil cases.

That sort of knot she knew how to attack and untangle. The Creeger angle she was much less sure about.

"I know that but I'm not sure I can keep this to myself."

"Can you get more proof?"

"I don't think so. Not on my own. Too big for that."

"Bring in the Feds?"

"Would that put me and my role in a better light?"

"Probably not," her father conceded.

Both of their phones rang at almost the same time. They glanced at each other.

"Adams. What? Yeah. Okay. Got it."

"Thanks," her father said and hung up.

"Fire at Carter's. There are bodies," Colleen said.

"That was Foxx. He had the same."

She could smell it from three blocks away. She'd worked a few wrecks as a trooper before moving into the detectives. It wasn't something you forgot. The odor of burned flesh permeated through the smoke and other chemicals from the fire. She showed her badge to the officer on the scene and ducked under the tape.

The active fire was out. Two groups of firemen were rolling up hoses and reloading separate trucks. The house's facade was a blackened shell, with most of the damage on the lower floor.

She found Foxx leaning against the door of his beloved patrol car.

"Detective Adams."

"Any idea what happened?"

"Beyond the fact that it clearly started in the basement with some sort of accelerant? No, not much."

"How many bodies?"

"They think two."

"Think?"

"Two very crispy lumps in the basement."

"ID?"

"Not yet. Haven't eyeballed them myself, not sure I want to from what I'm hearing, but it doesn't sound like any definitive ID will be fast."

"Is the ME or crime scene people here?" She looked around.

"Yes, they're around here someplace but everything is on hold. Apparently, the air quality is so bad down there from whatever started the fire that the smoke jockeys chopped out some ventilation and want to wait until morning to go back in."

"Pussies."

"That's exactly what I said, but after they confirmed everyone inside was DOS, staying inside wasn't a priority."

"Just because everyone is dead, doesn't mean things in there aren't a priority. Sometimes that makes it more of a rush."

"Preaching to the choir, Adams. Feel free to take it up with the white shirts over there."

Adams glanced over at a mixed group of command personnel from both fire and police. The address and potential victims had gotten the brass out of bed. She had no desire to stick her neck out over there.

"No, thanks."

"I knew you were smarter than you looked."

She briefly looked around for Creeger, but didn't see him. No reason for him to be here, really, and if the picture from Sullivan was accurate, even more of a reason to keep his distance.

She suddenly felt very tired. She was tempted to get Foxx's opinion about Creeger, but this wasn't the place to talk about it. Too many ears around. She asked instead, "You think they went out together?"

He knew who she was talking about.

"I honestly don't know, Adams, but we aren't going to find out tonight."

CHAPTER FORTY-FOUR

I t ended up taking three days. The fire in Carter's
basement had gotten so hot that the victims' teeth had
fragmented. They'd ultimately had to rely on DNA to
find out for sure that both James Carter and his associate,
John "Little John" Baggely, had died in the basement.

Foxx had gotten her a copy of the report. The fire department's investigation unit was able to determine that flammable liquids, likely a flooring lacquer, had combusted, likely
in an explosive manner and splashed on the two victims.

In an odd bit of editorializing, the investigator had added
that death was likely to have been excruciatingly painful.

Creeger was going down. It was only a matter of time.

Colleen would help, but it turned out she was late to the
party. Very late. A long and voluminous file already existed
and dated all the way back to Creeger's stint in the organized
crime unit in the '90s. Not only would he get charged with
helping Carter avoid the most recent indictments, but he'd
also likely face additional racketeering-related offenses, even

up to second-degree murder, for tipping Carter off to other gang and OC-related cases that led to Carter murdering various suspects.

Creeger would be in prison for a long time.

Eddie soon found out whose house he had hacked. Lawrence had been against Eddie helping further, but Max convinced him. Eddie didn't need to be near the house. He was able to find a way in from his own apartment. Plus, the job had been simple. Once he got the call, slowly raise the thermostat temperature to seventy-five degrees. The whole house was wired up in a comprehensive security and monitoring system. He could turn on and off lights, unlock doors and windows, check camera feeds. Turning up the temperature was the most banal thing he could do. But when he got the call, he did it.

While he was inside, he hopped on the wi-fi and poked around a little. He found a little walled off area that led to a laptop. It was an interesting security protocol and he bet it was a backdoor left by whoever installed the system. It turned out the laptop was rather boring, too. Just full of spreadsheets with long columns of numbers. It didn't interest Eddie, but he thought it might interest Lawrence.

The spreadsheets definitely interested Lawrence. The accounts and routing numbers for offshore accounts interested him even more.

Rory's mother and aunt didn't get to take that trip down to the casino, not right away, at least, but they did find an envelope of cash in their mailbox one morning. They were careful and made it last. It didn't make them forget Rory, but it did help.

Foxx got a new patrol car. He liked the new suspension but missed the old, broken-in driver's seat of his old ride.

Sean, the bartender, found a new gig at a wine bistro on Newbury Street. He kept his old hair.

There were two other anomalies tucked into the final report near the back that kept poking at Colleen like a popcorn kernel lodged in her gum.

The first was that the report noted a room on the second floor that appeared to be set up for long-term nursing care. The second floor was undamaged except for secondary smoke and some water damage. Follow-up interviews with the nursing staff employed by Carter had told them that description was essentially true and that Carter kept a man named Daniel, they never knew his last name, who suffered from increasing dementia, locked in the room but essentially well cared for. A third body hadn't been found. Neither had Daniel.

The second was just as strange. The report listed the items cataloged in the old-fashioned cold room in the basement. There had been some minimal smoke damage, but the door and seals to the room had held and it was largely undamaged and intact. Listed among the accounting of various jars of spoiled preserves was an item described as 'small oxygen tank and mask - empty.' No other explanation or note was added.

Get more free books, crime fiction news and other exclusive material.

I'm a crime fiction fan. I love reading it. I love writing it. And I love connecting with other fans about it. Talking with readers is one of the best things about writing.

Once a month I email a newsletter with crime fiction news, what I've been reading, special offers, and other bits of news on me and my writing. There might also be the occasional story or picture about my dog, Dashiell Hammett.

If you sign up for the mailing list I'll send you some free stuff:

1. A copy of the Max Strong prequel novella SLEEPING DOGS.
2. A copy of the short story collection OCTOBER DAYS, which includes the award-nominated short HOW TO BUY A SHOVEL.

You can get both books, **for free**, by signing up at mikedonohuebooks.com/starterlibrary/

Did you enjoy this book? You can make a big difference.

Reviews are the *most* powerful tools that I have as an indie author to bring attention to my books. Honest reviews of my books help bring them to the attention of other readers.

If you've enjoyed this book, I would be very grateful if you could spend a few minutes leaving a review on the book's Amazon page. It can be as short as you like.

Each review really makes a difference.

Thank you very much.

ABOUT THE AUTHOR

Mike Donohue lives with his wife and family outside Boston. He doesn't think reading during meals is particularly rude. Quite the opposite.

You can find him online at mikedonohuebooks.com.

Printed in Great Britain
by Amazon

15019363R00164